THE ROOM

Also by Hubert Selby Jr.

Last Exit to Brooklyn

The Demon

Requiem for a Dream

Song of the Silent Snow

The Willow Tree

Waiting Period

THE ROOM

Hubert Selby Jr.
a novel

MARION BOYARS
LONDON • NEW YORK

Reprinted in the United States and Great Britain in 2002 by
MARION BOYARS PUBLISHERS LTD
24 Lacy Road, London SW15 1NL

www.marionboyars.co.uk

Distributed in Australia and New Zealand by Peribo Pty Ltd,
58 Beaumont Road, Kuring-gai, NSW 2080

First published in the United States and Great Britain in 1972
Republished in the United States and Great Britain in 1989
by Marion Boyars Publishers Ltd
Reprinted in 1998, 2000

Reprinted 2002, 2004, 2007
10 9 8 7 6 5 4

A CIP catalogue record for this book is available from the British Library.
A CIP catalog record for this book is available from the Library of Congress.

ISBN 0-7145-3038-7

Printed in the UK by CPI Bookmarque, Croydon, CR0 4TD

This book is dedicated,
with love,
to the thousands
who remain nameless
and know.

*Defense counsel touched the defendants hand
before slowly rising and facing the jury.
He hesitated only a second before speaking.
I do not ask for justice for the defendant,
but mercy*

HE was conscious of the dark stillness in the corridor. He knew there was nothing to be seen, yet he continued to stare thru the reflection of his face in the small window. The corridor was only 7 feet wide and the wall opposite was dimly visible. He read the signs over the dirty-linen baskets—blue shirts, blue pants, blankets, bath towels, hand towels. He was just able to read the last two by pressing against the glass and standing to one side. Again he read them from left to right, standing first in the middle then moving to the left and straining his eyes to read the last sign. Shirts, pants—he could recite them without trouble. He closed his eyes. Hand towels, blankets, bath towels. . . . He didn't bother checking his accuracy. He knew he was right.

Turning from the heavy, locked door he looked in the mirror over the sink. Now that his eyes were accustomed to the night light he could see his face clearly, even to the small blemish on his cheek. He leaned closer and touched the red spot with a finger tip. The beginning of a pimple. He started to squeeze it, then lowered his hands. Why bother? Itll just bruise the skin. I/ll wait until it comes to a head . . . if it doesnt just disappear first. Who knows, maybe it will, touching it again with a finger tip. He stopped patting the spot and stood back slightly and just stared at his face, his eyes slowly closing to a squint, his face wrinkling into a frown.

He shrugged and turned from the mirror and sat on the edge of the bunk. He knew the room was only dimly lighted compared to the daytime when all the lights in the ceiling

were lit, but it seemed to be just as bright now. Of course
it only seems that way. But if it seems that way then it is
that way. Right? Right now its just as bright as a beach on
a sunny day.

But
you know it isnt. You know that it only seems to be, and
it only seems to be because youve become accustomed to
it. And when they turn all the lights on it will be so bright
you wont be able to open your eyes all the way, then after
a while it will seem like its always been that way until
they turn the lights out and only the night light is on and
suddenly it will seem very dark until you become accustomed to it and then it will seem bright just as it did
before. Its always the same—you get used to one thing,
then it changes. Get used to another, and that changes.
over and over. always the same.

O well, the hell with it. Its
not important anyway. Its not dark and im not tired enough
to sleep. Shouldnt have taken that nap this afternoon. If i
had something to read i could probably tire my eyes and fall
asleep. O well, it doesnt make any difference if i sleep at
night or during the day. Its all the same. The same amount
of time has to be passed each day

and night. The same twenty-four hours. But the
more you sleep the faster time passes. Like xmas eve when
youre a kid and you cant wait until morning to see what
santa claus brought. You know as soon as you fall asleep it
will be morning. Thats all you have to do. Just fall asleep
then wake up and jump out of bed. And there you are, under
the tree tearing paper off presents. It was hard to sleep then,
too. But you knew that as soon as you fell asleep it would be
morning, no matter how far away it was. And you kept thinking, fall asleep and it will be morning. But it was hard to
sleep. But the time did pass, and you fell asleep—eventually.

And it was just as hard to fall asleep even when you knew there was no santa claus.

What the hell.

Well, anyway, time has to pass. But sometimes its so goddamn long. Sometimes it just seems to drag and drag and weigh a ton. And hang on you like a monkey. Like its going to suck the blood out of you. Or squeeze your guts out. And sometimes it flies. Just flies. And is gone somewhere, somehow, before you know it was even here. As if time is only here to make you miserable. Thats the only reason for time. To squeeze you. Crush you. To tie you up in knots and make you fucking miserable. If only you could sleep 12 or 16 hours a day. Yeah, that would be great. It doesnt happen though. Maybe you can do it for one day. If you go a few days with only a little sleep. But after that youre right back where you started from. Trying to sleep so the goddamn time will pass.

And those crazy old bastards spent their whole rotten lives watching the stars, and all that shit, to figure where theyll be. All screwed up with time. No telescopes. No watches. Just trying to figure out time. Thousands of them for thousands of years. Just sitting on their asses staring at the sky. All screwed up with time. Just worrying about the stupid stars and planets. Crazy. How could they do it? Just spend all their dumb lives looking at the sky. And some of the nuts lived to be 80 or 90. And day after day. Night after night. All screwed up. They had to be nuts. And where did it get them? So they figured out where mars would be in ten thousand years. Big deal! Krist, what a stupid waste of time. And where did it get them? Where? After they figure all that shit out theyre either dead or still sitting on their ass looking at the goddamn sky. Right back where they started from.

You always end up where you started from. No matter what happens.

Right back in the same cesspool. Even if you do sleep for 24 hours youre right back where you started from. Sitting around for the next 24 hours waiting to fall asleep. Sitting on the edge of a bunk, or something, staring at a goddamn wall. The fucking night light blinking and your eyes open.

Well, at least the wall is gray.

Gray.

Yeah, it would be gray. Almost battleship gray. Its easy on the eyes anyway. Its bad enough with the night light on all fucking night without having some bright, shiny wall glaring at you.

Thats right. That's where battleship gray came from. i was wondering. How old was i.   About 8 or 9 i guess. Got it in my stocking at xmas.   What battleship was it.

Cant remember the name. But the glue sure did stink. i guess mom helped me put it together. She usually did. Took a couple of days i guess. Probably more. Think i sanded all the pieces real smooth. Think it was the kind of glue that took a long time to dry. Had to be very careful the pieces stayed in the right place while the glue was drying. Yeah, had to keep it by an open window while the glue was drying. It smelled so bad. Guess the battleship gray was my idea.

Or was it? Maybe the directions said to paint it gray.

O well. i remember buying the paint though. In the hardware store across the street. It was a small can and only cost a dime. Same as a ham and potato-salad sandwich in Kramers delicatessen. It really didnt look like much when it was finished though. i dont know, maybe it was the gray. Something was missing. Like the model airplanes. They never looked like they should. Not really. But it was fun to build them and then set them on fire. They sure did burn fast. Sure was dumb sweating over those fucking models. Spend all that time and what have you got? A model airplane. What dumb shit.

The hell with it, looking at the mottled concrete floor and trying to create images out of the variously shaped spots. Funny, but its easy when youre looking at clouds floating across the sky. He studied the floor carefully, but the more he looked the more the floor seemed to blend into one solid mass of gray. Eventually, after carefully studying every inch of visible floor, his glance reached the door. He looked up at the small window. Yeah, i know——shirts, pants——towels, blankets. Backward, forward—forward, backward.

He looked up at the wall, closed his eyes and bent his head back.   NORTH, NORTH NORTH EAST, NORTH EAST, EAST NORTH EAST, EAST; EAST SOUTH EAST, SOUTH EAST, SOUTH SOUTH EAST, SOUTH; SOUTH SOUTH WEST, SOUTH WEST, WEST SOUTH WEST, WEST; WEST NORTH WEST, NORTH WEST, NORTH NORTH WEST, NORTH. Yeah, that sounds right. Lets see NORTH, NORTH NORTH WEST, NORTH WEST, WEST NORTH WEST, WEST; WEST SOUTH WEST, SOUTH WEST, SOUTH SOUTH WEST, SOUTH; SOUTH SOUTH EAST, SOUTH EAST, EAST SOUTH EAST, EAST; EAST NORTH EAST, NORTH EAST, NORTH NORTH EAST, NORTH.

Yeah, lowering his head and opening his eyes. Can still box the compass. Front and Back. Krist, thats twenty-five years ago. More. Was the best in the troop. In tracking too. Could probably still tie those knots——sheepshank, stevedores knot, square knot, bowline, closing his eyes and studying the illustrations in the scout manual for a moment, then opening his eyes and nodding his head. yeah, can still tie them. there must have been more, but cant seem to remember them . . .

yeah, there was a half hitch and a clove hitch. thats right. almost forgot.   yeah.

Guess we must have had the smallest troop in the city. or at least in brooklyn. Used to have a lot of fun though, head tilted back, smiling, especially pom pom pullaway. Hanson sure got me that one time. tried to jump over him, but he tackled me anyway. We sure went down hard.

Like the time i tried to tackle Pee Wee Day. Should have dumped him for a 5-yard loss, but i hit his legs with my head instead of my shoulder. Sure did knock me on my ass. Damn near knocked me unconscious. Sure was stupid of me, going at him like that. If i had hit him from the side i would have stopped him cold. Would have been a great open field tackle. Nobody within 10 or 12 yards of us. Only one who drifted over with the play and then i blow the tackle and he makes 20 yards. Stupid sonofabitch.

Wonder if we won that game? Dont think blowing that tackle did us any harm. Shit. Whats the difference. So i missed a fucking tackle. So what? lighting a cigarette, an expression of defiance on his face as he watched the smoke floating through the room and spiraling up from the end of the cigarette.

Why in the hell do they bother putting those goddamn vents in here. The sons of bitches dont work. You can blow smoke right at it and the goddamn smoke just hangs there. Doesnt suck a goddamn bit of it up. Aint a goddamn bit of ventilation in here. They lock you up in a 2 x 4 room and the hell with you. Lousy bunch of chickenshit bastards. Who in the hell do they think they are locking a man up on this micky mouse shit? Never heard of such asshole shit. I/ll fix their asses. I/ll blow the lid off the whole goddamn police department.

And the rotten jail system too, tossing the cigarette into the commode in the corner. I/ll showem who theyre fucking with. I/ll fix their asses. The whole, lousy, stinking bunch of them, punching his pillow into position against the wall, stretching out on the bunk, clasping his hands behind his head and closing his eyes

To the Editor and Publisher:
Gentlemen:
I would like to bring to your attention, and the public at large, a condition that exists in this State. Actually, I should say I feel that it is my duty and obligation to bring this situation—*no*—flagrant situation to the attention, and conscience, of the people.
There exists—*no. lets see*

We are living in the midst of a Police State, a creeping neo-fascism. Wherever you go, whatever you do, you are followed by the eyes of the State in the uniform and guise of the police. *yeah, thats good, that should hit them real hard.*
Naturally, the average person is unfamiliar with the many and various laws in existence. As a matter of fact there are so many laws still on the books, some hundreds of years old, that even the members of the legal profession, including the judges on the bench, cannot possibly be familiar with all of them. For example—*no*—e.g.; how many people know it is against the law to spit on the sidewalk. And this is not the only ridiculous—*no*—the only inane law still on the books. There are literally hundreds equally as asinine. And why are such laws allowed to exist? I/ll tell you why. To provide the tools (the police) of this Police State the means with which to harass its citizens at will. They know that it is impossible for any citizen, no matter how law abiding, to walk the

streets 5 minutes without breaking a law of some kind.

Of course there are those who will say that such—— archaic laws will never be enforced. Let me here and now assure you that such is not the case. The average cop is vindictive and will not hesitate to use his authority and position to avenge a real or imagined grievance. Be subjected to a cops animosity and park a few inches from the curb; or drop a cigarette butt on the sidewalk and see what happens *yeah, youre damn right they will*.

Or suppose you are falsely arrested and you are able to prove it in court. Just see what happens then. Just see how they dog your every step just waiting for you to commit some sort of infraction of the law. *yeah, the bastards*. And it can be some obscure health law written in the days of sailing ships. They will continue to hound you and lock you up (knowing, of course, you will be released) until you are ready to have a nervous breakdown. And another thing—how many times can you call your employer and tell him you will not be at work that day because you are in jail. Just how long do you think you will have your job. And even if they have no right to lock you up, how many people can afford to continually retain a lawyer.

This too the police are aware——cognizant of. They know no individual can withstand their organized pressure. They have the power of the State behind them.

It is time for the people of this State to be awakened to the real and potential danger surrounding them. If something is not done soon to retard the growth of this fascistic cancer we may all be awakened some night to the sound of axes chopping down our doors and Storm Troopers will be dragging us out of our beds.

I know this to be true as I am one of the victims of this conspiracy.

yeah, thats a good idea.

This letter was written with great danger both to me and the individual who smuggled it out. For that reason I dare not sign my name or even mention where I am incarcerated.

He reread his letter, nodding with self-satisfaction as he emphasized particular words and lines.

That should do it. That should really stir something up. Theyll probably try to shut me up somehow, but I/ll be damned if they will. I dont care what they try. They can beat me all they want, and keep me in the hole as long as they want, but I wont break. Theyll never break me. Theyll have to kill me to keep *me* quiet.

And after the letter is published they wouldnt dare kill me. With that newspaper behind me theyll be afraid to put a mark on me no less kill me. The publisher will probably insist that they release me. Even if they raise my bail *they* will be able to bail me out. Be no trouble at all with *their* money and influence. *They* can even go to the governor. Theyll go to the governor eventually anyway. Therell be an investigation by the legislature and then the entire country—hell, the whole *world*—will know. Then theyll be sorry they locked me up. Theyll regret they fucked with me. I just hope they dont drop dead from fright or some damn thing. I want them all to live to regret it.

His door clanged open and the guard told him he had visitors. Smiling smugly he adjusted and smoothed his clothes as he followed the guard to the visiting room. He was led to a stool on the prisoners side of the partition. The room was empty except for the guard, two well-dressed men, and a captain. When the guard left the captain turned to him. This is Mr. Donald Preston, publisher of the Press, and Mr.

Stacey Lowry, the attorney. They nodded to each other over the partition. As you know, it isnt regular visiting hours, but im making an exception in this case. The captain smiled at all of them before leaving.

He looked at the captains back, sneering. Exception. He knows damn well a lawyer can come anytime. He waited a few more seconds, until the door closed behind the captain, before speaking to the two men.

I see you got my letter. Yes. It was delivered by your friend last night and my editor called me immediately. I immediately called Stacey—Mr. Lowry—and made an appointment to get here the first thing this morning.

Well, I am certainly glad you got here as fast as you did. I was not sure if he had been able to smuggle the letter out or not. I was afraid he might have had to destroy it. Or even been caught with it. It is a relief to know he made it all right, smiling briefly before resuming his look of serious intent.

Has anyone indicated, in any way, that they are aware of, or suspect, the fact that you smuggled a letter from here.

He looked at Stacey Lowry, wanting to convey, in some way, the fact that he was aware of his reputation as one of the finest criminal lawyers in the country, if not *the* finest. No sir. I am certain no one even suspected. We were extremely careful. And too, I do not think the captain would have been so unconcerned.

Probably not, but you cannot be too certain about that.

I hope you did not have too much trouble reading my letter. Well, my editor did have a little trouble with a few words, where the paper had been folded, but nothing really serious. By the way, whose idea was it to use toilet tissue.

That was my idea. I did not have any paper, or money to buy any—they took all my money—and I knew they would be suspicious if I asked for paper so I used the toilet paper. They do not check on that. And my friend was able to sneak a pencil to me and I wrote it at night. The only problem was sharpening it. I had to use my teeth. I imagine you could see, by the writing, that the pencil was not too sharp, smiling.

Well, that certainly was clever of you. It is obvious that you are one of those rare individuals who can persevere under adversity with ease.

He looked at Donald Preston and started to smile, but only allowed his face to relax slightly, not wanting to have them think he was conceited. Throughout their conversation he wanted to convey the impression of quiet courage.

You say they took all your money and refused to return any of it. Yes sir. Thats right. They would not even allow you enough for cigarettes. Not only that, I could not even get a toothbrush.

A warm glow flowed through him as Stacey Lowry looked at Preston, an indignant expression on his face. Why that is utterly ridiculous.

As you can see, I was not exaggerating when I said they were harassing me. Well, we will put an end to that immediately. We have already contacted the bail bondsman and you should be out in an hour.

I certainly am glad to hear that. Being locked up alone without even a book to read or

cigarettes can get to you after a while. Well, we are going
to sit right here with you until they finish the paper work
and release you. We are not going to take any chances.

Chances?

looking quizzically at them. Yes. The captain was very
curious as to why Mr. Lowry and myself wanted to see
you.

O, I see.

He adjusted his chair so the tape recorder was out of his sight.
Donald Preston sat behind his large walnut desk, Stacey
Lowry on the side facing him. He adjusted his chair again
so he was facing the area between the two men in such a
way that they were always in his area of vision. He enjoyed
the size and richness of the room. He stretched his legs and
sipped his drink.

He spoke deliberately and distinctly, concentrating on being coherent and knowledgeable. He related his story, going into detail necessarily omitted from
his letter. When he had finished they took a brief break before starting the question-and-answer session.

It was obvious
that the immediate rapport they enjoyed was due not only
to their singleness of purpose, but also because they accepted him as a man. They were complete equals. He
realized that they understood immediately that he was not
just another crank, or simply paranoid, but a man wronged
by the authorities. It was also evident that they understood
that he was not only fighting for his own rights and vindica-
tion, but for that of others who have been, are, and will be
abused by this same authority if something is not done to
check its malignant growth immediately. It was good to

know that they understood these things and realized the type of man he was.

He nodded as Donald Preston freshened his drink. You know, the more we discuss this matter the more mystified I am that an individual such as you should find himself in such a—shall we say—unusual situation. What I mean is it seems so incongruous that a man of your breeding—you are obviously cultured and, I might hasten to add, a gentleman—should find himself behind bars.

He looked at the publisher, and Stacey Lowry, as he leaned slightly forward in his chair. Well, frankly, so am I. It is all so nightmarish that I do not fully understand it. Their motivation that is. One minute I was free and the next incarcerated. At first I thought perhaps it was a case of mistaken identity or some such thing. Then, after I went through the ordeal of interrogation and being booked, I started becoming paranoid. It seemed as if they had simply, and arbitrarily, decided to subject me to these flagrant indignities for no other reason than that I was there—like the mountain and the mountain climber. He smiled as they recognized the appropriateness of the analogy. It was not until I spoke to some of the other inmates, and observed what was happening, that I realized that this was simply an extension and manifestation of a higher, unseen and unheard, authority. Well, I guess I should say unheard except through the lower echelon.

That manifestation, as you so aptly put it, is something we have been combating—or at least attempting to—for years. But, unfortunately, most people think that police brutality is autonomous, that it is simply an error of overzealousness, or corruption by association with criminals, on the part of a few officers. They just dont seem to be cognizant of the real basis of this brutality. We have tried, Donald and myself, to make the public aware of what the real causes are and, of course, their ultimate and logical conclusion. But, of course, I do not have to tell you this. You have already outlined the genealogy of this structure clearly and succinctly.

The world-renowned criminal lawyer smiled at him and he allowed a slight smile to soften the gravity of his expression as he silently accepted the compliment.

True.

True. Stacey has been lecturing for years on this selfsame subject and I have tried, from time to time, to awaken the public to the inherent dangers in this situation through editorials, but for the most part our words, or perhaps I should say, pleas, have fallen on deaf ears.

Well, the grave expression once again on his face, I do not know if its deafness or smugness. The it-cant-happen-here attitude. The old ostrich-in-the-sand routine.

Precisely. Thats why your letter was of such great interest and importance to us. Now we have something tangible to work with.

He looked at Stacey quizzically. I am not certain I understand.

It is this way. We have never had an individual, such as yourself, who was capable of presenting the case to the public in an intelligent and coherent manner, who had personally been subjected to this inherent corruption. I have met many men who have suffered unmercifully from this same evil, but there was always something to discredit them in the eyes of the public. Naturally most of them had criminal records, as these are the types of individuals the police love to prey on, and the public either discredits their testimony on the basis of this record, or simply says it serves them right, what can people like that expect. They do not seem to realize that it could just as easily happen to them.

How well I know, a broad smile on his face.

Precisely, both men returning his smile. And too, most of these men are incapable of presenting the situation clearly as they do not understand all the ramifications themselves. And even if they did, they are so pressured by the authorities that they are afraid to pursue an investigation to its logical conclusion for fear of being found dead in an alley. And frankly, I do not doubt that it can, and does, happen.

I know perfectly well that it can. And does. I have heard stories that would frighten anyone, emphasizing his words with his most stern expression. But surely there must have been others, like myself, who have been victimized by the system, in quotes.

Yes, of course, endless numbers of people have found themselves in the same situation you are in now, but even if they do come forward to protest they are only interested in voicing their own grievances, or, in some cases, they want to sue the state and get what they can. In any event, whatever their reasons may be, they are usually selfish—or perhaps I should say that they just do not seem to understand the overall picture. They just do not seem to be capable of realizing that this corruption perpetuates itself, and grows larger and larger each day, and that it not only constitutes a constant and continuing threat to them, but to their children and their childrens children. I guess they simply lack vision.

And even if we are successful in explaining the situation to them, and they understand it, they are afraid, for any one of many reasons, to attempt to destroy this cancer. They are afraid of recriminations and retaliations and feel they should leave well enough alone. In most cases they would rather move to another part of the country and start over again rather than try to do something about the problem.

I am certain you understand that my simply publishing your letter would be of no value whatsoever. It must be followed up vigorously. If not, it will just be another instance of a few people being temporarily—or perhaps I should say momentarily—(he nodded his agreement to the correction) outraged and then it will be forgotten as the many worries and responsibilities of everyday life push this from their minds.

Well, what exactly did you have in mind. I am certain you realize that I will cooperate in any way I can. There is just about nothing I will not do to help remedy this situation.

Well, Stacey and I have discussed that very thing and we were certain, after reading your letter, that you were the individual we have been looking for to assist us.

You see, we want to mount an all-out campaign, using your experience as a springboard. I—we—believe, with you in the foreground, that the results will be both beneficial and efficacious.

What we intend to do is coordinate our efforts. Stacey will speak before professional and civic groups—or any other group that will listen to me—and I will continue a daily barrage in the paper. We will dig out all our old files: statements, letters, depositions, photographs, rumors, anything and everything that will arouse the public and force a legislative investigation. We are willing to use any and every tool available, no matter how devious, to bring this evil to the attention of the public, and eventually have something done to rectify this situation. We will not stop until an aroused public forces the legislature to act.

Are you certain this can be done. I mean these very men, the politicians from the top to the bottom, are the very men who helped create this situation. And too, they are very jealous of their power. They will not want to relinquish one iota of their authority. And I am certain they are not overly sensitive to the injustices heaped upon an unsuspecting public.

That, of course, is quite true. But—and this is *the* but—they are sensitive to the reactions and desires of their constituents. They want to stay in office and will do anything to do so.

As soon as there is enough public reaction you just see how fast someone gets up in the capital and demands an investigation. To begin with, the opposition party, no matter which party it may happen to be, will use anything to attack the incumbent party—and do not forget that this is an election year. And, relative to that, of course, precipitating such an investigation will be good publicity for anyone running for re-election, regardless of what party he belongs to. And all this is in addition to the fact that politicians love to keep their names before the public especially in the role of crusader and protector of the public welfare. They all have visions of living in the governors mansion or going to Washington. And do not forget, our government, on all levels, is run by committee chairmen, and they will start an investigation over the size of a piece of penny bubble gum. Especially if there is the possibility of a protracted investigation with daily press and t.v. coverage.

And thats another thing. The campaign I referred to is to be a comprehensive one. Not just speeches by Stacey and editorials by me, but we intend to use television, mass-circulation magazines, interviews, personal appearances by any and all of us, and, if necessary, we will print and distribute pamphlets.

He shook his head and smiled at the two men. I must admit that I am a bit overwhelmed by all this. Of course I had hoped that something like this would happen, but I never dreamed it would become an actuality so fast. I am extremely grateful to you gentlemen for all this.

On the contrary. It is us who are grateful and obligated to you. You have enabled us to put into action a campaign that we have dreamed of for years. You are the one who is making all this possible.

With his eyes still closed, and a look of glowing satisfaction on his face, he reviewed the scenes and dialogue and found nothing that needed changing or improving. With their backing he would really show them. He would really shake the shit out of them.

And that goddamn Smith. *Public defender*. What the hell does he care. Probably trying to get a job in the d.a./s office anyway. All they want you to do is plead guilty. Yeah, they tell you if youre not guilty say so. But they do everything they can to get you to plead guilty. *Public defender*. ha. *Defender*. My *ass* defender. Couldnt even defend that, the rotten a.k./s. Afraid to bug the judge because they might get in front of him when they have a private practice. Just trying to make friends with every son of a bitch in court except their client. *Client?* Aint that a crock of shit. Just another bum to them. Dont even want to sit too close to you. Youre just a springboard to a jr. partnership anyway. A deaf mute could do a better job. With somebody like Stacey Lowry defending me I/d be on the streets right now. All it takes is money. And influence. And if you got the money you got the influence. You got that and you go free. Shit. Got the money and you dont even have to go to trial. They wouldn't bother taking a mickey mouse case like this to court if they knew I had a good lawyer. But as soon as they see you have to use a goddamn public defender they want to send you away for life. Just want to pad the record. Make it look good. Boy, look at all the convictions he has. He must be good. We/ll have to run him for d.a. next election, and then governor. And after that who knows. . . . Yeah, who knows. Ya wouldnt even make a good dog catcher ya rotten son of a bitch. They dont care who they destroy. Just all in a days work. Whats the difference who they do in as long as it helps their career. Nothing but a bunch of goddamn assassins. And they have the nerve to call other people leeches sucking the blood of society, or weeds that should be plucked out and destroyed. Where in the hell do they get the nerve to send a man to the gas chamber. Theyre no better than a professional assassin. They both kill for money. The only difference is that the pro only kills occasionally, but these bastards destroy as many lives as possible every day. Only they do it legally. At least the professional killer takes his chances. These bastards do it with immunity. Wearing their silk suits and hiding behind the courts and law books. And if you say anything they shrug their shoulders and tell you they didnt do anything wrong. They were just doing their job. They destroy and kill hundreds— thousands—every year, and theyre patted on the back. Good job. Thats the way herkimer. Great record you got there boy. Some stupid son of a bitch kills somebody and everybody wants to kill him. Hes an animal. The other ones a brilliant prosecutor. And what happens if someone is proven

innocent of a crime. Are they happy because an innocent
man was not unjustly convicted. O, no. You bet your sweet
ass theyre not. Doesn't make any difference to them that the
man was innocent. Krist no. The only thing that counts is
that they lost a case. Probably go home and beat up the
wife and kids. And then think of what they should have
done to get a conviction. So what if hes innocent. Cant mar
their wonderful record by having an innocent man going
free. Never get to the governors mansion that way. And
what do those fucking p.d./s do. Nothing. Just keep their
goddamn noses stuck up the judges ass. They dont even
bother to close their eyes. They dont have to. They just
make like the whole thing doesn't exist. They dont even
ignore it. They don't have to. aaaaaaaaaahhhhhh shit! The
hell with the whole goddamn bunch of them. Wipe out the
whole damn bunch of them. The whole rotten system. By
the time I'm finished with them everyone will know how
rotten the system is. I/ll beat them at their own game. Then
theyll sweat.

   Wiping the palms of his hands on his legs then
stretching out on the bunk. He put his hands behind his
head and stared at the door and unconsciously flexed his
leg muscles in time with the beating of his heart. For many
seconds his concentration was intense as he glared at the
locked door

                  then he
breathed deeply and adjusted himself on the bunk until he
was looking at the ceiling. He listened to his heart beating
for a moment, then closed his eyes.

He stood as the charges were read, recognizing a few of the
words, but for the most part it could have been a foreign
language: to wit; therefore; blablablabla. He stood hearing,

but not listening. Only the sound registered. He knew he was standing there and that it wasn't a dream, but that was about all he knew. Eventually the judge asked him how he pleaded and he simply answered not guilty. He had been only vaguely aware of the p.d. standing beside him until he told him to sit down. Sliding a piece of paper and a pencil in front of him he told him to write down any questions that came to mind, that he didn't want him speaking to him while witnesses were giving testimony, that he couldn't listen to them, the d.a. and him at the same time. He accepted the paper and pencil silently and blankly. He knew this was the man who was going to defend him, some sort of someone whose name he didn't know, someone he had never seen before, someone who had passed him a piece of paper and a pencil, spoken a few words then ignored him completely as he glanced at papers. And he just sat as his defense counsel looked at papers and spoke, from time to time, to the d.a. He knew that whoever it was sitting beside him had already sold him out, so he leaned forward, pencil in hand, as the first witness was called.

He wanted to listen intently and absorb every word, every gesture. He held his pencil poised, ready to take notes, and when his attorney failed to notice discrepancies in testimony he would make note of them and provide the ammunition necessary to destroy the prosecutions case.

The first witnesses were the arresting officers and, from time to time, he would start to make a note, but he couldnt find the proper words to define exactly what was going through his head. His frustration increased as the testimony proceeded and he leaned further and further back in his chair, and soon the pencil was lying on the piece of paper. He listened to stipulations being made and agreed to for purposes of the preliminary hearing and then the judge would say so stipulated and it would be entered in the record. And then they started waiving. This was waived and noted; that was waived and noted. When they finished the stipulating and waiving the p.d. asked for a dismissal of the case on various grounds, citing various cases and decisions and the prosecuting attorney asked that they not be and cited cases and decisions. There was a brief recess while the judge retired to chambers to decide on the motions for dismissal.

When the judge returned he spoke briefly to the attorneys, referring to their citations, then quoted a few himself before denying the motion for dismissal. Then there were questions and answers and a lot of other dumb shit and his goddamn lawyer just sat on his ass letting everything slide by, never once doing a fucking thing for him. Not once did the son of a bitch try. It was bullshit. The whole fucking thing was nothing but a bunch of bullshit.

He had no idea how long he sat in that fucking courtroom, but time and the bullshit were endless. Finally the bullshit ended and he was led from the courtroom. Then, eventually, he was back in his cell.

He sat on the edge of the bunk almost apathetically as the door clanged shut behind him. His eyes burned and felt heavy. They ached from the enormous weight that seemed to be pressing on their lids. The light seemed to scrape them. Yet there was energy in his body. It wanted to move. It craved some sort of action. It was waiting to be directed against something. . . . . . . .someone. It wanted to leap out and away from the hollow feeling deep inside that seemed to come from the burning and aching eyes, the weighted and drooping lids. His head lowered itself to the pillow, and his legs rolled out on the bunk. His eyes fell closed and an arm covered his eyes.

He tried thinking about the day but everything was confused. He knew he should have grabbed the guard when he opened the door this morning and smashed his head against the wall and opened all the cells and let everyone run mad and kill every uniformed prick they saw, but the pressure on his eyes would not allow him. He tried to grab the guard around the neck and snap his spine, but when he moved his arms they seemed to float with imperceptible slowness and years and years later they were still miles away from his neck. He could see himself watching his floating arms and he screamed at them to hurry, hurry, get him, and he twisted and knotted his body trying to urge the arms to move faster, but they continued to float, seeming to be suspended in a weightless space. Then after a passage of endless time, he felt a tingle in his hand, and his arm slid from his face, and the darkness lightened slightly and he squeezed his eyes open and became aware that his hand had fallen asleep and he was trying to shake it awake. He blinked rapidly as his vision was filled with the overhead light. His legs swung over the side of the bunk and his body raised itself to a sitting position. He sat for several moments, rubbing his face with his hand, then rose and went to the sink and splashed cold water on his face. He dried it then looked in the mirror, examining the blemish on his cheek. It seemed a little larger, more tender, a little redder. He examined it closely, touching it tentatively at first, then more firmly until he felt the needle-like pain. He removed his finger, continued to stare at the inflamed blotch, then went back to his bunk.

He sat on the edge of the bunk wondering, at first, if he had slept, then when he realized that he must have, he wondered how long. O well, it didnt make any difference. Time was all the same. 3 meals a day and an occasional shower. The time of day was meaningless. And night. Lights always on so you never know. Except that its noisier during the day. All the same. No difference.

He leaned against the wall and put his feet on the edge of the bunk. It seemed like just a short time ago that he was awakened to go to court, yet he knew it had been about 5/30 and that he didn't get back to his cell until after 7/30. 14 hours. Fourteen long hours, yet he could remember very little of it. He had stood and waited; sat and waited; paced and waited with time seeming to be endless, yet now it seemed like such a short time ago that the guard awakened him and threw him a set of blues and said, court time.

He reviewed the day, thinking of specific incidents, trying to remember all the details, every word said, reliving every gesture, yet he could review it all in minutes, yet those minutes added up to 14 hours. He sat on the bench for a while, then they went down on the elevator to the holding tanks. Then he waited for his clothes in one tank, then waited to be cuffed to the chain in another tank, and then they got on the bus and went to the courthouse and went to another holding tank and were unchained and then to the courtroom, then back to the holding tank, then back on the chain and on the bus and back to the jail and another series of holding tanks until eventually he was back in his cell. And it added up to 14 hours. At the time endless and now a matter of minutes.

He knew he had been in the court-room a long time because the other guys asked him why he was there so long when he got back to the holding tank under the courtroom, yet, now, it seemed like minutes. All that talk. All that stipulating and waiving. All the stupid questions and answers. Only minutes. Hours of bullshit that end up being minutes. It was like a church ritual, or some fucking thing. Nobody knew what the ritual was about, or cared, they were only interested in keeping it going. Thats all. Keep it going. Like a perpetual-motion machine. Just give it a push and it keeps going on and on and on

until

you stop the sonofabitch. Thats all you have to do. Just stop it. Thats what I should have done. Just stuck my hand out and stopped all the bullshit. Just tell them where its really at. Shove all their words and ritual right down their fucking throats. Show them up for the assholes they are. I should have just shoved that stupid p.d. out of the way and took over myself, the dumb bastard. The do-nothing sonofabitch. Just twist their ritual around and shove it up their asses.

Screw

it. Its not important anyway. Just a preliminary hearing. I/ll get them the next time. Theyre not going to screw me around with their rules. Itll be different the next time. When it really counts. They cant play their games with me.

BANG, bang. I gotya. Ya did not. Ya missed. Youre a liar. I gotya right between the eyes,

smiling, chuckling aloud, stretching out on the bunk, running through the park, slapping the side of your leg with your hand, clucking your tongue against the roof of your mouth, horse and rider all in one. Getting shot on top of the hill and rolling down then crawling behind a tree or bush and shooting the dirty redskin, or owl-hoot or sheriff or whoever else was chasing you. Hiding behind the tree or bush and using the rifle you slipped from the saddle holster as you slipped from your horse and shooting at your pursuer and missing an occasional shot and the bullet kachanging off a rock and the other rider slides from his horse and returns the fire and soon everyone is crawling, running, hiding, shooting. And every day, before the game started everyone yelled Im a bad guy—Im a good guy, and, somehow, in a matter of seconds there were two sides and they were running, riding and shooting. And the whine of bullets followed the leg-slapping, tongue-clicking, galloping of the horses as they pounded over the grass, in between and around bushes and trees, suddenly leaping over gopher holes or logs, suddenly yanking on the reins to avoid the strike of a rattler and eventually stretching out on the grass beside a small stream or water hole and looking up at the clear sky as the horse quenches his thirst, and the smell of grass was sweet as horse and rider renewed their strength to continue the chase or retreat.

And those battles on 72nd street. Seemed like there were hundreds of kids packed in the street with guns made of the corner edge of an orange crate, the joint of the 2 pieces cut at an angle and a rubber band stretched from end to end, and square pieces of cardboard shot at each other as everybody ran, screamed, and charged or attacked pushing a scooter made from an old skate, a 2 × 4, and an orange crate. And old Mrs. McDermott. She thought it was real and called the cops and when they came everyone ran screaming like a madman.

They sure were some great battles. Days were spent making the guns, cutting every piece of cardboard that could be found, and then the street was packed with kids. And the battle would go on and on, and when you ran out of ammunition you just picked up what you needed from the street. There was cardboard all over. From curb to curb, hahahahahahahaha. The street cleaners sure must have hated it. Those old italian guys with their little hand trucks and brooms and shovels. But they probably didnt mind sweeping up the cardboard as much as they did the dog shit and horse manure. But old Mr. Leone used to help them. He used to come out with his shovel and pail and select only the best pieces of manure. But he always waited until the birds had eaten what they wanted. Sometimes he/d stand there for an hour waiting until the birds had finished, then he/d inspect the pile, select the choicest lumps and carefully put them in the pail. He sure did have a nice front yard, but it sure did stink sometimes, especially in the summer. Everybody said he had a real great garden in the back. Mostly tomatoes. But who knows. No one ever saw it. Anyway, the rosebush in front was nice. Smelled so good you couldnt smell the manure in springtime. That was always a good time. But June sure was long. Waiting for school to be over. It seemed like years before it was time to sing, no more pencils, no more books, no more teachers dirty looks. And then home to mother to show her the report card and tell her you got promoted. And she was always happy to see good marks, but then she wanted to know why the D in effort and D in conduct. And there was never an answer. Youre such a good boy. Why cant you get A in effort and conduct, the hurt look on her face. And you try shrugging and mumbling the question away, but it doesn't work. And you get all knotted up and sick to your stomach and you feel hotter and hotter and theres nothing to say. Not a goddamn thing to say. Nothing that anyone would understand. You talk on line, or laugh in the classroom and some asshole teacher tells you to write a demerit slip, and you whisper again, or chuckle and the dumb bitch hands you another one and another one and then youre supposed to explain why those assholes give you D in effort and D in conduct. As if it was your fault or something.

Fuckit. Who gives a shit. The dried-up old douche bags. Why in the hell do they teach school if they hate kids so much. Stop that giggling. Dont you know youre disrupting the class. Shit. They just cant stand to see people laugh. They got their rules and a sour face and thats it. They dont want to know anything. If you dont do it their way theyll screw you up. Too bad we couldnt get them in the middle of one of those battles. And get them with one of the Baileys guns. Or slingshots.

Yeah. . . . . .they were good slingshots. It was the rubber bands. Their old man made them out of the inner tubes of tires. They were really powerful slingshots. And they made their ammunition out of old pieces of oilcloth and it hurt like hell when you got hit with one of them. Really was dirty fighting. John killed a cat with a slingshot once. Put a big hunk of steel in it and hit the cat right in the head. Really smashed it. But those battles were great. The screaming, the running, the clogged streets and stalled traffic.

But cops and robbers was a good game. Even when it was raining and you had to stay in the house. Especially that apartment on third avenue. It was on the fourth floor and was perfect for shooting it out with the cops,

kneeling beside the open window. Pow. Pow. He was Dillinger. Or maybe Pretty Boy Floyd. Pow. Pow. The street was filled with cops—behind buildings, cars, lampposts, in the doorways of buildings. And the rain flooded the streets and splashed off his window sill onto his face. They yelled at him to give himself up. Youll never get me alive copper, pow. Pow. He knew they had him surrounded, that there were hundreds of cops out there just waiting to riddle him with bullets, but he wasnt going to give up. He/d fight to the death. And if they got him he was going to take a few of them with him. Yeah, they might getim, but he wasnt going alone. He ducked below the window as the sashing was splintered with bullets of all kinds: pistol, rifle and machine gun. He twitched his lips and flipped his cigarette out the window, cursing the lousy coppers. He crouched against the wall, looking at the bullet riddled walls, snarling. When the shooting stopped he slowly raised his head and once more emptied his gun at the cops.

Then it happened. He took a slug in the shoulder and fell on his back, still holding his gun.

His mother jerked up in bed in the next room. Whats wrong son, scrambling out of bed and wrapping her bathrobe around her. He jerked around, startled by the sudden voice, and stared at his mother who struggled with the robe as she ran to her sons side. The fear in his

mothers voice and the panic of her movements made it
impossible to answer. He was fascinated by the size of her
breasts. He had never realized they were so large. When
her body turned they seemed to take many minutes to
follow. He never realized that she had large, dark nipples.
Even after they were covered he could see them sticking
in the robe, and could see their movement as his mother
knelt beside him and put her arms around him. What is it
son? Whats wrong? Nothin. Nothins wrong. I was just playing. She hugged him and she felt unusually soft. He never
remembered his mother feeling so soft. His mother held his
face in her hands, smiled, and kissed him on the forehead
before getting up and going back to the bedroom to get
dressed. He started to continue the game, but decided
against it and instead he leaned against the window sill
and watched the rain splash on the street and on the tops
of cars.

Yeah, the goddamn rain. Always coming at the wrong time.
You plan on doing something, or going somewhere and it
rains. Every goddamn time. Like the fourth of July they let
me buy fireworks and it fucking drizzles all day. What a
bunch of shit. One fucking day out of the whole fucking
year and it has to rain. Probably the only time it ever rained
on the fourth. The only time I can remember. Just my fucking luck. Had to worry about keeping the punk dry so it
wouldnt go out so I could light the firecrackers. Wouldnt
have been so bad if it had rained like a bastard for a while
and then cleared up. No, it had to drizzle all day. And of
course the next day was nice. The goddamn sun shined
like a sonofabitch all day.
                        Fucking shit, sitting on the edge
of the bed, his muscles tensed and teeth clenched, staring

in front of him and shaking his head. Fuck it, fuck the whole
rotten mess, jerking up and wishing to krist there was something or someone to smash. He stood in front of the mirror
and stared at his reflection for a moment, his arms half-
raised, then leaned closer and looked at the red spot on his
cheek. He jabbed at it with his fingers, but the sonofabitch just hurt. Nothing happened. Nothing came out of it.
It didnt get bigger. It didnt get smaller. It just hurt.

He
turned around and looked at the cell just waiting for it to
say something. Anything. Go ahead you sonofabitch, say
something and I/ll smash your fucking face in. I/ll crush
your fucking head. He looked a wall right in the eye and
defied it to make a move. Just one single move. Or say a
word and he/d tear it apart. He/d pulverize the cement
into powder. If only there was a face to scream into. A face
that would say something and he could take the words and
shove them down the faces throat. Or beat his fucking
breast, or kick the fucking door

o shit, staring at
the wall

shit!
He sat on the edge of the bed and let his body slowly
relax and shook his head in disgust. It was a bitch. A goddamn bitch. He knew where he was. Youre fucking well
right he did. There was no bullshit about that. He was right
where he was. And so was that wall. And that one. And
the door and the ceiling and the floor and the bars on the
window and the commode in the corner and the sink on the
wall and the goddamn pimple on his cheek. And the rats ass
bunk he was sitting on. Real. All of them. Yeah, he knew
where he was. Just as sure as krist made little apples he
knew where he was. But if only he could dream the sonofa-

bitch away. Just close your eyes and dream it away. Not even lay down or anything else. Just close your eyes and let the bastard disappear. Open your eyes and walk through the fucking door. Open or closed just walk right the fuck through it. Thats all. Bye, bye baby.

O fuck, stretching out on the bed and covering his eyes with an arm. I wish theyd turn the lights off for a while. Just for 5 fucking minutes. Thats all. Just 5 minutes so maybe you could get some rest.

Rest? Aint that a fucking joke. Theyd rather die than let you get any rest. Just a little darkness. Thats all. Just a little darkness. Is that so much to ask for. Theyd even save money if theyd turn off the lights. Just complete darkness so you cant see a thing. No corners. No walls. No window. No nothing. Just a big black nothing. Thats all. And they act like youre asking for the world. And all I want is a big, black nothing. And I wont even whistle. But they love the light. Krist how they love it. Theyll give you every fucking shade of gray in the world, but just dont ask for black. No shadows. Have to have a little light in those corners. Just has to be. Just enough so you cant rest. Thats the whole idea. Just enough so you cant rest. They dont want you to lose any time. Dont want you to slip through a few hours by sleeping—the cell door clanged open—the rotten motherfuckers.

He got up and went to the mess hall. It was bright. The trays were bright and shiny. He leaned against the wall with the others, slowly moving an inch or so every now and then. And everything was dull. The talk. The food. The people. Dull. All dull. When he finished he went back to his cell, threw some water on his face, dried it, then sat on the edge of the bed waiting for the door to be locked.

He didnt know what he was thinking, if anything, but he could feel something moving around inside him. He could feel his arms and legs getting tingly. He wished ta krist theyd hurry up and lock his door. Theyre always right on your ass making sure you dont go this way, or look that way, and now they take their own sweet time about closing his door. What in the hell is taking them so long. The goddamn thing should be locked by now. For krists sake. How fucking long do you have to sit around waiting for some dumb sonofabitch to lock your door. The meal was over hours ago for krists sake. If the sonofabitch was locked and you wanted it open they damn sure would keep it locked. But now, all of a sudden, they wont lock the sonofabitch. Anything to break your balls, the *rotten* motherfuckers, his fists and jaw clenched, getting tighter and tighter. Krist, no matter *what* you ask them to do they wont do it. Doesnt make a *fucking* bit of difference what it is, they wont do it if—the door clanged shut.

He stared at it for a moment,

then swung his right arm around and smashed the pillow. He growled as he grabbed it with his left hand and pounded it with his right again and again and again and again then put both his hands around its throat and squeezed and twisted as his voice growled in his throat and his stomach knotted. Then he flung it against the wall and leaped after it and punched it back to the bed and pinned it with his left hand around its throat against the mattress and pounded and pounded the face into a pulp then raised it above his head and slammed it against the wall and punched it against another wall but his fists kept sinking into his pillow, meeting no resistance, so he pinned it again to the mattress and pounded and pounded hearing his fist thud and thud and thud over and over and over again and again into his pillow.

Then he stopped and looked at it with disgust and flipped it to the other end of the bed with the back of his hand. He was panting, but his stomach and chest were loosening. The bastards. The rotten, fucking bastards. His breathing slowed and he reached down and grabbed his pillow, jammed it into a ball and stuck it behind his head and stretched out on the bed. He let his eyes close when they wanted to and then he put his arm over his eyes. He squirmed his head into his balled pillow, while the deepening gray soothed his eyes. He rested.

He was sitting in the courtroom with Stacey Lowry. He was well-dressed and confident. When his case was called he followed his attorney to the counsel table. He stood erect and calm as the charges were read, pleaded not guilty, then sat and listened as the preliminary hearing proceeded. The opening formalities flowed smoothly and quickly. When the prosecution finished questioning the first witness, one of the arresting officers, Stacey Lowry rose and walked halfway to the witness stand. He only questioned the officer for a few minutes, his voice smooth and moderate at all times. When the witness had been dismissed he addressed the court and asked for a dismissal of the charges, citing the State v Rubens (1958; 173,20.5). The motion was granted and he followed his attorney from the courtroom.

They were joined by Donald Preston in the corridor and they shook each others hand. Preston put his arm around his shoulder and asked him how it felt to be free. Frankly, its a little bit bewildering. It all happened so fast. Its hard to believe its all over.

They sat at a rear table in a quiet and dignified restaurant. It was a small room off the main dining room and the walls were oak paneled. The linen was white and sunlight filtered through stained-glass windows. He was naturally excited, yet had no trouble retaining his composure. When their cocktails were served they toasted their success and their forthcoming campaign. He smiled and said he would drink to that and they all laughed. Then Preston congratulated him on his courage, and his responsive smile was filled with humility.

As they sat in Prestons impressive office he tinkled the ice in his drink from time to time. He felt completely at ease and energetically discussed the forthcoming campaign. He was most anxious to hear their plans and to offer his suggestions. Now that the legal formalities were over his mind was formulating ideas with concrete clarity.

As I mentioned previously, one of my reporters, one of the best, was at the hearing and is writing a report of it. When he is finished he will come up here and interview you. It wont be too long, just long enough to enable him to give our readers your thoughts and reactions. The actual reportage will appear in tomorrows paper and the interview will be in the Sunday Supplement. As I say, it wont be too long, just 2 or 3 pages. You see, we do not want to hit the public with everything at once. If we do they will tire of it too quickly (he nodded in agreement) and we will lose their enthusiasm. In between there will be a statement by me—a manifesto if you will—explaining the campaign and its purpose. This naturally will be followed up at least 2 or 3 times a week with something new, and hard-hitting, on the subject. In that way it will always be before the publics eye.

And, in the interim, I will be writing articles for the law journal and making as many addresses as possible to civic and professional organizations.

That sounds very good. Really marvelous. There is one thing, however, that I would very much like to mention. He paused for a second, then leaned forward in his chair. I think we should make this campaign against all forms of authoritative despotism. What I mean is, there are all forms of abuses of authority—police, politicians, unions, bankers, schools, prisons—and god knows how many others. Also, it seems to me, if you continue a campaign too long people will become immune to it, but with the proper lapse of time between them—and when other news is scarce—you can always go into another aspect of the campaign and expose any one of the authoritative evils in the world.

It was obvious from the manner in which they agreed with him that they not only appreciated his suggestion, but were aware of the fact that it was not offered because of any personal vindictiveness.

The reporter sat across from him, the microphone for the portable tape recorder between them.

Q. First, let me ask you how it feels to be free once more?

A. Fine (smiling) just fine. And I cannot thank Messrs. Preston and Lowry enough for helping me.

Q. Just how did you manage to get in touch with them?

A. Well (leaning back in his chair slightly, a thoughtful look on his face, not wanting to be too mysterious, but wanting the reporter to understand that this was a serious question, and not one to be answered without due deliberation. When he noticed, by the expression on his face, that the interviewer was aware that he was not just acting a part, but that this was an extremely serious and delicate question, he leaned forward) I am afraid I cannot go into detail as to how I was able to get in touch with these gentlemen. However, I can say that I did manage to get in contact with the paper and that is how Messrs. Preston and Lowry became involved.

Q. What, exactly, made you feel it was necessary to contact the paper?

A. Because I was unjustly arrested and detained. Actually, as Mr. Lowry proved today, I was not only unjustly arrested, but illegally.

Q. Why didnt you contact a lawyer or a friend?

A. Well, you see, I do not know anyone in this city. I decided to spend the summer driving around the country and I had just gotten here the day I was arrested. I had gotten in late that morning after driving all night, and checked into the first hotel I noticed. I realize, now, that it is far from the best in town, but I was too tired to look around so I simply stopped at the first one I saw. I washed, had something to eat, then slept. When I awakened I dressed and decided to walk around until I found a good restaurant. When I did I had a leisurely meal, then went to a late movie. When I got out I decided to see what the city looked like at night. I walked along the streets looking—you know, more or less like a tourist I guess—and because I slept during the day I was not tired and was unaware of the time. Eventually I became conscious of the fact that I was almost the only one walking the streets. I was a little surprised to find myself almost alone, except for an occasional person passing by—as I said, I had more or less lost track of time—but I continued to stroll along at a leisurely pace. Then I realized that I did not know exactly where I was so I started looking at street signs and trying to orient myself with some sort of landmark.

Q. In other words you had strayed from a familiar part of the city to one that was unfamiliar?

A. Precisely. I did not know where my hotel was with respect to where I was at that particular moment. I was standing on a street corner looking around and trying to figure out which way I should go when a patrol car stopped in front of me and the next thing I knew I was arrested.

Q. What were the charges?

A. Suspicion. I do not know of what, but they said I was acting suspiciously. I tried to explain, and even showed them my drivers license and other identification, but they still locked me up.

He was 12, or maybe 13. He and 2 friends were shooting crap under a light in the park. It was a cool evening and they were completely involved in the game and in keeping their hands warm. There was 2¢ on the ground and he was shooting for a point. As he was reaching for the dice someone yelled, cop, and they ran. He grabbed for the 2¢ and before he could get up and start running a cop came out of the bushes behind him and hit him across the reaching hand with his club. He ran, never knowing what the cop looked like. Not even feeling the pain until an hour later. The cop didnt pursue them and a block away he met his friends and they walked the few blocks home together. They asked him about his hand. He

*said it was all right, but it was starting to burn. When he
had been home in the warmth of the house for a while,
the pain started to increase. He was afraid to tell his parents
as they would want to know why he had been hit and he
was afraid to tell them what he had been doing. In the
middle of the night the pain became acute. He moaned in
his sleep and his mother came into his room to wake him
and ask what was wrong. He told her he had fallen while
playing a game and had hurt his hand. Early the next
morning they went to the hospital and the hand was
x-rayed. Three bones were so sharply broken it looked like
a razor cut. He had been hit so hard there wasnt a trace
of splintering. The break didnt even need to be set or put
in a cast. It was that clean a break. A small roll of gauze
was put in his palm and the hand was wrapped. It was
that simple.*

In retrospect I guess it is difficult to understand. Perhaps I was naive, but at first I did not take them seriously. I mean I was annoyed, naturally, but I never
believed for a moment that they would actually take
me to a police station—*in handcuffs.*

Q. What happened then?

A. Well, to be perfectly honest, it is a haze of confusion
until I was locked in that room. All I can remember
is sitting in one room for hours, then another, and
another and being fingerprinted and having my picture
taken and being asked endless questions. I was in a
state of utter and complete confusion. It all seemed
so unreal somehow.

Q. Were you subjected to any form of physical punishment?

A. Well, in a way that is hard to answer. What I mean

is they did not beat me or actually threaten to—that is verbally—but the way some of them walk around and look at you, as if you are some kind of animal or something and they would like nothing better than to get you alone in a locked room. . . . . . .well, under those conditions you always feel threatened. But to be more specific, no, I was never actually threatened with bodily harm.

The pain in his hand started to subside after it had been wrapped, but he was afraid to tell his mother that it felt better. When they had been home from the hospital a short time she asked what had happened. I dont know. We were just playing and I hit it and it broke I guess. But how could you have hit it so hard, son. I told you, I dont know. All I know is that we were playing and it hit something. Nobody did it. It just happened. But I didnt ask you if anyone hit you, I only —yeah, yeah, I know. But thats what you were thinking. That somebody hit me because I did something. But I— jesus krist mom, cant you leave me alone. It hurts bad enough without you bugging me about it.

Q. Were you subjected to any other kind of duress?
A. Yes. Most definitely. In addition to the hostility of their looks—perhaps sadism is a better word—there are many other ways in which a man can be humiliated. Or should I say subjected to inhuman punishment?
Q. What, specifically, do you mean?
A. Well. . .let me put it this way. After I was finally booked, sent upstairs to be interviewed by the medical depart-

ment—if thats the proper phrase—and x-rayed, they
sent me to the—what is their phrase again. . .o yes,
the t.b. suspect ward.

Q. Why there?

A. I am not really certain. They said I had a spot on my
lung. I told them that I had a slight touch of pleurisy
many years previously and that it was just a scar from
it. But they said they had to check it out. So I literally
shrugged. I had no idea I was going to be put in
solitary.

Q. They put you in solitary?

A. Well, no, not exactly. That is, it was not what the others
refer to as the hole. But I was locked in a 9 x 6 cell
in the t. b. suspect section of the jail.

Q. That sounds very uncomfortable.

A. To say the least (smiling) Its quite an experience to be
locked up all by yourself in any size room, no less a
little cell. But I managed to survive (looking around
the room at the others) and here I am.

He slowly opened his eyes
and looked at the ceiling, still seeing the look of complete
and absolute approval on the faces of Donald Preston and
Stacey Lowry. He swung his body up and around and sat
on the edge of the bed nodding his head slightly from time
to time and feeling contented.

He got up and went to the sink. He
looked in the mirror and stretched the skin around the
pimple. He squeezed it gently then touched it with the
tip of a finger. It seemed to be a little more tender than
the last time he touched it. But it still wasnt ready. He
went back to the bed. He stared at the wall creating images

with the cracks. He lay on his back and shielded his eyes from the light with his arm.

He was indignant when the cops put him in the car and demanded to be allowed to call his attorney as soon as they arrived at the police station. He called Stacey and told him what had happened and then refused to say a word until Stacey arrived. They conferred briefly then Stacey went to the Captains office and demanded that his client—friend—be released immediately. The Captain told him he couldnt do that, that only the courts could release him. And anyway, I dont even know what the situation is or why the man has been brought in. Stacey told him he did not care what the Captain knew or did not know about the circumstances, that he was a friend of Staceys for many years and he knew he was an honest man and that it was ridiculous to arrest him on suspicion for simply standing on a street corner. When the Captain repeated what he had previously stated, Stacey called the Police Commissioner and explained the situation. The commissioner spoke to the captain and in a few minutes they were in Staceys car.

I am sorry I had to bother you Stace, but I did not know what else to do.

That is perfectly all right. After all, that is what friends are for. I would have been highly insulted if you had not called.

Well, anyway, thanks, slapping him lightly on the back.

You know, I was really surprised to hear your voice. I thought you were not getting into town until tomorrow.

Well, I did not expect to, but I got an early start and made good time. I got in town a few hours ago.

Then you can come over the house tomorrow night for dinner.

I am looking forward to it. It has been a long time.

I bet the kids have grown.

Grown? You will not recognize them.

They both smiled and continued to his hotel.

He stirred slightly, adjusting his body to a new position, smiling contentedly.

After the commissioner ordered his release he conferred with Stace about having the 2 arresting officers reprimanded in some manner. You see Stace, it is not that I want to be vindictive, but I would like to see them be more careful in the future. It is not right to allow them to do such things. If they can do it to me they can do it to anyone—and probably have. You understand.

Completely.

You know how I have always been fighting injustices of all nature—just as yourself—and especially the misuse of authority.

They went to the captains office. He asked the captain if he could speak to the 2 officers. He could see by their faces that they were worried and he felt a slight twinge of joy inside him. He told them that he had no intention of pressing charges or taking any form of official or formal action, but that they should be more careful in the future. There are times when overzealousness can be just as dangerous as dereliction of duty.

When he and Stace left the office the 2 officers were still standing in front of the captains desk looking extremely worried, the captain upset and angry. The door had been closed many seconds before he started to speak. Whats the matter with you assholes? You trying to have me kicked off the force, or put out in the sticks someplace? You have to be a first-class imbecile to arrest a friend of Stacey Lowry that way. But we didnt know—then youd better learn, pounding the desk, his red face thrust at theirs, and real fast. You ever cause the commissioner to get on my back again I/ll throw *your* ass in a cell. Now get the fuck out of here.

He put his arm even tighter against his eyes so he could see their faces more clearly. The red of embarrassment turned to a white of fear and panic. The joy surging through his body was so intense his throat constricted and he sat up as he started coughing. He sat on the edge of the bed trying to restrain the image of those frightened faces, his anger increasing as the coughing continued to destroy the image. Eventually the coughing subsided and he lay down and tried to bring the faces back, and though they were blurred, he could see enough of them to allow the pleasure to once again flow through his body, but then he started coughing again and the beautiful scene dissolved.

He sat on the bed, back against the wall, his body still tingling with the feeling of joy. He glowed as he watched the startled look increase and increase on the captains face as he listened to the commissioner; and the look of utter and complete rage as he yelled at the 2 cops.

Even after he opened his eyes and stared at the cracked, gray wall he continued to feel good for many minutes. Then the cracks became closer and larger, as did the walls.

He got up and started pacing. He looked at his feet and the floor as he carefully paced from wall to door (step on a crack and break your mothers back) and door to wall. For a time he was void of feeling, then slowly his body tightened with anger. He stared into the mirror for a moment then continued his careful pacing. It was a stupid game. Dont know why in the hell we ever played it. Hopping all over the goddamn street. Wonder if we ever believed it?   Balls.

He sat on the bed and covered his eyes with his hands.

The officers looked concerned and frightened as he chastised them and they were visibly shaking as they left the captains office and the captains face blew up with rage as he laid down the law to the 2 cops and then had a wonderful evening with Stace and his family before everything blurred with light and he got up and started pacing again.

1, 2, 3, 4, 5, 6, the door. 1, 2, 3, 4, 5, 6, the wall. 1 and 2 and 3 and 4 and 5 and 6 and the door—glance through the little window—no one, nothing, just walls and floors. 1 and 2 and 3 and 4 and 5—almost took too short a step, lengthen final stride—and 6. Back and forth. Back and forth. Forth and back. Count the goddamn steps from the fucking wall to the sonofabitching door. Again and again. Make sure each foot falls in the proper place in each direction. Keep in own footprints. Dont vary. Always the same. Just like everything else is the same. Always gotta bug ya. 1 step and 2 steps; a tick and a tock. Back and forth, a tick and a tock. Dont step on a crack, youll break your mothers back. I/ll fix them when I get out. I/ll fixem all. Even that sonofabitch that broke my hand. Someday I/ll even get him. I/ll wrap his fucking club around his head. Who does he think hes fucking with the rotten mothafucka. And those other 2 pricks. I/ll getem kicked off the force. You bet ya sweet ass I will. Cant fuck with me.

                    He stopped pacing and sat on the edge of the bed for a moment before stretching out and covering his eyes with an arm. He had to wait for the beating of his heart to slow before the image could form.

He was playing catch with a few friends in the alley behind the apartment houses. Angelo came over to him with his 2 older brothers and said he hadda fightim. What for. I doan wanna fightya. Whats amatta, ya afraid to fight my brudda? Na, Im not ascared. I just doan wanna. Aaaa, youre yella. Wont even fight a guy thats smalla thanim. Yeah, but hes oldern me. Hes 9. So what? Hes still smaller. Ah, go on. Youre ascared. Yeah, hes a mommas boy. I aint not. I AINT NOT! Ha, ha, hes a mommas boy. Ha, ha, hes a mommas boy. I aint. I AINT!

                    They continued to chant as they formed a ring, Angelo standing in the middle as he continued to back away screaming he wasnt afraid. The others kept shoving him forward as he stumbled away, face red and tears forming in his eyes. Finally Angelo hit him and he screamed and lunged at Angelo, his arms flailing, fists clenched so tightly his knuckles were granite white. Angelo couldnt recover or repulse the sudden rush. Angelo fell down and he fell on top of him, still screaming furiously. He was dragged off, only fighting for a few seconds against the restraining grips. When he stopped resisting he felt weak and was almost happy he was being held. He stood like that for many moments while Angelos 2 older brothers inspected red puffs on Angelos face.

Look whatcha did? Yeah, ya giveim a shiner. We just wanted to box a little. Ya didnt have to hitim so hard. Ya no good hittin a guy thats smaller thanya. . .

the voices and jeers continued, but he no longer understood the words. He broke free and ran home, crying. When his mother opened the door he ran past her and into his room and fell on his bed. His mother quickly followed him and sat on the bed beside him and put her arms around him and rocked him back and forth listening to his sobs. Its all right son. Dont cry. Mothers here. Mother will always be here.

He removed his arm and allowed the light to filter through his closed eyelids. He opened his eyes then sat up on the bed. He stared in front of him for many minutes then smiled slightly. They just shouldnt have pushed me. But I sure did teach them a lesson. Cant fuck with me.

Then the smile started to broaden as an excitement started to build up within him. Then he heard the door clang open and a voice yell, chow time.

He was almost oblivious to his surroundings, the clanging of metal trays, the babble of voices. He was aware of eating, but not the taste of the food. He stayed in the mess hall as long as possible, savoring not the food, but the feeling within him.

He sat on his bed after having walked slowly from the mess hall. He heard the door clang shut and the grinding of the lock as the bolt was shot, but it didnt bother him right now. Now he had something to look forward to. A dessert of sorts. He would sit and enjoy the anticipation as long as possible. It felt good. So good he could taste it. He waited and waited, the excitement and enjoyment almost painful. Yet still he waited. And the pleasure increased until it was almost critical.

He luxuriously lowered himself on the bed and put an arm over his eyes.

H E was standing on the street corner looking up and down the avenue and street. Which way to go? Which way to go? Think I/ll stroll up the avenue. Can I see your i.d. 2 officers behind him. Hard hats glowing from faint street light. (no. no.) Hey buddy, what are you doin here. The cops had a hard scowl on their faces. Nothing. Just looking around. I am afraid I am lost. Lost? Dont give me that shit. Well, it is the truth. I just got into town and went for a walk and I do not know how to get back to my hotel. Cant you think of a better story than that? Lets see your i.d.—get against the wall. He was shoved hard against the wall. Now see here officer, I am not doing anything and you have no right to do this to me. O, we dont? We/ll show you what rights we have. The back of a hand against his head. Are you crazy or something? You cannot do that. I know my rights. Listen wizeass, you do like youre told or we/ll split your goddamn skull open. I am advising you against hitting me again. Hit you, we/ll kill you. 1 of the officers reached for his gun and he suddenly hit them both on the side of the head with open hands, their hard hats clanging loudly in the night. Their eyes rolled and the gun fell from the officers hand. He banged their heads together again then took their helmets off before thudding their heads together once more. He stepped back and calmly watched them crumble to the ground. He then put them in their car and strolled away. Yeah   hahahahahaha   thats the way to do it.   Wonder what they would think when they came to. Bet they wouldnt fuck with me if I ever met them again. Just slam them around.

Riding the subway during rush hour. Morning. Lousy mood. A lousy weekend. Crowds all jamming and pushing. Smells of newspapers, clothes, breath and bodies. Woman with 2 large bundles standing by the door. She has scraggly hair and lumpy clothes. Shes stained and has large, hairy moles on face. Looks like she stinks. An old guttersnipe. Wont move when people want to get off or on. Like she owns the goddamn subway or something. Have to squeeze past her. Shes big. Heavy. Repulsive. Should at least stamp on her foot. Kick her shin. Still there when he wants to get off. He body checks her as hard as possible. Shes propelled from doorway. Hits the wall of the station. Bundles fly from cruddy arms and contents are strewn on platform. He smiles as he walks away

he watches her bounce off the wall and fall to the ground. Makes believe he stumbles over her. Steps, hard, on ankle. Falls and knee hits her in stomach. Hand hits her throat. Adams apple. Presses hard on stomach and chest when he gets up. Shakes head sorrowfully. Sorry. Aglow inside.

When the cop drew his gun he chopped him hard on the wrist with his hand, and with almost the same motion he kicked the other one in the groin. Even before the gun hit the ground he hit the first one on the back of the neck and he fell to the ground, then the other as he was curled in a fetal position holding his stomach. Just a few karate chops and it was all over. He leisurely put them back in their car and looked at them for a moment then took their badges and guns. Walked to the corner and dropped them down a sewer. He strolled away, his grin wide.

His grin was still complete as he lay on his bed, his knees

bent and legs crossed. Let them explain that to the captain. Yeah. Especially when they dont answer their radio.

It was an all-car alert. A gun fight with robbery suspects just a few minutes from the corner where the 2 officers were slumped, unconscious, in their car. Their number was blasted from the radio over and over. 1 officer killed. 3 wounded. Assist immediately. Repeat. 1 dead. 3 wounded. Assist immediately. Repeat. Assist immediately. Please respond. Please respond. Pleas unheard as they remained slumped in the car. Still unconscious, badgeless and gunless. Pleas from radio roaring down the street. When questioned about failure to respond they were afraid to tell the truth. Eventually they were forced to stammer and stutter the truth, but their story was not believed. They were loathed and despised by their brother officers. The heros funeral of the officer killed that night was covered by the television and radio networks, and many times during that day, and the days that followed, reference was made to the 2 officers who were only a few blocks away at the time of the killing, but did not respond to the pleas for help. They were suspended and allowed to resign from the department. Their faces and story were known everywhere they went. Silence and disgust greeted them when they applied for jobs and when they got home at night. Their wives were ashamed to go to the store. Their kids had to leave school. Soon their families left them, unable to bear the burden of shame. The ex-cops finally disappeared and the story forgotten until the body of one is found, slightly decomposed, in a junkyard.

Yeah, yeah. With maggots and rats guzzling away. Beautiful. Beautiful. A deep smile eased through his face. He felt a happiness and contentment that was immeasurable. He could taste it and roll it around on his tongue. He could inhale it and feel it caressing him. He looked more closely at the rotting flesh and gnawed bones and eased into an ecstasy. And with the ecstasy came a brief semiconsciousness. Not a sleep, but an exciting relaxation that he immersed himself in.

But to stay so immersed too long, too deeply, would deprive him of his ecstasy and if he lost it he might never experience it again. He was too excited to remain on the bed. His eyes opened and he went to the sink and rinsed his face many times with cold water and blinked his eyes completely open. He rubbed his face hard with the towel and felt the tingle of his skin. He examined the pimple briefly then went back to the bed. An arm covered his eyes.

When the officer pulled his gun—first he warned them he was a karate expert—he hit him on the wrist, the gun falling, and jabbed his finger tips in the others adams apple. He then shoved his finger tips in the first ones solar plexus, chopped the second on the back of the neck and did the same to the first one. They fell unconscious to the ground and he disarmed them. He then went to the pay phone on the corner and called the newspaper and related the events that had just occurred and requested that a reporter be sent to the scene. Not many minutes later a reporter and cameraman arrived and they called the authorities. In the few minutes before three squad cars arrived he quickly repeated his story to the reporter while the cameraman took many pictures. When the other officers arrived, including a sergeant and lieutenant, he was asked many angry questions and looked into many angry faces. As he said later, they were incensed. He was bumped slightly and not treated too gently as they rode to the station house. He made the remark about them being incensed during an interview in the publishers office where he told the interviewer, and others who were there (the publisher, managing editor, a leading criminal attorney, a representative from the a.c.l.u., and leaders from many civic organizations) that he was certain that he would have received a terrible beating if the reporter and cameraman had not been there. As a matter of fact it would not have surprised me if they had found some way to send me to prison for many years. They undoubtedly would have accused me of attempted murder and god knows what else.

Q. Just what made you call the paper rather than just walking away?

A. Well, actually, I made that call for a few reasons. I was afraid that if I were to simply walk away I might be picked up at some future time and then I would have no way to defend myself. You see, there were no witnesses. So I decided the wisest thing to do would be to call a reputable paper, tell my story, and ask that a reporter be on hand to prevent what I am certain would have happened if he had not been there. Of course, sending a cameraman added even more insurance. And too, I did not want these so-called, quote, officers of the law, unquote, to go unpunished. They were grossly abusing their authority and that is not only wrong, it is dangerous. And that is why I called your paper. I know Mr. Preston has always concerned himself with the rights of others and is an honest and courageous individual.

Q. Well, what was it that made you do what you did to the officers?

A. Well, I guess I just got fed up with their bullying. I

spoke properly to them and they continually abused me, insulted me, pushed me, and all the time I was giving them straightforward and honest answers. I even warned them to stop hitting me because I am a karate expert and would feel compelled to defend myself. Then when one took his gun out of his holster I simply decided I was not going to take any chances on being killed.

Q. What are your plans now?

A. Well, I am going to press charges against them. I do not think anyone should be allowed to abuse anyone else. I do not believe in allowing the criminal element to simply run around the streets doing whatever they want to whomever they wish. And I certainly am thankful for a police force to help protect the honest citizen. But—and this is a big but—I do not think a police officer should be allowed to do so either. There is nothing more dangerous than irresponsible authority. (yeah, thats a good one)

Q. Are you planning to sue the city for punitive damages?

A. No. Definitely not. And that is something I want completely understood. I am not doing this to make money. Of course, like everyone else, I could always use a little more (smiles and nods), but that is not the reason. I am doing this because I believe it is my duty to do so.

Q. What other plans do you have for the immediate future?

A. Well, I am going to work with Don and Stace to see if we can do something that may help prevent this from happening again. I do not imagine it can be prevented completely, but perhaps we can at least diminish the frequency and in so doing we may help save some innocent persons life. Or as far as that goes, anyones life.

Thank you very much.
It was my pleasure.

And more pleasure at the trial, orgastically squirming slightly on the bed. No, not just pleasure, or even ecstasy. This was something sublime. Yes, sublime to destroy them in a public trial with newsmen watching, the public watching, the cameramen from newspapers and t.v. watching. All watching and listening.

The first witnesses called were from the newspaper. The first was the switchboard operator who answered the call and was told that he had just knocked out 2 cops who had abused him. She said she referred the call to the editor.

He testified that he answered the phone and was told the story of what happened, briefly, and that a request for a reporter had been made.

The reporter testified as to what he was told and what he saw.

The photographer testified in the same vein and then authenticated the pictures he had taken and they were placed into evidence.

Then he took the stand and clearly and precisely related the chain of events that led them to all being there in the courtroom. And then he did a magnificent job of making the defense attorney look like a damn fool. Time after time counsel tried to intimidate him, trap him, bully him, belittle him, but he simply and calmly foiled all attempts. Of course Stacey Lowry made many objections, which were sustained, but actually it was not necessary. No matter how, and in what way, defense counsel attempted to discredit him or his testimony he was steadfast and said not one single word that conflicted with his original story. Eventually defense counsel, baffled and frustrated, gave up in disgust. He was magnificent on the stand.

And when the officers testified he made short notes and passed them to Stace showing the discrepancies in their stories. The cross-examination was brutal (all the news media commented on what a strong impression he had made while on the stand. Especially under cross-examination). Stacey had the officers contradicting themselves and each other in 5 minutes. There were times when there was so much laughter in the courtroom that the judge had to pound his gavel for silence. It took the jury 30 minutes to reach a verdict. It was a joy to see the look on the officers faces when they were pronounced guilty.

It was sublime.

And there were columns of print in the paper the next day about the trial stressing how the entire case had been won by him the way he made the defense counsel look ridiculous; and what a profound impression he made on the jury. There was even an editorial about the trial praising him for his courage to stand up to the authorities in the name of justice, and he watched the jurors filing in and taking their seats. The verdict was handed to the clerk who handed it to the judge. The defendants stood and he watched. He stared and that warm glow filled him as the judge read the verdict and they turned white or gray or maybe green, but it didnt matter, he felt good; and he stared politely into defense counsels face, fully composed and relaxed and soon he could see that counsel was aware that he had met his match and the questions were thrust, hurled and screamed, but his composure remained constant, his demeanor relaxed, calm, and the judge thanked him, personally, for bringing the case to court and hoped that more citizens would have the courage in the future to follow the example he set; and he heard the muffled splash as the guns and badges hit the water and the captains face was red as he screamed at the 2 officers and he and Stace and his wife sat in the living room sipping brandy and talking and he felt the side of his hand crash against the back of the cops neck and heard the clanging of the helmets, and he tossed them in their car and

    the tumbling was starting to interfere with the enjoyment so he got out of bed and paced the floor, but not as he had before. There wasnt the previous tension. It had been replaced with an intense joy, almost a euphoria. Perhaps not as sublime a feeling as he had experienced, but none the less a euphoric one.

    Actually he didnt pace, but leisurely walked the feet from the door to the wall, without counting, without trying to follow his own footsteps, without worrying about breaking his mothers back.

    He looked in the mirror at his pimple and touched it gently. It seemed to be a little larger and perhaps a little more tender, but that was nothing. He simply shrugged then walked leisurely from the door to the wall not trying to regain the images or recapture anything, but just remembering and enjoying.

The first time he was ever in a police car was when he was 8 years old. The bell rang and his mother opened the door then came into his room and told him 2 policemen wanted to speak to him. He was suddenly covered with sweat. He knew why they were there. They were going to arrest him for beating up Angelo. But he only had a red mark on his cheek. Didnt he? Cant remember. Seems so. Couldnt see so good. Ran so fast. They yelled and he kept running. Somethin musta happened. Maybe he hurt his head. Maybe he was bleedin after he ran. Maybe blood was comin outta his nose or his mouth. Suppose his eyes was bleedin. Please God, not his eyes. He didnt wanna hitim. They made him do it. Maybe the cops was gonna hitim. They were gonna beat him up. Then they would take him away. He/d never see mommy again. Never.

Son. . .son (2 huge blue giants stood behind her. Couldnt see the doorway. They were up to the ceiling. Couldnt put his head back far enough to see their faces. Just a doorway filled with blue. And mommy standing in front. Why is she gonna let them take me away? He/d never see her again. never). Son. The police officers want to talk to you about the dog that bit you yesterday. . .

Dog? Yesterday? Yesterday. (he was roller skating with friends on the grainy sidewalk. They laughed and yelled as they raced down the block, their metal wheels grinding and buzzing. Suddenly a small black dog ran from a yard and bit him on the heel ((right one? left one??? yeah, the left one)). He screeched and started crying as the others yelled at the dog and a woman hurried from the house calling to her dog and yelling at the boys to stop yelling, youre scaring him, and he continued to cry still not feeling any pain and the same hysteria propelled him home as the woman called to him to come back so she could look at his leg but he skated as fast as possible and when he reached his house he didnt stop to take off his skates but clanged up the stairs, clinging to the banister, half-pulling, half-thrusting himself up the 3 flights of stairs until he reached his door and rolled into it hitting it with both hands open still yelling mommy, mommy, and when she opened the door he fell forward but mommy caught him, her face strained as she responded to his yells and hysteria as he panted and sobbed, unable to tell her what had happened.

no matter how much she soothed and questioned until she finally half-carried and half-dragged him to his bedroom and put his head on her lap as he stretched out on the bed and she rubbed his head with her hand and kissed away his tears until he buried his face in her lap and put his arms around her clinging desperately to mommy until the sobs stopped and she lifted her darlings face and continued to rub his head while he told her the story, then sat for many minutes until he was calmed enough for her to take off the skates and walk him to the bathroom and wash his face with cold water, comb his hair and take him to the doctor.

He wasnt nervous until the doctor told him that it might sting a little. He said nothing. Just looked at his mother. She held his hands and soothed him as the doctor cauterized the wound. Its not bad, and shouldnt give him any trouble, but I do have to notify the police so the dog can be tested for rabies.

When they got home she put him to bed and told him to rest for a while, doing all she could to comfort him, yet the look of panic would not leave his face. When he was finally able to stop his mouth from trembling he said, rabies. Do I have rabies like that boy in the movie and they gotta give me big needles in the stomach? No. No. Dont worry son. You will be all right, and she could feel his body trembling and shivering as she cradled him, rocking him back and forth as his mind whirled with images of foaming mouths and huge spikelike needles squealing into the soft flesh of his abdomen.)

They want to know where he lives. She entered his room and sat beside him and held his hand. The doorway widened and he could see their faces. (its only about the dog. they werent after him.) The cops and his mother talked with him for a few minutes and assured him that they wouldnt hurt the lady that owned the dog, they only wanted to test the dog.

As they left the building he could see a small crowd of people standing near the patrol car. He could see that many of his friends were there and staring at him as he walked, with the 2 cops, toward the police car. He felt as huge as the cops had looked. He knew none of his friends had ever been in a police car and he tried to look deadly serious as he walked to the car, wanting to wave to his friends but holding back, wanting to maintain the aura of mystery. He wished the walk could have been a hundred feet long, or even a mile, but the patrol car was only a few feet away.

One of the cops opened the door and he got in the back seat. He looked straight ahead as the 2 cops got in front, but adjusted his head just enough so he could see, from the corner of his eye, the gaping crowd. One of the cops asked him where the dog lived and he told them. As the car pulled away he could feel the stares and was sure he could hear their voices.

Then a jolt of panic almost made him bolt from the moving car. Suppose they searched him. Suppose they found it. They might send him to jail. They might tell his mother. How could he get rid of it. If he tried to sneak it out of his pocket they might see him. And if he did get it out what would he do with it. They kept talking to him. Telling him not to worry. Must be something wrong with the way he looked. Cant let them know. Maybe they do know. Maybe they saw it when they came downstairs. Maybe theyre not going to the dogs house. Its only half a block. Should be there. The car stopped and one of the cops asked him which house it was. He wanted to yell he was sorry. He wouldnt do it again. He just stared. The cop asked him again and he pointed. One of the cops got out and went into the house. The other cop sat in front, silent, and he thought everything would be all right. Maybe they didnt see it. But the cop was gone so long. Maybe he would have to go in the house and they would see it in his back pocket. Please God, dont let them see it. I/ll be good. I/ll never do it again. He was afraid he might wet his pants.

Then the cop came out with the woman and she was holding the small dog. He could see their lips moving and heard voices, but didnt know what was being said. He just sat rigidly in the back seat hoping God would protect him. The cop got in and he vaguely heard her say something about the dog just got scared by the noise—sorry little boy—good dog—tried to catch the boy. . . .

It seemed like he didnt breathe as they drove the half a block to his house. The cops stopped in front of his house and let him out. His friends came running over. They yelled. Asked. He remained silent until the cops drove away. He ran around the corner. They screeched questions over questions over questions. In between he shot out a word here, there, wherever, whenever. The story was told. Understood. And the whole time I had my slingshot in my pocket. But they didnt see it. They had me cold, the dumb cops, but I got away. Wow!

And he knelt on the floor and looked out the open window. Pow. Pow. Gotya. The dirty coppers had him trapped on the 4th floor and the window was flooded with lights. A voice over a loud-speaker told him to surrender. You cant get away lefty. Go tahell copper. Pow. Pow. Gotcha. Pow. Then a shot from a sharpshooters rifle hit him in the shoulder and he fell on the floor, clutching his bleeding shoulder and his mother suddenly sat up in bed and ran to him. Whats wrong son. What is it. And she bent over him, feeling soft, but he had to kill a whole bunch of coppers.

Balls. Too bad it wasnt real. Wouldnt mind having shot a few. (1, 2, 3, 4, 5, 6, the door. 1, 2, 3, 4, 5, 6, the wall.) O fuck it. Cops and robbers. (find the spot you stepped in before. dont miss it. each foot where it was. follow your footsteps. 1 and 2 and 3 and 4 and 5 and 6. about face. 1 and 2 and 3 and 4 and 5 and 6. sometimes 1 is 6 and 6 is 1. and 3 is always 3. so that would make 5 the same as 2—no. wait. . . . lets see. 1 is 6. 2 is 5. 3 is 4. 4 is 3. 5 is 2. 6 is 1. and vice versa. but its its own vice versa. 1 to 3—6 to 4. and 4 to 6—3 to 1. it goes up and it goes down. theres no middle. except maybe 3½. thats always the same. yeah thats it. only the ½, of 3½ is the same. all the rest goes up and down, up and down. hahaha. its just like screwing. up and down. up and down. oh fuck it. There were 3 full flights of stairs to the house. 6 half-flights. 8 steps in each half-flight. Go up 8 steps in one direction. A small landing. Turn around and go up 8 more steps in the opposite direction to the floor. 5 doors. 5 apartments. Then back the first way to the next landing. Opposite to the next floor. . .O balls.

motherfucking cops. Should have spit in their faces. He lay on his back, an arm over his eyes.

The mist persisted. Or was it light seeping through his arm and the closed lids of his eyes? No, it wasnt light. It was just a blur. Had to hunt. Hunt a fucking cop. Play a new game: hunt a fucking cop. 2 faces hung with crape. Guilty. The wives weep. The mothers of their children. Mothers. Mothers, all of them. The tumbling of turned backs. Despair. Pain. Pain. Hungry baby sucking on a dry tit. Swollen bellies.

Despair. No direction. Only death. A gun. Pills. No. A rope.
A kicked stool. Slow. Agonizing. Very slow. Pain. Yeah, pain.
Slowly blue. Very slowly. Tongue swollen like the bellies.
Eyes pop from sockets. A gurgle. So slow. Blood. So very
slow. A little sleep

and then a
little wakefulness.

Then
a slipping to some soothing place in between.

Mary used to baby-sit on Saturday nights. After the people
had gone he would join her. They would sit on the couch.
Afraid to mess the bed. Werent sure what to do anyway.
After kissing for a while he would put his finger in her
snatch. Then she would open his fly and play with his joint.
They would sit like that for hours, his finger up her snatch,
her hand around his joint. From time to time he would push
her head down and she would put his joint in her mouth.
And, from time to time, he would stand and make her kneel
in front of him and he would shove it in her mouth. And so
passed another Saturday night with her hand around his
joint, his finger up her snatch, and, from time to time, him
shoving his joint in her mouth.

Then he would wash his
hands and leave before the people came home, and each
Saturday night when he went home he was always afraid
his mother might smell his hand.

A. Well, when they told me to lean against the wall I refused and told them they could not search me, that they
did not have a warrant. That is when they shoved me
and I literally bounced off the wall.

I should have played stinkfinger with the motherfuckers. Take their goddam guns and shove them right up their asses. Stupid fucking assholes.

No one heard the shot over the rattling of the trolleys and the noise of the cars and trucks. The woman just fell under the marquee of the movie theater. A few people just looked for a second then went over to help her. An ambulance came and the police. She had been shot with a .22 caliber rifle. Soon after the neighborhood was swarming with cops, uniform and plainclothes. He was in his room when 2 came to the house. They explained a woman had been shot and they were searching the neighborhood for guns. They came to his room and found his toy shotgun. You broke the barrel, closed it, pulled the trigger and it went pop. He looked at them as they inspected it very carefully, minutely. They then inspected his cap pistol (tom mix) very carefully and minutely.

When they left his mother explained what had happened. He quickly grabbed his cap pistol and ran down the 3 flights of stairs. He met several of his friends in the alley behind the apartment houses. They slinked around corners, looking both ways before advancing very carefully. They could see the cops on the roof tops and tried to stay in any shadows. It was the best game of cops and robbers they ever had.

A regular bunch of Sherlock Holmeses. (brass buttons, blue coat, couldnt catch a nanny goat.) Just like that motherfucker that broke my hand. Wish I could have grabbed his goddamn club and shoved it up his fucking ass. Right the fuck up until it came out his head. No wonder judges wear black. They should be in mourning. The goddamn assholes. Wonder what happened to the kid that shot that woman.

Said he was shooting at the marquee. Trying to hit the lights, but missed. Funny, when he heard that the kid was shooting from his house 3 blocks away he couldnt believe it. Didnt think a bullet could go that far—o shit. Who gives a fuck. She was probably a fucking bitch anyway.

No. Have to push that away. Cant think of it. Get rid of the smell. Oo something to get rid of it. Maybe get up and walk. Not in the mood. Feels nice just drifting. But can smell it. Maybe its time to eat or some damn thing. Maybe the door will clang open. N, NNE, NE, ENE, E. Theres a girl scout in the grass with a boy scout up her ass. Bowlines, sheepshanks, square knots. Got kicked out of the boy scouts for eating a brownie. Theres a boy scout in the grass with a boy scout up his ass. Fuck it. Mary had a nice tight cunt. Wonder what its like now. Yeah, thats better. A nice tight cunt. Get a hard on. So hard it hurts. Something to do. Mary had a nice tight cunt. Mary had a nice tight cunt. Wonder if I/d recognize her now? Seems she wasn't too bad. Too young to screw. Afraid of jail. Mary had a nice tight cunt. Wonder what *that* broads name was. Good thing she was cherry. Yeah. That will keep the smell away. Away. Providence. Good name. Providence. He was 15 and had run away from home again. This time he got a job on an oil barge. It was during the war and very few questions were asked. All they wanted to know was if you were able to do the work. They had docked in Providence and he and the other deck hand got the night off and went into town. They walked around for a while, then went to a movie. It was a big movie house. No idea what the picture was. Came out and started walking around again. They were walking through a park and they met a girl. They walked and talked and Tom suggested they go behind a small house in the park.

Tom led the way and went first while he waited. Then Tom said its your turn. He kissed her and squeezed her tit, wanting to do so much more but ignorant of what and how. Scared, with a painful hard on. Then the 3 of them went behind the building together and felt her up until they were sated with what they were doing, but afraid to go any further. So they started to walk to the bus stop to go back to the barge. They werent sure how to get there so she walked with them to show them the way. They were walking down a dark, narrow street when suddenly a car stopped beside them and 2 men jumped out and grabbed them and told them to get in the car. He trembled as the man held his arm. He tried to ask what was going on, but couldnt speak. The men showed them badges and told them they were police officers. He was told not to worry, that they just wanted to check up on the girl. We think shes a runaway. They rode to the station house in silence. The girl was taken to one room (guess I never did know her name) and they to another. Their pockets were emptied and the contents put in envelopes. Then they were separated and questioned. them where he came from, what he was doing in town, etc. He was asked what he was doing with the girl.

Nothing. She was showing us the way to the bus stop.

You were picked up at 2 in the morning. What were you doing all that time?

Just walking. We went to a movie then walked around.

With the girl?

Part of the time.

Dont bullshit me, punk. I know what you did. Your friend already told us. You took turns with her. Didn't you?

He almost cried with panic. He tried to speak but only stammered. He knew he was wrong and his shame made it impossible to say anything. He nodded his head.

You punks make me sick. Im personally going to see that you get 20 years for this.

The tears started to well in his eyes, but he couldn't let them see it. He could only think of his mother. What would she say. Twenty years. What would his mother say. He wasnt aware of them taking his belt and the laces from his shoes. His daze didnt start to clear until he heard the door of his cell clang shut.

He sat on the steel slab that served as a bunk. He looked out the bars up at the window in the wall across from his cell and could see the faint glow of a street lamp. He stared at the bars for many long, long minutes. What would his mother say. Twenty years. The tears finally seeped from his eyes and rolled down his cheeks. He didnt brush them away. He couldnt feel them. He stared and the tears rolled as he tried to imagine what it meant to go to prison for twenty years. It seemed like he had been alive for so very long, yet he was only 15 years old. He tried desperately to conceive of twenty years yet couldnt. It was an eternity. He soon stopped trying as he no longer had the energy. He sat with his head lowered staring at the floor watching it darken as the tears fell from his face. There was no reason to stop them from flowing, even if he had been fully aware of the fact that he was crying. He was alone. All alone. And as the tears flowed from his eyes, the energy flowed from his body. He slowly, unknowingly, lowered himself on the slab and lay on his side and slept.

He had to fight his eyes open as the light from the streetlevel window opposite his cell scraped his eyes. When he adjusted his eyes to the light he became aware of a stinging cold in his body. The steel slab felt like ice. He sat up trying to convince himself it was just a dream, but the truth was undeniable. He was sitting on that slab and there were bars on the door. It was all as real as the light coming through the window. He sat.

Then a jailer came around with a small cheese sandwich and a tin cup half-filled with black coffee. He took them, set them on the slab and stared at them for many minutes. The bread was hard as was the cheese. He put his hands around the cup to warm them and wondered if he should drink the coffee. He had never had coffee before except for a few drops in his milk as a special treat. He warmed his hands then rubbed his body with them. Then warmed them again. He didnt know why, but he forced down the sandwich. Not through hunger, but some sort of habit. He sipped the coffee. It was worse than medicine. He took a few sips then left it, just using the cup to warm his hands.

He looked up at the window and could see a small portion of the legs of the people who walked past. For a while he simply stared then he started noticing the small portion of leg and wondered what the people looked like. He wasnt really interested, but it was something to do. It helped pass the time. Twenty years. How could he pass twenty years? How could he live twenty years? It was beyond comprehension. Too far beyond. It was unreal. But what would his mother say. He had to play a game. What do those people look like? Those people who belong to the 18 inches, or so, of leg he could see. How could you tell how tall a man was, or how heavy he was, or what color his eyes and hair were. How could you tell what he looked like when all you could see was a few inches of his pants leg. There was just no way of knowing or imagining. But it was different with the women. Of course he couldnt really tell, but at least he could see the shape of the leg and could imagine. He could even imagine what type of shoe they were wearing, especially if he could hear the click, click of heels. They had to be high heels. And if the leg were attractive, exceptionally attractive, then she was young with a nice figure and large tits. Firm and round and soft. The kind you rest your cheek on. The kind that had large, dark rosy nipples. And some had dark hair, some blond hair, and some had to be redheads. And they all had red lips and long painted nails, and their asses wiggled when they walked. But what color snatch hair does a blonde have? Redheads and brunettes were easy, but blondes???? Was it blond like their head or was it darker? Could they have black snatch hair or was it just sort of brown? If he could get close to the window he could look up their skirts and maybe some of them wouldnt have any pants on. He had heard of girls who didnt wear pants. But even if they did he might be able to see something. Anyway, that wasnt too important, the color, it would be great just to look. And they wouldnt know. He could just stand there all day and look. But not for twenty years. But he could look for now, anyway. He continued to watch those inches of leg walk by, then slowly became aware of a slight pain in his groin. He had a hard on. It scared him. Suppose the guard came and saw it. He had to get rid of it. He pushed it with his hand, almost shoving it back up in his crotch. It seemed to be made of the same steel as the slab he sat on. It ached, but he had to push. He placed both hands on the head of his prick and pushed even harder. For a brief second he thought it would put a hole in his hands, but eventually it started to bend and slowly it softened. He stood for a moment to make sure there was no visible bulge. All was flat. He sat down on the slab and turned his back to the window and didnt move until the guard called him and gave him another cheese sandwich and a tin cup of hot coffee. He slowly ate his sandwich, taking small bites and chewing as long as possible before swallowing, his back still to the window. He waited as long as possible, then took another bite and chewed and chewed. When his mouth was as dry as sawdust he took a few small sips of coffee. Then back to the sandwich. Cheese and bread dry and hard, coffee bitter, but it passed the time.

Sometime in the afternoon his cell door clanged open and the guard told him to come out. They went to the office he had been in the night before and Tom and 2 detectives were there. He sat in the seat pointed to. Sweat seemed to cascade from his armpits. He could feel it dripping down his sides.

The doctor examined the girl and shes intact (he stared at the detectives face, conscious only of the sweat covering his body. his scalp itched with it.) So we/re going to let you go this time. But if I ever see either one of you in here again I/ll break your head. The detective looked directly at him.

Why did you say you fucked her?

He blinked his eyes and it took him many seconds before he could mutter he didnt.

You calling me a liar?

He shook his head and blinked more rapidly. No sir. (He was trying to think, but his mind just wouldnt function. He tried to remember if they had asked him if he had fucked her, but couldnt. He was sure they didnt, but he couldnt remember.) He started to stammer something, but the detective cut him off.

Never mind the bullshit. Here, take your stuff and get out of here. I have work to do.

The envelopes with their personal items were dropped on the desk and Tom said his was the one with the most money. He stared at Tom and the smirk on his face, and almost panicked again. He felt like telling him to shut up. All he wanted to do was get out of there. Nothing more.

The detective looked up at Tom. Dont give me any lip punk or youll find yourself in the hospital.

They signed the receipts, put their stuff in their pockets and left as fast as possible. All the way back to the barge Tom joked about it, but all he could think of was he was going home. She would never know.

Couldn't get rid of the smell. Still there. So strong he could taste it. He couldnt tell her. How could he tell his mother. He didnt know exactly what it was, but he sensed it somehow. He knew it was her and it was something he couldnt, or shouldn't, talk about. All he could do was sit at the table toying with his cereal, pushing it around with the spoon. Whats wrong son, why dont you eat your breakfast. I dont know mom. Just not hungry I guess. Do you feel all right? Are you sick? No, I feel all right. Just dont feel like eating. Maybe I/ll be hungry later. But you havent even taken one spoonful. Why dont you try some and maybe youll feel like eating? Im not hungry I told you. Why dont you just leave me alone, jumping up from the table and going to his room. He sat on his bed knowing his mother was still sitting at the table staring at his empty chair with that look of sadness in her eyes. The smell was still so strong he could taste it.

Shit. Stupid son of a bitch. Didnt know. Just didnt know. O fuck it. FUCK IT!

The car stopped in front of them and 2 men got out and one grabbed him and he hit him, knocking him against the car and was about to hit him again when the other one took out his badge and said they were police officers. He stood still and looked at them. Why didnt you say so. What do you want with us. We just want to check on the girl. We think shes a runaway. O.K. Im sorry I hit you, but I thought you were trying to rob us. The cop he had hit stared at him and he stared back, unafraid.

He sat on his bed with the smell. He was getting sicker. He wanted to go out in the fresh air and rid himself of it, but he would have to go through the kitchen, past his mother, to get out. He didnt want to, but he had to leave the house. If he didnt he/d be sick and his mother would start worrying and be all over him. The desperation forced him to his feet. He wanted to run out of the house, but he forced himself to walk as slowly as possible, telling his mother he was going out for a while and hurrying on before she could protest too much. He walked rapidly along the street breathing deeply and exhaling completely. Why didnt she know? Couldnt she smell it? Its hers, why didnt she smell it? Worse than Mary.

The cop he had hit glared at him and continually dabbed at his face with a handkerchief. He could see, from the expression on Toms face, that he was afraid, and he smiled at Tom reassuringly. When they arrived at the police station the cops started shoving him in front of them so he just stood rigidly still, and silent, and stared them in the eyes until they walked away and told him to follow them. He answered their questions calmly and firmly. When they asked him again about the girl he repeated that nothing had happened. Why dont you have her examined, now, and save all of us a lot of time and trouble? They yelled at him to just answer the questions and he simply stared at them, calmly. Either have her examined, *now*, and release us, or charge us with something and let us make a phone call. They continued to yell and threaten, but he simply told them he had nothing further to say. When they were released, a few hours later, he looked at the cop he had hit, coldly, and said goodbye, chuckling as he left the police station.

H E drove to the Capitol Building with Don and Stace. He was calm and confident. The interviews with reporters and on t.v allowed him to gain additional poise. When the campaign first started he was a little apprehensive, but now he knew he could cope with any situation. No, actually the real starting point was not so much the campaign and interviews, etc., but the way he handled the defense attorney at the trial. Yeah, that was the real beginning. On the stand for days and never once faltering in any way. After that he knew he could handle anything. Not that he ever really lacked confidence, but that certainly left no room for doubt. That was real concrete evidence.

As they drove along the highway they discussed the forthcoming hearings and senate investigation. They were elated. All their labors had at last been fruitful. They had not only reached the public, but had, at last, reached the State Legislature. They realized they would have to work twice as hard from now on, but at least now they could see the goal that they had been working so hard to reach in sight. This was not the end, but just the beginning.

The Sunday after the trial the interview with him appeared in the Sunday Supplement. The interview was augmented with pictures taken in various jails and detention homes graphically displaying the deplorable conditions under which accused individuals were forced to exist. (No. No. That would be the following week.)

The response to the interview was greater than expected. Reading, and acknowledging, the letters was a full-time job. The following week the first of a series of articles appeared, shockingly illustrated with photographs. The point was emphasized over and over again that the people forced to exist under these conditions were not convicted criminals, but people who had only been accused of a crime and were, under the law, assumed to be innocent until proven guilty.

The most shocking article of all was the one dealing with juveniles, where they were forced to sleep on the floor and were literally suffering from malnutrition and many of them were not even accused of a crime, but were there because their parents were sick or unable to care for them for one reason or another and they had no place to live. Their only crime was homelessness. (an angry nod of satisfaction. that was good. he nodded again.)

He knew there would be reporters, news photographers and t.v. cameramen at the Capitol Building and that he would be asked many questions before he even entered the building, but he was well prepared. He would simply continue to tell the truth and rock the foundations of the authority that had abused him. The coverage of their campaign was so extensive throughout the country that the State Legislature almost begged him, and Don and Stace, to testify. Although Don and Stace had attaché cases filled with photographs and documents of all kinds, he knew that he was the nucleus around which the entire campaign revolved. The depositions, statistics, articles, photographs, etc., were important, but it was his testimony that made it all real to the people. Theirs were facts, but they were cold to the average person. He was living proof. He gave those facts significance.

When they reached the State Building in the capital, there was a group of newsmen waiting for them. He approached them with self-assurance. All the media were represented and many of the newsmen were known by name because of the many conversations they had. He waved to those who were familiar and answered questions calmly for the press, radio and t.v., while cameras clicked and rolled. Then, after many minutes with the newsmen, he entered the State Building flanked by Don and Stace.

The interior of the building reminded him somehow of the courthouse. He wasnt sure just why. Perhaps it was the marble or the long corridors, or the way footsteps sounded and resounded; or perhaps it was the high ceiling and massive wooden doors; or maybe it was simply the coolness of the atmosphere that was reminiscent of the court building. In any event it wasnt necessary to define why this building reminded him of the other as long as he could enjoy the feeling. And with each click of heels on marble the flood of feelings increased. He enjoyed and savored remembering how he felt the first time he went to court, how the stone coolness penetrated his bones and how he was led around like a dog on a leash being forced to be subservient to everyone in the courtroom, even that goddamn idiot who told him he was his lawyer and then turned his back and did nothing. He wanted to remember that day, the day he stood before the judge as a defendant vulnerable to the blindness of justice. And those fucking cops lying their asses off and that stupid sonofabitching public defender doing nothing but kissing the judges ass. O, how he wanted their asses to roast in hell. How he wanted to peel the skin from their bodies slowly, inch by inch, listening to them scream; then yank the fucking balls right out of their bodies. How often had he clenched his teeth with anger until he thought his teeth and jaw would snap, or clench his fist until it felt as if his fingers would go right through the palm of his hand. Even now he could hear the hinge of his jaw crack and feel his knuckles turning white as the old rage seeped through his body. But this time was different. You bet your sweet ass it was. The stone is just as cool, the ceilings just as high and the doors just as thick and heavy, but this time there was a beautiful warmth flowing through him along with the bitterness and hate. Things were different now. Much different. He was no longer an unknown, insignificant and impotent nobody being shoved around by sadistic slobs and an impersonal law. Now he was someone. Someone that had to be reckoned with. Just getting those 2 motherfucking cops thrown off the force wasnt enough. That had been the beginning. He had started to shake the state to its very foundation and he wasnt going to stop. He/d continue fighting until the day he died if necessary. The entire world would see how rotten and corrupt the system is. Even if Don and Stace wanted to stop he would continue. He would never stop fighting. Never.

Here we are. He nodded and entered the hearing room as Don held the door for him. They walked to the front and sat. He looked around at the tables, chairs, microphones, the members of the press and t.v. and the people who filled the chamber. While still remembering his first visit to the courtroom he enjoyed the atmosphere he was in now. He knew all the people would be watching and listening to him. He was the reason for this hearing. The cameras would be on him. And the eyes of the people sitting behind him would be on him. He knew that if he did nothing more than nod his head to a question that that nod would be news. And he knew, too, that not only the people in the room, but people everywhere were sympathetic toward him, that they understood what he was trying to do. He knew they were aware that he was doing something millions of people wanted to do. Something millions dreamed of and prayed would happen and he was making it happen. He was not just going to fight city hall, he was going to burn the motherfucker down.

As he felt the warmth of all those eyes on his back he

was vaguely aware of Don and Stace taking papers and photographs from their attaché cases, sorting them and placing them on the table in front of them. The sound of their voices was a hum of approval. When the papers were arranged in the desired manner Stace asked him how he was doing.

Wonderful. Just wonderful.

Good. I guess it is a little difficult to believe that we are really here.

Well, I guess it is in a way, but I will tell you Stace, it sure does feel good to be here. I have never felt half—one-tenth—as good in my life as I feel now. I just cannot describe how good I feel.

Stacey Lowry smiled at him and patted him on the back. I can imagine. It has been a long and difficult struggle, especially for you (he shrugged slightly), but we are finally getting some real results. A great many good things have already been realized by our campaign, but this hearing will really provide the opportunity to get at the foundation—the very core—of this thing. And this is not the end, but rather just the beginning of another phase of the campaign.

Well, I am ready for it Stace. Ready, willing and able. Nothing can stop me.

They smiled at each other again then turned toward the front of the chamber as the senators entered.

He watched them intently as they walked to their seats, growing in stature with each of their august steps. He sat taller and straighter in his chair as he felt their eyes single him out from the hundreds of people in the room, yet he was void of tension and his composure and calmness increased as did his excitement. And as his eyes continued to focus on the members of the senate committee as they took their seats and adjusted their papers in front of them on the huge oak table, he listened to the musical humming of the t.v. cameras behind him. Nods and various greetings were exchanged and then the chairman of the committee gaveled for quiet and attention (he lay on his bunk with eyes shut tight and the scene vivid within and before him. He could see their conservative and well-fitting clothes and could even sense the colors. He admired his blue, single-breasted suit that fit so perfectly on his shoulders and hung softly, wrinkleless, with half an inch of the soft, white shirt collar showing above the smooth line of the jacket. And though he was viewing himself from behind, he could see the concerned and relaxed expression on his face and the not too tight overhand knot in his tie, and the small gold tie clip. He could see too, under the table, his black socks and shoes, the shoes polished so they just barely reflected the light from the massive window on his right. All was as it should be. Vivid and impeccable. The scene was so vivid he could smell the newness of his shirt, the wool of his suit, the papers on the table in front of him, the table itself, the polish on the many newly shined shoes, the drapery on the windows, the ink on the ribbon of the reporters stenotype machines, the wood of the just-sharpened pencils and even hear the humming of the cameras. He was so deeply involved in the scene that it remained static for many minutes, or hours, and he just stared and stared, the images and smells coming singly and combined; simultaneously and overwhelmingly. He suddenly became aware of a creeping drowsiness and was almost tempted to open his eyes, but didnt for fear of losing the image. He couldnt and wouldnt lose this. He had fought too hard for it and now it had become more than just an image, more than something conjured up in his mind, something that was now real, more real than the bunk upon which he was lying but could not feel, the cell in which he was locked yet did not exist. He relaxed ever so slightly and let the scene continue to its logical conclusion. It had to.) and the voices quickly silenced and for a second the only sound was that of the humming cameras.

And then the sound of the chairmans voice. The committee was in session. Above the hum of the cameras he could hear, again, the rustling of paper, the scraping of shoes on the floor and the various squeaks and creaks as people adjusted themselves in their seats. He carefully and casually crossed his legs, leaned back in his chair slightly and looked intently at the chairman as he spoke.

And I feel it incumbent upon me to state, at this time— and I speak not only for myself, but for the other members of this committee as well—that this is not a pleasant task we have before us, but, regretfully, a most necessary one. And, I might add, a most urgent one. I would also like to comment, at this time, on the insinuations that have appeared in a few minor publications. I want to state categorically that this investigation will be neither a whitewash nor indictment of any political party, but rather a fearless search for the truth and let the chips fall where they may. I would also like to state, and again I speak for my colleagues as well as myself, that we very much appreciate that the gentlemen here today to assist us in our inquiry have made themselves available to this committee. He nodded his head, along with Don and Stace, in acceptance of the compliment.

As the proceedings started Stace read a prepared statement, with the consent of the chairman and the other members of the committee. Actually it was more than a statement—it was their manifesto. It stated the humane reasons for their campaign, referring briefly to the facts that would be presented. Their statement/manifesto ended with

a note of thanks and appreciation to the commitee for re-
plying so rapidly to their request for an opportunity to
present the results, to date, of their investigation. When he
finished reading Stace removed his glasses, putting them
carefully on top of the statement, and said that he would
like to extend his and Mr. Prestons appreciation to the
third, and most important, member of their campaign. No
praise can be too high or too complete. What this brave and
fearlessly honest man has done to help try to correct so
egregious a wrong is unparalleled.

He modestly lowered his
eyes and listened, half-dozing and not trying to maintain
the crystal clarity of the image, but rather letting it float
around him, being warmed by the tribute being paid him,
wanting to prolong the statement being made by Stace, but
then people were taking his picture and shaking his hand
and the chairman and other members of the committee were
talking with him and those fucking cops were asking for
help—begging for his forgiveness—and his body felt luxuri-
ous with the weight of tiredness and he and the image
became one and he drifted gently into a sleep.

He stirred as
the door clanged open, but the sound was muffled by his
sleep and as he fully awakened even the sounds in the
corridors seemed almost gentle. He stayed on his bed
vaguely aware of the sounds and commotion, ignoring what
he was aware of. Nothing bothered him. He felt light,
detached and strong. He wasnt smiling, but all his muscles
were relaxed and he knew his eyes reflected his feeling of
quiet fearlessness and strength. His body didnt pulse with
this feeling, nor did it flow through him. It was simply
there, his entire body alive with it.

He got up and washed
and inspected his pimple after drying his face. He looked

at it briefly, touched it with the tip of his finger, aware that it was more sensitive, but quickly turned his attention to his entire face. Actually it was his expression, his countenance, that he examined. He studied his face from various angles, noticing the angle of his jawbone, the slope of his cheeks, the shallow lines on his forehead and all the time aware too of his eyes, knowing from the inside that their expression never changed, but continually confirming the fact from the outside. No matter what part of his face he examined or what aspect of his expression he scrutinized, the reflection of secretive knowledge in his eyes never changed.

He didnt walk to the mess hall with buoyancy in his step, but with a very conscious awareness of solidity. Each step was firm with knowledge and direction. Just as firm as the concrete upon which he walked.

As he stood in line in the mess hall, aware yet undisturbed by the noise and commotion, he knew that the others were aware of him, glancing at him from the corners of their eyes, yet he didnt feel self-conscious. He realized he was conspicuous, as much so as if he were 7 feet tall with orange hair, yet he wasnt disturbed. He simply accepted it. He realized he had no choice. There was no hiding how he felt. He knew too that the buzzing of voices was due to their speculating about him and he was almost tempted to tell them who he was and what he was going to do. He wanted to tell them how he was going to help them beat the fucking law, but realized this was not the time or place. And anyway, they would know. Someday. So he moved along in line hearing his own distinct steps above the shuffling of the others.

He picked up his tray and passed along the line silently accepting the food then walking to a table and sitting at the end. He ate slowly almost ignoring the taste of the food, but enjoying the eating of it. He also enjoyed his hunger. It wasnt a panicky hunger, but a very natural one that was easily satisfied, diminishing slowly with the swallowing of each mouthful of food. It was a hunger of strength, a strength that increased as the hunger ebbed.

As he ate he raised his head imperceptibly and glanced around the room and as his eyes passed from face to face he noticed their expression change to one of hope and understanding readily recognizing the glimmer of understanding in the many pairs of eyes that met his. He allowed the faintest of smiles to alter his expression, knowing that those eyes were looking to him for reassurance, for strength. Even the eyes in the most distant corner of the mess hall were looking to him sensing somehow that he would be their salvation. He knew he was the focal point of their despair and frustration. And he knew, too, that though he sat there silently and slowly eating in the midst of the clanging of tin trays and cups that they found the reassurance they needed in his eyes. He was the hope of the hopeless.

When it was time to go back to the cells he could feel the dignity in the way he stood and walked, and when the door was clanged shut behind him it was just another sound, a sound he didnt have to ignore because it was no longer important.

He sat on the edge of his bed and looked at the wall with an amused look of indulgence. The wall was there, more or less, but it didnt matter because the distance between him and the wall was vast and temporary and easily tolerated for now. And that door that clanged open and shut from time to time was nothing. A big nothing. And just as far away as the wall.

Actually he enjoyed sitting in

his cell, his little 9×6 room. It was all a part of something, his being here, sitting on the edge of his bed. He felt a comfort and a sense of power. It was hard to describe to everyone just how he felt, but the feeling was strong and confident. His feeling of enjoyment didnt simply come from the knowledge that he would soon be out, but what was going to happen when he got out. And who was going to get him out.

Actually he hoped he didnt get out too soon. It would be a good idea if he stayed there a while. It would add more power to his story. He was glad he didnt simply bail himself out immediately. It was much better this way. He would stay here as long as necessary and endure all the hardships and privations necessary to help him accomplish what he had to. And they would pay many times over for what they did to him. For every second of misery spent in this hellhole he would see to it that they spent a year in hell. A living hell. They would suffer torment and anguish so deep they would plead for mercy. They would beg him to let them die. O no. They werent going to die. Not yet, the fucking bastards. They had to suffer. When those fucking cops go home and tell their wives they got kicked off the force and all the newspapers and magazines and television networks carry the story and their pictures theyll wish to krist they were dead. When their kids go to school and all the other kids point at them and laugh, and their kids come home crying, I hope they think of me. I hope they never forget that Im the one that did it. I hope they live a long, long time and spend every minute of every day hoping to die and remembering me. *Me*, you rotten pricks. Dont ever forget me because Im never going to forget you. Not as long as I live. Yeah. Thats a good idea. Every xmas I/ll send them xmas cards. On easter too. Maybe even on columbus day. Or maybe some nice picture post cards from Hawaii or Acapulco or Paris or the Riviera. Having wonderful time. Wish you were here.

Yeah, wish you were here. Right here. O would I fix your fucking asses. A nice long, thin hot needle in the eardrum. Or maybe a hot cigar in the eyes. Nothing fancy. Or maybe some of that old indian shit of cutting the eyelids off, or some hot lead up the ass. And then listen to them scream. O what sweet music that will be listening to those fucking pricks screaming. Should really do it in a hospital with doctors and nurses to make sure they dont die. Yeah, that would be great. With microphones and the volume turned all the way up so it would sound even better. And all the time theyll be seeing my face. Yeah, with their eyelids cut off they cant close their eyes. Theyll have to look at me. At me with wide-open eyes. Eyes that cant close and a nice bright, hot light shining in their eyes. And every now and then a light gets a little closer and a little closer and brighter and hotter. Burning hot until theyre almost blind. But not quite. And then some nice cold water on their eyes to soothe them. One drop at a time. Maybe every 5 seconds. Yeah. Every 5 seconds for a while until they get used to the timing and then every couple of seconds. And then none for 10 or 20 seconds or even longer until they think its all over and then let the water start dripping again. Just until theyre almost out of their minds. Have to be sure they dont go completely out of their minds. They have to last a long, long time. And they have to know Im doing it. And then we can dry their eyes with a nice bright, hot light. And then cool them. And warm them and cool them. Just for a couple of weeks. A little vacation in the country. A nice quiet little rest home. A private sanitarium. Yeah, that would be nice. Just long enough to make them a pair of vegetables. Yeah, and I/ll water the vegetables, hahaha. A couple of lumps with their tongues hanging out and spit dripping down their chins. And maybe put a dog collar around their throats and lead them with a leash. Yeah, after all, theyll need some exercise. Have to keep them away from trees and fire hydrants though. Yeah, on a fucking leash. With their fucking badges stuck through the tips of their noses. And their fucking wives can greet them with open arms. Here children, say hello to your father. This is daddy. Woof, woof. O, what a nice daddy you have. Comeon. Say hell to

the fucking sons-abitches. O I/ll get those rotten motherfuckers it its the last thing I do. I swear to krist I/ll get them.

Fuckem, the rotten pricks.

His fists were clenched and his nostrils flared. He could hear the grinding of his teeth. He stood for a second, shook his head, then walked to the mirror. He stared into the mirror for many minutes until he felt his body relax. His finger patted the pimple and toyed with it, teased it, then he nodded and walked back to his bed. He sat on the edge and stared at the wall. The wall slowly moved back. He smiled and nodded again. I/ll just bide my time. Theres plenty of time to get those pricks. And when I do I/ll getem good. The longer I wait the better itll be. O, you bet your sweet ass its going to be good.

He stretched out on the bed, hands behind his head, and let the overhead light penetrate his eyelids. He could feel the light on his eyes and now and then he would open them for a second and look at the light and when they started to water and smart he closed them and smiled. The water from his eyes felt cool and smooth as it gentled itself down his cheek. He squeezed his eyes tight until it was as dark as possible then opened them suddenly and let the light slash into them and scrape them with heat then closed them and felt the caress of the water on his cheek. He played the game over and over until his eyes started to pain and then he just closed them and relaxed, flowing deeper and deeper into himself and the comfort of the future as the pain slowly subsided. The bed was soft. The breeze cool and gentle. The moonlight peaceful. He flowed deeper and deeper into himself, wrapped in the comforting strength of hate.

It didnt take too long to train the dogs. At least it didnt seem to take very long. Actually he wasnt certain how long it took, but it seemed like a short time because he enjoyed it so much. Especially forcing them to sit still, absolutely still without so much as a twinge or a whimper, as he pinned their badges to their noses. Of course it took quite a while, now that he thought about it, to get the palms of their hands and their knees calloused and hardened. God, what a supreme joy that was. To watch them crawl on all fours over gravel and broken glass and then when their palms were hardened so they could plod along as rapidly as possible the callouses were peeled off and they had to start all over again.

And the races on the cinder path chasing a mechanical bitch and a spotlight following them around the small track, their naked bodies shining in deep-dimensional relief and every time they passed the small box their families were sitting in—every living member of their families jammed together as tightly as possible—they stopped and assumed their begging positions and barked and then he would whip them on their bloodied and bared asses and the race would start again. And sometimes he would trot after them whipping them, laughing, and urging them on and sometimes he would declare a rest period and they stayed on all fours, their heads hanging, their tongues hanging, and he could see the pain as they struggled for breath, their chests constricted with unbelievable pain, and he would rub salt and vinegar into the slashes on their asses and into their bloodied hands and knees and then the race would resume with the lashing of his whip and they would once again race around the cinder track until they fell from exhaustion and were dragged to their kennels, unable even to whimper as their skin, from the tops of their heads to the tips of their toes, was ripped, scratched, burned and torn by the cinders, gravel, the glass and concrete they were dragged over and through.

And every day, or quite often many times a day, he would inspect their fingernails and their toenails. He would start with the fingernails, saving the toenails for last, squeezing them with a pair of pliers and rapping them with the butt end of his whip. And he measured them carefully, making notes in his little black book, to see how much further down they were worn. Sometimes he couldnt inspect them, or measure them too accurately because of the clotted blood and dirt so he cleaned them thoroughly with a wire brush, lashing the dogs repeatedly when they cried out with pain. And as he inspected and measured and brushed he wondered how long it would be before he could see a bit of bone thrusting itself through the mangled flesh. And, too, with each inspection he spent longer and longer on the finger tips saving and savoring the toes for last as a gourmet would relish each delectable bite of the entree while looking forward to the exquisite dessert that would be the culmination of the feast. He would crack the caked blood and dirt with the butt of his whip, one finger tip at a time, then peel and yank at scabs before wire-brushing and measuring and inspecting. Then a long thin needle would be pushed slowly into the tip of the finger until it hit the bone and the depth carefully measured. And then through the top of the finger where the nail had been worn away. And then when he had spent as long as possible on each and every finger tip iodine was poured slowly, drop by drop, on each one. He had to take proper care of his dogs. He didnt want them to get an infection. O, no. He wanted healthy dogs. He wanted his dogs to be able to frolic and cavort. Yeah, they should be able to traipse and romp over hill and dale. And too, if they didnt have strong and healthy front paws how could they dig for buried bones and cover their turds when they shit. When he finished dropping the iodine on the front paws, he stood for a moment and surveyed his animals with a smile of complete and consuming joy before once again kneeling and examining their hind feet. He would just stare at them for a few moments making a mental note of how far back on the toes the skin was now starting to rip and tear. This examination took time to do thoroughly as there was much more to be inspected and measured. There was not only the wearing down of the nail and the tip, but also the wearing away of the skin on the joints of the toes.

No matter how they ran or tried to keep their toes off the ground it was inevitable they eventually would have to drag their paws over the gravel, the cinders, the glass, the concrete. He would watch them joyfully, timing them with a stop watch, as they ran, trying to keep the tender paws elevated, watching their faces contort with the sudden pain as they lost the battle. And the more he ran his dogs the sooner the battle of the hind paws was lost. At first he inspected them every few minutes to see how long it took for the hairs on them to be worn off. And when the paws were completely bald he made careful note of how long it took for the joint to peek through the scraped skin. And he took polaroid pictures constantly to see if the bone would really turn whiter with wear. And then with each running, more and more of the bones would be exposed and as he measured and noted and added with metric precision his stomach would glow as the figure increased. And then the needle where the nail had worn away and where the tip of the toe had worn away.

He also played a little mathematical game of trying to

determine the ratio between the wearing away of the tip of the toe and the nail. From careful measurements he knew how much of the tips of the toes and fingers had been worn away and also how much of the nails had been worn away and, too, just how far away from the tip of the toe or finger was the edge of the nail. He could not develop a formula that would determine exactly what the difference would be, but he experienced great joy and stimulation in seeing just how close he could predict the measurements before each run. And naturally, as with the forepaws, the cracking and peeling of scabs and wire-brushing were done slowly, deliberately, and with great relish and joy.

Obviously the examinations were extremely painful and the fucking animals screamed and yelled until, with constant and considerate lashings, they learned to howl and yelp with great canine artistry. And too, they would jerk and thrash about so it was necessary to restrain them so the necessary and various measurements could be made accurately. He employed various methods depending upon his mood. If he wanted to hear the yelping and howling loud and clear he would simply shackle their limbs to the floor of their kennel. That way they could constantly thrash about and howl and yelp piercingly, especially when slowly pricked with the needle. Naturally he was well aware of the danger of infection from needle pricks, especially tetanus, so he carefully heated the needle in the flame of a candle to be certain it was completely and thoroughly sterilized.

But there were times when he wanted a different sound accompanying his examinations so he added strangulation collars and attached the other end of their leashes to the wall. Then as they thrashed and yelped and howled the collars would slowly tighten and their music would be muted until with a sudden stab of pain there would only be a barely audible croaking deep in their throats. He would then stand and look at them as their tongues protruded and swelled and darkened, their eyes bulged with absolute and uncontrollable terror and their skin slowly turned blue. Then he would loosen the collars and start the process all over again. This was his favorite means of inspecting and measuring. He could slowly toy with their paws and see how long their howls and yelps would remain at their highest pitch and then he would see how long he could prolong it while the pitch slowly descended until he heard the ultimate croak from their throats. And there was also the added thrill of watching them twitch and writhe as their contorted bodies starved for air. And each time he loosened the collars he would measure the dents in their necks to see just how tight the collars had gotten. The ultimate goal was to see how far he could go without them dying. But he would have to wait to determine that, however. That would come if he ever tired of the game. Then he would simply let them die and then measure the dents in their throats and see how close he had come the previous times. Maybe someday he would just let one of them die and save the other one. But that was in the future. No need to worry about that now. There were many more games to be played and enjoyed.

And like all good dogs they should learn to beg for their food. How in the hell do you teach such goddamn dumb animals to do anything. Well, I guess I/ll just have to start at the beginning. A little flogging and prodding with cattle prods should help. Now beg you sonsabitches. No. No. Not like that. He stood back and looked at them for a moment, shook his head then flogged them and prodded them in the balls with the cattle prods. Keep your hind fucking feet flat on the floor. Now bend your knees. No. No. For krists sake.

He shoved the cattle prods up their asses and kept them
there for many long, painful seconds. Keep them at a 45-
degree angle. Goddamn stupid mutts. He shoved the prods
up their asses and flogged them, then stopped and surveyed
the scene for a moment, thinking. I guess youll just have to
learn the hard way.

A wonderful surge of excitement flooded through his
body as he made the preparations to teach those fucking
mutts how to beg. They would know just how much to bend
their knees and let their hands hang limply and get the
proper mournful look in their eyes. By Jesus he would teach
them.

His hands trembled with excitement as he twisted one
end of a wire around their balls and the other end to an eye
bolt in the floor. He then tightened the wire until their
knees were bent at precisely the proper angle. Then he
twisted one end of another piece of wire around their balls
and attached the other end to the ceiling, tightening it
until it was impossible to move ½ inch without feeling that
their balls were being crushed in a vise. He walked around
them as an art critic would a statue, studying every little
detail of his work. His excitement was so great that he could
feel his stomach trembling from his guts up to his throat.
Yes, everything was ready. The knees were bent at just
the proper angle and now he could concentrate on teaching
them the proper attitude of their front paws, the proper
attitude of the holding of the head and the mournful hound-
dog look that should be in their eyes.

But first it might be best if they knew what it would
feel like if they moved. He shoved the cattle prods up their
asses and listened to them scream and watched their bodies
twitch and struggle to find that one minute point at which
the pain would be relieved. He screamed at them that they
were dogs and were supposed to howl and whimper and not

scream like men and jammed the prods deeper then flogged them with the cat-o'-nine-tails until they started howling then stopped flogging and yanked the prods from their asses and stood back and watched the desperate twitching and jerking as their eyes bulged with the pain of their balls being twisted, the electric pain jabbing through their guts.

He sat on the floor in front of them so he could see their eyes bulge with pain, their tongues flop and the spit dribble from their mouths. He laughed and laughed, but not so loud as to drown out the sound of their howling. After many long and torturous years they found the position that relieved the pressure and pain. Their breathing was rapid and labored and he yelled at them to pant properly. He picked up the prods and their eyes started with fear and their tongues quickly hung from their mouths and they panted like hounds. Thats better. Thats the good dogs. He continued to sit in front of them staring at the wires and their balls. Then he noticed an almost imperceptible movement of their knees, as they strained to keep their painless positions, and his mouth tightened with joy. He noticed the straining and taut muscles and tendons in their legs and thighs and could feel the painful battle going on within his dogs as they strained to maintain the position, hearing their prayers that their muscles wouldnt cramp, feeling the endless time they were experiencing, as they prayed desperately that the wires would snap or that their master would die or go away and leave them alone. Praying for anything that would relieve their torment. And o god, it was good to feel their desperation and hopelessness. To see the pain not only in their eyes, but in the very flesh and muscle and sinew of their bodies. And the more he felt the painful immobility of their time, the more time, for him, was nonexistent and sublime. And the more their guts were knotted and tortured with pain, the more his body felt weightless and free. And the more he watched them groveling in their hell, the more he embraced and caressed his heaven. He didn't bother trying to think of new tricks to teach his animals. He was simply and fully content to wallow in his sublime joy as they wallowed in their endless and painful time.

But then his reverie was interrupted by the buzzing of a fly. He waved at it with his hand, but it kept coming, buzzing around his face until the spell was broken and he swatted at it angrily, cursing the sonofabitch for bugging him. But then he suddenly stopped and broke out into a loud laugh that startled his wired animals and he laughed even louder as the look of pain on their faces was mixed with complete and utter confusion and apprehension as he stood up and told them you can catch more flies with honey than you can with vinegar. He watched the contortions of their faces as his face broke into a huge grin and he stared at them for long moments, chuckling. I/ll be back in a few minutes, my mans best friends. Dont get lonely while Im gone. I wont be long. He laughed aloud and left the kennel, returning quickly with a jar of honey. He stood in front of them and held the jar in their faces, then took off the top and passed it back and forth under their noses. See? Honey. His grin was larger than his face as he stared at them, then slowly tilted the jar and poured honey over their balls, pricks. Its true. Believe me. Its really true. You can catch more flies with honey than you can with vinegar. He sat down a few feet away from them, then leaned back on his elbows and waited with the excitement of happy anticipation.

There was almost a gentleness in his smile as he stretched his legs out and tilted his head to one side and looked at their faces and into their eyes. And as he looked at the beautiful expression of terror on their faces he could feel the tension of their bodies. Every muscle, tendon and sinew straining with all possible power and control to remain immobile. He studied their faces and eyes carefully and minutely, digesting with every cell of his body the beauty he saw there. The most exciting beauty he had ever viewed. And they truly were beautiful animals. Their tongues were thick and wet and their panting was an extremely musical accompaniment to his excitement. And then over the deep and constant beat of their rapid panting there glided then soared the lyrical melody of a quartet of flies, their beautiful cello-like sound strongly punctuated by the bass accompaniment and their shimmering, iridescently lovely forms were watched with bulging and screaming eyes. Aaaahhhh. . . . . . . such a wonderful and beautiful sight to behold. He started humming in a low counterpoint then relaxed beyond belief as excitement continued to beat through his body. His head swayed slightly and lightly back and forth to the music and then his face burst into an endless and complete grin as he sang the words to his song—a trip to the moon on gossamer wings. He laughed and laughed as he sang the line over and over. He stopped laughing and sat up and looked at his animals and spread his arms. Its just one of those things. He laughed again, but quickly controlled it to a chuckle as he saw the flies zeroing in on the honey. Now the fun begins.

His face quickly hardened with intense concentration as he tried to observe every inch of his animals simultaneously. His eyes flew from face to body to crotch to legs then crotch then face, but whatever parts of their bodies he focused on he was afraid of missing something important in another part. He quickly eliminated the portion below the hips because he could feel the tension there, the jerking and straining. Instead he adjusted his vision to take in the area just below their balls upward, raising his sights occasionally to note the difference in their bulging eyes and gasping tongues. He thought briefly of trying to measure the bulge of their eyes and tongues, but dismissed it for fear of missing something important.

When the quartet stopped playing and rested, refreshing themselves by sucking the succulent honey, he watched with fascination as muscles twitched spasmodically in time to the continuing accompaniment of the ever louder and deeper panting. But now there was a new sound. One that punctuated the panting accompaniment and the lyrical melody still heard in his head. The staccato beating of their hearts. And then the muscles tightened and the music was replaced with the most beautiful sound of all. Their screams.

He listened joyfully for many minutes then slowly picked up the cattle prods and walked toward them, his eyes never looking anywhere but in theirs. Now, now, we cant have all that noise. What would the neighbors say? A series of giggles jerked out of him. How many millions did they pay for that rembrandt? Whatever it was, and however beautiful that painting is, nothing could be more beautiful and exciting than this picture. What could be more excitingly beautiful than the blatant terror in their eyes. He chortled as he stared into their eyes, his swimming with ecstasy as he nestled in the beautiful sight and listened to the heavenly music of the flies sucking the honey from their pricks, the soothing cacophony of their strangled screams, the throbbing beat of their panicked hearts. Dont you know that beauty is in the eye of the beholder, and his laugh soared and prevailed through the music as he jammed the cattle prods into their scrotums again and again as their screams and howls infused him with more and more energy and he jabbed harder and harder, then stood back and surveyed this masterpiece of sight and sound, his body trembling with such an abundance of excitement and energy that every cell of his body and being tingled and vibrated and the music inspired him to wave the prods like batons while his eyes sucked in every minute detail of the living canvas he painted—the beauty of the bulging eyes, the distorted and distended tongues, the flush of the flesh, the little beads of sweat that glistened and glimmered and dripped, drop by drop, into the bulging eyes and burned with joyous intensity, and the dribble of spittle. He waved his batons and brushes until the music built to the point of needing a crashing crescendo and he twirled behind them and thrust his instruments of creation into their fucking assholes and twisted and shoved until the crescendo lifted him from himself and his body trembled with such exquisite joy that his hands slid from the instruments of joy and his body was slowly and softly lowered to the floor, his eyes fixed on the animated prods hanging from their asses, and was delivered by the heavenly music to a peaceful slumber. He turned on his side and put his folded hands under the side of his head, his legs slightly bent at the knees, his body as completely relaxed as ever a body could be by the soft murmuring of a lullaby.

He wasnt certain how long this part of the training program lasted—days, weeks, but however long it was glorious and extremely effective. Pain is such an effective teacher. During the other phases of the indoctrination he would flog them when they erred, but didnt waste too much energy with the cat-o'-nine-tails, but simply put them back in their basic classroom. As he said many times, he simply wired them for learning.

Teaching them to be good watchdogs, to be ever alert and vigilant, was another phase of their training that required much wiring. It was not only necessary from the point of view of their training, but also to allow him to obtain the proper amount of rest. It eventually boiled down to teaching them always to be half-awake no matter what time of the day or night. At first he would simply walk up to their kennel in the middle of the night, not trying to be quiet. But they continued to sleep until he flogged them awake. He then left and returned later warning them that they must bark and howl at the first sound. It was a very tedious job, but necessary. At first he flogged them and returned in an hour or half an hour, but when he was still able to open the door of the kennel without them barking he simply wired them and retired for the night.

In a few days he had a schedule that allowed him to obtain the maximum amount of rest and training time. He simply left them wired during the day and slept. After a few days of this they became more alert and most of the time they barked before he opened the kennel door. He started making notes of how close he was to them before they started barking so he would have a constant record of their improvement. Finally, one night, they barked and howled each time he approached them and each time he was further from them, so he allowed them to rest and one wire was removed from each. He told them what good dogs they were and patted them on their heads. He studied them closely as the relief flowed over their entire beings and they collapsed on the floor and groveled into a sleep. He quickly flogged them and told them to keep their tongues out like the good dogs they are or I/ll just have to wire you again. Or maybe I should just nail your tongues to the floor, that way it would be much easier to keep them out. He burst into laughter as panic swallowed them and their tongues were shoved from their mouths. He threw them both a bone and left them to their rest, still laughing.

An hour or so later he walked quietly into the kennel and stood over them as they continued to sleep. He shook his head and smiled as he thrust the prods up their asses. I guess youll never learn. When he left later they were wired and strained all through the remainder of the night to hear the approaching steps so they could howl and bark and be once more relieved of the torturing wires. He slept soundly, and peacefully, until early in the afternoon.

Eventually, because of his mercy, and the boredom of playing the same game over and over, he allowed them to sleep through an entire night, as best they could, and the next day went on to another phase of their training.

What happened was that he suddenly realized that they just werent eating properly. They had learned to beg, with the aid of the wires, as they should, and when he threw them scraps from his table they were able to catch them most of the time, but they hadnt learned many things as yet. Up to now he had allowed them to more or less sip their water from their bowls, but now it was time for them to do it properly. He explained what was expected of them then led them to their bowls and told them simply, lap you bastards, lap. It only took a few hours and a few jabs of the prods for them to learn. He continued to check on them from time to time, but for the most part they were good dogs and learned their lessons well. Or, as he told them occasionally, youre wiry, and laughed.

It took a while for them to learn how to bury and dig up a bone, but that was less difficult than getting them to eat a piece of gristle that had been buried for a day or two. But he felt it was important for them to learn how to do this as soon as possible. After all, who knows what the future might have in store. They might get lost in the woods and be forced to eat the rotten remains of some dead animal. A dog should be able to survive no matter what the circumstances. And too, it was a good way to remind them that they were dogs. And there was another advantage to a diet of rotten meat. When he gave them a can of succulent dog food it was a rare treat and one to be relished. At first they didnt seem to realize that he was doing this for their own good no matter how often he told them and gave a detailed explanation of the situation. For some reason the rotting and dirt-covered gristle sickened them and they insisted upon puking on their food. He empathized and thoroughly understood, but he also knew it was his duty to train his animals properly. So he sighed, with a slight chuckle, and adjusted the wires so they couldnt move their faces more than a few inches above their food. Im sorry, but I guess you just have to learn everything the hard way. You get nothing else until thats finished. He wasnt certain how long it took to finish, but eventually they got it all down. At first he tried leaving them alone and letting hunger force them, but that would take too long, and there were many things yet to be learned. So he simply prodded them into finishing their meal. A most delicious repast he referred to as gristle à la puke, as he shoved the prods deeper into their asses, laughing and coaching, eat, eat. Soon they accepted everything with relish and gratitude and wolfed it down as rapidly as possible.

One day, toward the end of this particular training period, something happened that made him laugh so much he almost loosened the wires holding one of his animals. When the meat was dug up there were usually many little friends of various kinds still munching on their dinner, and at first this created a bit of a problem until they finally realized that they too were part of their dinner. As he explained to them, you cant get fresher meat than that. But one day there must have been an exceptionally large amount of rather tenacious ants on one piece and a few of them lost their sense of direction and crawled up the nose of the eater. The dog howled pitfully and threw its head in insane gyrations, its balls straining at the wires. He laughed and watched with utter and complete fascination as the animal went through a series of contortions that were unbelievable. The ants must have panicked when they found themselves stuck in his nose and ran crazily to free themselves from the sticky mucus, but continued to lose the battle against the great rush of air that sucked them further and further into the darkness. And the more the dog fought against the minute giants in his nose the more he yanked on the wires twisted around his balls. The scene was so funny that he almost fainted with laughter. He wanted to ask his dog which was worse, the itch in the nose or the noose around his balls, but couldnt stop laughing long enough to speak. Finally he just staggered out of the kennel, his eyes and nose dripping from laughter.

He now decided that it was time for them to learn to make love. His dogs were different in many ways from most dogs, but he realized that the sexual drive in all animals was very strong and so he thought it only proper that he should teach his dogs the proper way to screw. He didnt anticipate any problems with the actual screwing itself, but he thought the mounting might prove to be a problem and he was certain that there would be certain objections to the pre-liminaries. But he loved his animals and was willing to be patient and help them in any way he could. After all, they were rather large animals and might need more guidance than the ordinary dog. But they were well wired for learning so he didnt anticipate too much trouble.

When he explained their next lesson to them they seemed to be repelled by the idea, but he patiently explained that they had to learn to be good dogs, and all good dogs start with their nose. He told them he didnt think it was necessary for him to lecture them about the proper procedure, after all everyone has observed animals and is familiar with their particular overtures and preliminaries to the act of love. You are no different from any other kid in the streets or on a farm, giggling and laughing as you watched a male sniffing a bitches snatch. Shit, how many times have you sniffed your old ladys snatch and given it a few healthy laps with your tongue. This is no different except now your old lady looks a little different and you have a nice tight asshole to sniff and lap. And dont tell me you think its a shitty idea, HAHAHAHAHAHA-HAHAHAHA. . . . . . .hahahahehehe. Just think of the advantages. You dont have to fight your way through a rough bush. Its like having a nice young bald pussy. haha-hahahahahaha. Dogs love to chew up pussies.

o.k. Lets get going.

He stretched out on the floor and leaned against the wall and gave a gentle tug on the wires. You must be the mommy and you must be the daddy.

He gave another tug on the daddys wire, reminding him to start with his nose. He watched quietly and calmly as his bitch stood frozen with terror as she awaited the cold nose and wet tongue of her mate. He stood behind her staring at her wide expanse of ass deeply cleaved, all lines of light and shadow leading to her dark, wet hole. He made a halfhearted attempt to narrow the gap between his nose and her tightened ass, but automatically stopped and waited for the inevitable tug on the wire.

But their beloved trainer tugged not. He watched the scene with complete and penetrating awareness that made tugging the wire unnecessary, now. Instead he watched with quiet pride at the evidence that his long and patient work was fruitful. They stood on all fours like dogs, their tongues hung and quivered like dogs. They panted like dogs. They looked and smelled like dogs. And he knew they werent acting a part. They were dogs. A prideful joy warmed him. And while he luxuriated in the soothing time-lessness of the scene his joy and warmth multiplied and multiplied over and over with the realization that for them time was endless and alive with paralyzing dread and terror as they awaited the inevitable yank of the wire that would propel them into the repugnant act. It was beautiful to look at their outsides and feel their insides. It was too bad he hadnt kept a constant photographic record. But actually that wasnt necessary. He could remember, vividly, what they were like when he started training them and appreciate the fruits of his labors as he leaned against the wall, wires in hand, and watched his animals.

He continued to drift weightlessly through infinite time as they felt the crushing burden of impending time. . . .

O.K., you fucking faggots, yanking the wires, get that nose up her ass-hole.

His hounds howled and he kept a slight pressure on the wires as he guided their movements like a puppet master. Go on sniff it, sniff it you sonofabitch, tugging, guiding, jam your fucking nose in that bitches snatch. Thats it, sniff. Sniff you bastard, sniff. Take a good deep whiff. Comeon. Comeon. Get it in there. Bury it you bastard. Bury it in that bitches bumgut. . . . Thats it. Thats a good dog. Now take a good deep sniff. . . . Yeah. Thats the way. Now kiss it so she/ll know you love her. . . . Good dog. Again. Yeah. Again. A nice big soul kiss. Comeon. Get that tongue in there. In. In. In. Deeper. Deeper. I can still see part of it. Deeper you mangy, fucking hound. Deeper. Bury your face in that bitches cruddy ass. Hahahahahaha. Thata boy. Thata boy. Enjoy your taste of honey. Hahahahahahahahaha. . . . .

Now its time for the lovers circle. Comeon. Dont look at me like that. You know what I mean. Youre dogs. Dogs! Theres a nose and tongue for each asshole. Comeon. This is a lovers circle, not a fucking square dance. Thats it. Thats it. Now you got the idea. And dont worry about those dangling dongs or hairy balls. Just concentrate on the assholes. Hahahahahah. . . . Thats it. Concentrate on the assholes, you assholes. . . . . . hahahaha

O.K., its lapping time. I said its lapping time, yanking on the wires, so get with it. . . . Thats better. Yeah, much better. . . . Now harder. I want to hear it. Make pretty music for daddy. Thats it. Slurp it up you mangy, mongrel mother-fuckers. Hahahaha. A taste of honey. Hahahaha. A taste of honey. Thats a good one. Isnt it, you lap-happy fucks. Hahahahahahaha. . . . . .

O.K. Fuck-time. The dogs stopped instantly and stood frozen, their heads and tongues hanging, their eyes bulging from their heads and spit dribbling from their tongues. He smiled as he surveyed his kennel and listened to their panting. Whats the matter with you. Why do you have such a shitty look on your faces? Hahahaha. . . . What a shitty looking pair of hounds. Hahahahahahaha. . . .

He leisurely unfolded himself from his sitting position and picked up the prods. Tell you what Im going to do. Youve been a couple of good dogs. Im really proud of you. So just to show you that I appreciate good dogs I/ll help you out a little bit this time. After all, whats right is right and whats fair is fair. And Im a very fair person. I dont believe in punishing my dogs to teach them. I mean, you can see that from the kind way Ive trained you. No. I just dont believe in hurting dumb animals. I believe a good performance deserves applause, clapping his hands and whistling, and so far youve given a pretty good performance. And whenever my dogs do what theyre told I like to reward them. I dont have any dog yummies, but I do have something that will make the next performance a little easier. He dipped the tip of a prod in a bucket of axle grease. I/ll just grease up this bitches ass for you boy. He smeared grease on the cheeks of the bitches ass then jammed the prod in her asshole and pressed the button that shot the juice through the rod. She yelped and howled, almost drowning out the soothing buzz of the electric prod, but he didnt allow that to prevent him from keeping his promise of greasing the bitches ass. He rotated the prod slowly in widening circles. I dont know what youre howling about. I really dont understand you bitches. Try to do you a favor and you complain. Hahahahaha. I just want to make sure youre in a wide, receptive condition. Hahahahahahaha.

He yanked the prod out and stepped aside. O.K. boy, go geter. A few low grunts belched from them as the bitch was mounted and the hounds cock fumbled its way into her asshole. Thats it boy. Thats the way. Now a little this way. Now a little in that direction, nudging the guiding wires. Thats it boy. Get it in there. Comeon, shove. She cant go nowhere. Thats a strong wire around that bitches balls. Hahahahahaha. Thats a good one, aint it boy. The bitches balls. Comeon boy. Sock it toer. Goddamn it boy, cant you do any better than that? Jesus kay-rist. Dont you know how to fuck a bitch. Sink your teeth into her neck and hold on. Thats it. Sink them in. Yeah, thats it. Now just hold on. She cant go nowhere. Just listen to that pretty howling. Just like a dog in heat. Hahahahahaha. Yeah, she loves you boy. You hear her howling with joy? Hahahahahahaha. You know what shes saying when she yelps like that? Heh, do you know? Shes saying, I love you. Yeah, thats right boy, shes saying I love you. She wants you to sink those teeth in her neck, boy. Thats it, getem in there. Get a good firm grip on her cause youre gonna ride that bitch boy. Youre gonna ride the shit out of her. Hahahahahahaha. Thats it boy, youre gonna ride the shit out of her, shoving the prod deep into his ass and listening to the juice buzz through the prod as his dogs yelped and howled with the pleasures of love.

He left the prod jammed in the dogs ass and caressed the tip of the bitches prick with the other. Hey now, we cant have any of that. Dont you know a bitch cant have a hard on. Hahahahahaha, letting the prod roam up and down the bitches prick and balls, finally burying it in her scrotum.

He chuckled as he watched the frantic and involuntary movements of his prize pets, and when their passions were spent he arranged the wires so they would remain locked in their lovers embrace and went for a walk. The air felt soft and clean.

BUT everything has its own fucking stink. Like trying to eat that breakfast with her smell. It was the same as Marys, and all the others, but different. All her own. I dont know, maybe she didnt know. You dont always know your own smell. You know it, but you dont know it the same way as somebody else. I dont know. I guess it was different to me. Maybe she didnt smell it. Maybe she was used to it. But she always knew where I was by the smell. As soon as I walked into the fucking house she knew if I was in the poolroom, the diner or who knows where else. She/d sniff me like a fucking dog. Like some kind of fucking blood-hound or something. She/d look at me and her goddamn nose would twitch like a sonofabitch and ask me where I was and then tell me. Youve been here, youve been there. Twitch, twitch, twitch. Just like a fucking dog. Shouldve told her why I couldnt eat that fucking breakfast. Shouldve twitched my nose and told her. All their own stink, and all the same.

Just like Mary, only different. Her stink didnt bother me. Wonder why she didnt sniff my hand when I came home from the movies. Maybe they think its their own smell. Maybe it was the soap in the movie bathroom. Pretty hard to smell cunt juice after washing your hands with that soap. Krist, my hand sure did smell funny after washing with that soap. Shit, I dont know what it smelled like, but it sure was weird. Guess they were the only times I washed my hands in the movies. Never did like that soap. But my hands sure did get washed on Saturday afternoon. I guess going to the movies with Mary was the closest thing I ever had to a date when I was a kid.

He would meet her on the corner and they went to the same theater each Saturday afternoon. It didnt make any difference what might be playing, he never bothered to find out or try to determine whether or not he would enjoy the movies. That had nothing to do with his being there. The theater was wide and the front section had two wings on the side where they wouldnt be noticed. All morning he got more fidgety, and his gut got tighter and tighter, as he anticipated going to the movies. He always wore the same blue, corduroy pants. They were his lucky pants. The zipper seemed to be a little longer in them and could be opened with comfort while he was sitting. The only trouble with them was that if any scum got on them you could see it a mile away so he had to inspect them carefully in the bathroom before he left the movie and wash any spots before they turned to a stiff white. But it was worth the trouble. He always scored when he wore his blue corduroy pants.

By 11/30 he had finished his lunch and had gotten a quarter from his mother for the movie. She always asked him what he was going to see and when he told her he didnt know she always said, well, whatever it is, enjoy it. She kissed him and told him to have a good time and be home in time for dinner. He walked as rapidly as possible up the streets to the theater, his excitement knotting his gut and spreading throughout his body until the tip of his joint squirmed like a dozen ants were crawling around inside it. He started slowing down as he approached the theater just in case Mary might be there waiting, but she never was. She always got there about 10 minutes after he did, wearing her long, pink jacket. He looked at the stills while he waited, vaguely wondering what the movies might be about, then leaned against the corner of the building until Mary got there. When she did they got on line with the rest of the kids. When they got inside they walked down the far right side to their seats and got Marys jacket adjusted on their laps then waited for the lights to go out.

The screen lit up, the music blared and the theater was darkened and they adjusted themselves in their seats. He put his hands under the jacket, down her thighs to the end of her skirt, then worked the skirt up to her hips, their eyes watching the images on the bright screen, then tugged one side of her skirt under the cheek of her ass as she lifted it slightly, then the other, back and forth slowly, inch by inch, always staring at the screen, their heads immobile, until her skirt was over her hips, Mary keeping her hands on top of her jacket, continually adjusting it so she was always covered. When he was sure her skirt was out of the way he paused for a moment then hooked his thumbs inside the top of her pants and started working them down, first one side then the other, their eyes always looking to the left at the screen, feeling the soft, warm flesh of her ass against his fingers, Mary lifting one cheek just barely enough to allow him to slide them under, and then the other until they were down to her knees. They kept the upper part of their bodies almost rigid as he rubbed the inside of her thigh with his hand for a moment then pushed against the inner part of her other thigh with his finger tips, and she spread her legs so he could get his hand between them. He felt the heat of her crotch on his hand and her hairs on his fingers as he wiggled his middle finger between the lips of her cunt, pushing them aside and spinning his finger between them until he felt the warm, moist lips around the tip of his finger and then, with the images still appearing before his eyes and the sounds still tapping at his ears, he continued to rotate his finger as he slid it up and down until he found her hole and prodded his finger in as far as it could go as Mary kept her arms on her jacket so it wouldnt slide from her lap and kept her legs spread as far apart as her pants would let her. He stopped moving his finger for a moment and just let it rest in her tight hole. It was warm and moist and so was her entire crotch and his hand. He shoved it in deeper until he felt the hairs bristle against the back of his hand and the moistness of her snatch around his knuckle. He held the edge of her jacket with his other hand and told her to take it out. Moving only her hand and part of her arm she reached under the jacket and searched briefly until she found the top of his zipper. She opened it as he stretched his legs to help her, his finger still buried in her twat, their eyes still staring at the screen, then slid her hand into his open fly and hunted for the opening in his shorts with her finger tips. She felt his long hairs wrap themselves around her fingers then moved down until she felt the base of his cock, then tightened her hand around it and tugged it through the opening. They remained motionless for a moment, he with his finger buried in her cunt, she with her hand squeezing his cock, the both of them holding on to her jacket and staring at the screen.

Then he started shoving his finger deeper and deeper into her hole with short, quick prods, feeling it get warmer and wetter, feeling her juices warm against his knuckle and the back of his hand rubbing against her patch of hair, feeling his hand, and the inside of her thighs getting warmer and wetter, his hand moving easier and faster as her snatch and crotch became lubricated with her juices and sweat, his excitement growing and growing with each jab of his finger into her hole and the tightening of her hand around his prick as she responded to each prod of his finger going deeper into her belly, and his knuckle rubbing against her lips as they unfolded and swelled, and his hand slid along her sweated thighs and she didnt have to force her legs apart but simply let the movement of his hand create the necessary room, and she continued to squeeze and squeeze and squeeze the stiffened prick in her hand and she could feel the juice and sweat tickle her crotch as they were mixed and spread through her bush by his hand and they kept their eyes and heads directed toward the screen as they squirmed slightly in their seats, squeezing their assholes tighter and tighter as their excitement increased.

He stopped moving his hand when it got tired and started to cramp slightly, but continued to wriggle his finger inside her hole and told her to play around. She milked his joint a few times then spread the fluid around the tip of his joint with her thumb. He stopped wiggling his finger and just enjoyed the feeling of her thumb caressing the tip of his cock, feeling the slightly sticky film between the flesh. He told her to go down and she moved her head slightly to look around and he told her it was all right, no one was looking, and she moved her jacket then bent over and put her mouth around his prick and started sucking on it as if it were a straw. He reached around her with his other hand and started squeezing her tit as she sucked on his joint. Her mouth was warm and wet around his joint just like her cunt around his finger. It was different, but the same. They were both part of the same thing. He stared at the screen as he felt her tit in his hand, felt her mouth sucking his prick, felt his finger up her hole and his hand clamped between her legs, and wondered if she liked to have his prick in her mouth and what it was like and how it felt and he wanted to shoot his load in her mouth, but not now, maybe later at the end of the show and even if she couldnt keep it all in her mouth that was all right because most of it would probably go on her jacket and if he got some on his pants he could always wash it off in the bathroom before it dried stiff.

He suddenly felt the cool air around his joint as she raised her head, but it was only for a second then her jacket was covering him and she slid her hand up his cock to the tip and squeezed it and rubbed it with her fingers. He moved his arm as she sat back in her seat, and held the edge of the jacket with his hand. She spread her legs and adjusted herself in her seat and when she was settled he started jabbing his finger in her hole faster and faster, his finger and knuckle going deeper and deeper and she leaned back in her seat and held tightly to his prick as finger and knuckles moved faster and faster, her lips getting larger and unfolding further and he lowered his head slightly to listen to the clicking, squishing sound as his hand pumped rapidly against her wet crotch and juiced cunt. When he stopped she continued to cling to his prick and remained stiffened in her seat. Something happening on the screen caught his attention so he watched for a few moments, letting his hand rest between her legs. He could feel the tenseness in her body, but he thought she was just stretching, or something, so he continued to watch the action on the screen until he became aware that the hand around his prick wasnt moving.

Jerk off. She adjusted her hand slightly and started jerking him off, slowly, with short, uneven strokes. He moved his hand so his finger went deeper, then pushed and twisted until it was in as far as it could go and his knuckles were buried in the swollen lips of her cunt, and continued to just push as her thighs tightened on his hand and her hand moved more rapidly in longer strokes, and the faster and longer the strokes the more he pushed and twisted, the tighter he squeezed his asshole, and the tighter she squeezed her legs until he couldnt move his hand and she stopped jerking him off and milked his prick a few times, slowly, then spread the thin, slightly sticky film around the head of his prick with her thumb. Around and around her thumb went, the film getting thinner and thinner until he eventually felt the skin of her thumb on the head of his cock and it started to twitch inside, and she continued rubbing and he could feel it in his balls and down his legs. When both thumb and cock were dry she stopped rubbing and kept her hand loosely around his prick and he rested his finger in her cunt.

He watched the movie for a few minutes as she squirmed slightly in her seat, pushing lightly against his hand and squeezing his joint. He felt her movements and waved his finger around a bit in her snatch until he became annoyed with the action on the screen then jabbed his hand into her cunt faster and faster as she tugged harder on his prick and continued even when he stopped. She was rigid again and was pumping her thighs together and he looked at her out of the corner of his eye, puzzled, then inwardly shrugged his shoulders and told her to go down. She sucked as hard as she could and he could feel the pressure of her thighs on his hand and the tingle of her teeth against the head of his cock. His groin and gut ached with excitement and his mind pleaded for more, but more of what? His joint was in her mouth and his finger was up her cunt yet there was a confusion of more and what and all he could do was sit as quietly as possible feeling the tingle of her teeth and pressure of her thighs, vaguely aware of movement on the screen and the sound of voices and music, as she sucked as hard as she could.

When her jaws forced her to stop and she sat up and spread her legs he moved his hand in her sodden crotch, as they both stared at the screen, bewildered by the screaming urgency for more, more of some damn thing, but what? His hand stopped moving and he watched whatever it was that was happening on the screen. His hand was a little stiff and tired, but he left it where it was. There was no sense in taking it out, hed only have to put his finger back in again, so why bother taking it out. It felt good where it was. It would smell when he took it out, but he could always wash it. And it was nice and warm and wet in there. And on the outside too. It was good to think of his hand being there. To think of her pants being down around her knees and her legs spread apart and his finger in her pussy. To think of his finger in her bush and his prick in her mouth. He moved his finger in a circle and shrugged off the more and what and told her to jerk off, then play around, then go down and in between she squeezed and tugged and he jabbed and thrust and they sat as still as possible and stared at the screen as she jerked off, played around, went down and he kept his hand and finger moving as fast and long as possible vaguely aware of her stiffening from time to time and tugging a little harder on his joint, but he ignored it and kept his hand and finger moving and kept her jerking off, playing around and going down until the second show started and he told her to jerk off and she jerked him off harder and faster until he said he was ready to shoot and took his hand from her snatch and she cupped her hands between his legs and he pulled back her jacket and grabbed his joint and yanked it off until he shot his load into her cupped hands, his body twitching as he strained to keep the stream directed properly, then milked the final drops and rubbed them off on the sides of her hands.

When he finished he let the head of his joint rub against her jacket, then shoved it in his pants and closed his fly as he watched her open her hands and let the scum drip to the floor then told her to rub her hands together and watched as she rubbed his scum into her hands sensing how it felt and aware of the smell coming from his finger. When he told her O.K. she stopped rubbing and wiped her hands off on the seat in front of her. After she got her pants back on they got up and went to the bathrooms. He went directly into a stall, locked the door, then inspected his pants carefully, opening his pants and belt to be certain there were no telltale spots anywhere, either in or out. When he finished he flushed the toilet then washed his hands. He washed them many times, filling his hands with soap each time, sniffing his finger between washings. When he was satisfied that all he could smell was soap he washed them once more then left the bathroom. She was waiting for him at an exit and followed beside him as he left the theater.

They strolled down the street and he asked her if she was going to baby-sit tonight and what time and told her to look out the window when the people had left, that he would be waiting downstairs in the courtyard. He left her in front of her house and went home. He quickly and vaguely answered his mother when she asked him how he liked the movies, and went to his room.

He sat on the edge of his bed for a while just sort of wondering. It seemed like he always felt like this when he got home from the movies. Like there was something missing or something. He never could quite figure it out. Just some little something missing, or just not right. It puzzled him, but thinking about it got him nowhere and anyway he couldnt wonder about it too long because of the itchy feeling in his crotch.

He went to the bathroom, closed the door quietly, let his pants and underwear drop to his ankles, then sat on the commode and toyed with his joint, his eyes closed tightly trying to create a new image in his mind, one that would give meaning to the more and what he was feeling, but always ending up with the same one, the only one that seemed to satisfy his needs. It consisted almost completely of a single frame from a story in a comic book he had read a few years before. He couldnt remember anything about the book, or the story, except the one frame where an ancient and evil looking oriental had a white woman chained to a pillar in a large hall. He was thin and bony with a pointed chin and goatee, a large sharp nose, long droopy mustaches and red evil eyes. The woman was young, very white and her arms were stretched above her and chains were wrapped around her wrists and around the pillar. Her feet were bare and the tips of her toes barely touched the floor, her evening gown was ripped and her left tit was hanging out. And she was terrified. And the evil oriental stared at her and you knew he was going to do something horrible and whatever that something horrible was satisfied the more and what and made his balls tighten with excitement and he beat his meat faster with the sharp image in his mind of the young white and beautiful woman chained to the pillar and the evil red eyes staring at her and the tit hanging out of the torn gown and he focused on that evil face, the horror on her face and the tit hanging from the chained body and he reached over and grabbed a handful of toilet paper and held it in his left hand as his right hand moved faster and faster and a feeling of satisfaction drifted through him as he could sense what was going to be done to the young white woman as she was chained to the pillar with her left tit hanging in the yellow face with the red evil eyes and he felt the warmth of her terror in his hand as his body jerked with the forced final strokes and he milked and wiped the drops on the paper and stared briefly at the heavy, yellowish white fluid in his hand. He milked his joint one last time, wiped the tip on the paper, then dropped it in the bowl and flushed it.

He went back to his room and sat in his chair, waiting for his mother to call him for dinner. He felt slightly more relaxed, yet still puzzled, discontented. It had been a good day so far, like many saturdays. Saturdays that were looked forward to from sunday morning on, yet there was always something missing or not quite right. At least nothing got screwed up today like it sometimes did. At least not yet. Sometimes she couldnt go to the movies, or didnt baby-sit for some damn reason, but so far everything went the way it should. And tonight hed go up the block after dinner and hang around with the fellows for a while, talking or doing something, then make some sort of excuse to get away without them knowing where he was going and he would see Mary again. He just hoped nothing would happen to stop those people from going out. It wouldnt be so bad if he knew ahead of time so he could meet Mary in the park, but he didnt want her coming around the corner and telling him that she wasnt going to baby-sit. The stupid cunt did that one night and he almost didnt get away from his friends without them knowing where he was going. Shit, that was a ballbreaker. Almost screwed up his whole week. But it should be all right tonight. They were going to some sort of a special party or something. The park was all right, but in the house was the best. He could see. He liked to sit on the couch with her and have her lift her skirt and then take her pants off. He always got a look at her bush and when he held his head right he could see his finger going into her box and he could watch her when she played with his prick and put it in her mouth, especially when he stood up and she knelt in front of him. And he could put his hand in her blouse and squeeze her tit and feel the nipple and even see it sometimes and when he shot in her hands he could see it and watch her wash her hands with his scum and hear it squish between the palms of her hands and then they would sit on the couch and start all over again. All week he planned and dreamed of a good saturday. From class to class, day to day, he dreamed and planned. . . .

But sunday morning always followed with that oppressive weight on his chest, that irritating gnawing that he tried to relieve by taking deeper and deeper breaths that always seemed to be just about to give him relief, yet never did. And everything always seemed to be so goddamn gray and heavy and his mother always asked him if he wanted to go to church with her and he always told her no. Every fucking week it was the same shit. Do you want to go to church. He felt like telling her to take her stinking church and jam it up her ass, but he gave the same answer to the same question. No, not today, and he would leave the house and wander up the block to meet his friends and screw the day away and he would go to school monday and tuesday and wednesday and thursday and friday and then would come saturday and if things went as they should he would go to the movies with Mary and they would baby-sit at night. But sunday always followed.

Yeah.

Yeah, that Fu Man Chu really knew where it was at. He sat on the edge of the bed with his hands clasped between his knees. I wonder if her name was Mary? Seems like it was. Yeah, Mary, Schmary, whats the difference. Whats in a name. By any name she smells the same. Anyway, she was better than nothing. He chuckled. He really knew where it was at that insidious son of a bitch, sitting on the edge of the bed with his hands clasped between his knees, looking. just looking. . . .

Shit. He stood up and stepped to the door. Fuck it. Fuck all that shit, thrusting his face at the small window, a dim reflection thrusting itself at him. He stared at the face, then through it at the wall and the signs over the baskets, yeah, yeah, yeah, blue, green, yellow, purple and shit brindle. He turned from the window and looked into the mirror over the wash basin, at the face and the wall behind him, staring for many minutes at the bloodshot eyes.

He leaned closer and stared at the goddamn pimple on his cheek. It seemed to be twice as fucking big as it was the last time he looked at it. It was red and angry and seemed to be spreading like some kind of fucking rot. He touched it with his finger tip and fucking pain shot through him as if someone had jabbed him with a hot wire. His body snapped rigidly and his eyes screamed as his body paralyzed itself to keep his hands from clawing the fucking thing from his cheek. His body shivered with rage as his screaming eyes glared at themselves and his hands inches from the sonofabitching cheek and that motherfucking pimple that was driving him out of his fucking mind, wanting to rip and tear the flesh from the side of his face and destroy the rotten cocksucker and the poison that was driving him out of his mind.

Suddenly his hands were at his side and his body jerked around and he leaned against the wall, rigid. Those fucking bastards. Those motherfucking bastards. I wish to krist I had those pricks here now. I/d fucking killem. I swear to krist I/d killem. I/d tear the eyes out of their heads. Those miserable bastards. Those miserable cocksucking bastards. He stormed thru his cell, his voice roaring in his head, YOU ROTTEN SLIMY PRICKS. YOU NO GOOD MOTHER FUCK ING BASTARDS strangling air with each hand, snapping his body around as he slashed his way through his cell, I/LL KILL YOU   I/LL KILL YOU,   YOU ROTTEN   SONSABITCHES.   I/LL   KILLYA KILLYA   KILLYAAAAAAAAAAAAAAAAAAAAAAAAAAAAA AAAAAAAAAAAAAAAAAAAAAAA his fists grinding into the corner over the commode, pounding his head against his hands, the bones in his chest being shoved apart by a growing lump that was slowly strangling him, kill you, kill you, slowly staggering down the wall, kill you, kill you, kill you, sitting on the commode, face buried in hands, kill you

rotten

son of a bitch. Thats all, just a rotten son of a bitch. Do you know that god? Youre no good. No fuck   ing good. A no good   fuck   ing   son   of   a   bitch. Do you hear me god? DO YOU HEAR ME YOU LOUSY BASTARD? YOURE NO FUCKING GOOD. YOURE A ROTTEN LOUSY SON OF A BITCH AND I FUCK YOU WHERE YOU EAT, AND YOUR MOTHER TOO, turning to the barred window and the hint of light coming through the milky glass, youre no fucking good, lowering his head and staring at the gray concrete floor. His feet were on the floor and his arms were on his thighs and his head angled forward from his neck and he looked at the gray concrete floor. There were spots and cracks and blemishes and areas where the concrete showed through the paint and that was just a slightly different shade of gray. How many shades of gray were there? The fucking cell seemed to have every shade of gray in the whole fucking world. Gray fucking walls, gray fucking ceiling with cracks going down the walls and into the gray fucking floor. Gray fucking bars. Jesus krist, youd think theyd run out of cracks and gray

maybe it was the North Carolina. Yeah, I think

that was the name of it. Put it together with that stinking glue. Krist, did that glue stink. Worse than rotten eggs and old farts. Painted the whole damn thing battleship gray. Should have painted it different colors. Probably would have looked good with some white and blue or something. Maybe even camouflage colors. Shit, I dont know. Dont even know if camouflage was around then. Fuck it. So what. Gray was good enough. And then to xmas services. Always so fucking cold in the church on xmas. Couldnt have the services at the regular time so the fucking joint could heat up. Had to have them early in the morning when it was cold enough to put icicles on a whores ass. Or freeze a whores tit, or whatever it is. Who gives a shit. At least on xmas we didnt have to sing jesus loves me. Every week in that fucking sunday school, jesus loves me this I know, and the rest of that horseshit. Loves my fucking ass. Jesus loves me this I know. Sure did fuck people up with that chemistry set i got one xmas. Krist, those stink bombs were ugly. Smelled worse than a skunks ass. Sure did fuck up the old Ridgeway movie house. Especially when I put them by the big fans.

JESUS loves me this—what a crock of shit. Theyre out there now riding around in their fucking prowl car talking about how they fucked me up. Bragging to all their friends how they put the fucking screws to me. Just riding around laughing their fucking asses off and stopping women drivers and threatening to give them a ticket if they dont let them pinch them on the ass or squeeze their tits. Cruising around the street looking for some young broad driving alone so they can turn on their fucking red light and force her over to the curb and get out of their fucking prowl car and hitch up their guns and adjust their hats and swagger like a couple of baboons and stick their fucking heads in the window and come on with the same old shit. Excuse me miss, but I have to ask for your registration and drivers license.

Why? Is there something wrong officer?

We/re not sure mam, but your car matches the description of a car reported stolen a few hours ago.

But there must be some mistake, this is my car.

Then there shouldnt be any problem in proving it. Would you take the key out of the ignition and give it to me please, shining his flashlight on the dashboard and the woman, peering down the front of her blouse as she leans over to get the key. He lowered the light as he took the key from her hand, slowly, and looked at the bottom of her skirt, just a few inches from her hips, and her long thighs. He shone the light on her license and registration then on her face. You Mrs. Haagstromm?

Yes officer, I am. But I really dont see what this—thats all right Mrs. Haagstromm. We/ll just call in and see if we can clear this up. He went back to the prowl car and leaned in the window. What did we get this time Fred? A living doll Harry. 5,5, a hundred and 25 lbs, and all tits and ass. How old is she? What the fucks the difference. Shes a good piece of ass. They laughed. I/ll drive her car and you follow. The place in the hills? Yeah.

He walked back to the car and leaned on the window. Im sorry Mrs. Haagstromm, but there seems to be a discrepancy of some sort. Im afraid we/ll have to drive to the station and try to straighten this out, opening the door and letting her know she should slide over by pressing against her. But I have to pick up my little girl at the baby-sitters. I really dont understand what this is all about. Thats all right Mrs. Haagstromm. It shouldnt take too long. You just relax.

After they had driven for a mile or so and the area became less and less populated, she asked him where they were going. It doesnt look like theres a police station anywhere near here. We/re not going to a police station Mrs. Haagstromm. We/re going to a special office of the motor vehicle bureau thats open all night for this kind of emergency. Theyll be able to check out your registration and license in a matter of minutes. I hope so. My little girl has a cold and Im late now. Soon they were driving along completely deserted streets in a heavily wooded area. He suddenly turned down a side road through the trees and parked in a small, flat area just off the road. She stared at him with her mouth open. The door of the prowl car slammed shut. You just keep quiet and everything will be all right Mrs. Haagstromm, looking through her purse. I only have a few dollars, but you can have it, all of it, her head and body trembling. Thats very kind of you mam, but I dont need your money, taking a handkerchief and tissues from her pocketbook and shoving them in her mouth as Harry reached through the window behind her and grabbed her by the arms. You just relax mam, and everything will be all right. Tape was put over her mouth and the bulb taken out of the overhead light before the door was opened. Harry continued to hold her, as they stood in the small clearing, Fred unbuttoning her blouse. Now you just stay still, mam and it will make everything a lot easier. You keep wiggling around like that and Im liable to rip the buttons off your blouse. Harry squeezed her arms harder and she stopped wiggling and stood still and trembling as Fred slowly unbuttoned her blouse, tears whimpering from her eyes and muffled sobs coming from her taped mouth. When Fred finished opening her blouse he cuffed her hands behind her back and unhooked her brassière. They stood in front of her, smiling. Fred lifted one of her tits in his hand, moved it around a bit then bounced it up and down in the palm of his hand. I told you she had a nice pair. Yeah, youre right. You sure can pick them. I gotta hand it to you, they laughed, she whimpered, and Fred tweaked the nipple of the tit, hard, with his fingers. Lets see what the rest of her looks like. That sounds good to me. She started to fall away from them and Harry grabbed her and kept her tilted back against him as Fred continued to remove her clothes. He took her shoes off and tossed them aside then unbuttoned her skirt and pushed it down as he slowly slid his hands down the sides of her thighs and then her legs, feeling the trembling of her flesh. Then he slid her pants down, slowly, and when he stood up he tossed them to Harry. Chew on them a while. Shes just what youve been looking for. A blonde with a black lace garter belt. Well, how about that. She sure has got a black lace garter belt. Its about time. Yeah. Now you can fuck a broad without taking her stockings off. Yeah, I wish my old lady would get rid of that pantyhose shit and start wearing garter belts, staring at the garter belt and light pussy hair while he massaged his crotch. He flipped a tit around a few times then twisted the nipple hard, digging his fingernails into her flesh. A groan gurgled in her throat and tears dripped from her bulging eyes as she staggered back a few steps. Dont go way honey. Im gonna fuck the ass off you. Fred laughed. Lets save that for later. O.K. hahahahahaha. Dont get shitty about it. They laughed as they pushed her toward a clump of small bushes. This looks like a good spot. Yeah. Harry kicked her feet from under her and she thudded on her back. Now thats what I call a groovy broad. Just cant wait for the action to start. They laughed and Harry rolled her over on her stomach and opened one of the cuffs. They put another pair on the other wrist then flipped her over on her back, spread her arms and cuffed her hands to the bushes. Careful there, you dont want her to get a run in her stockings, do you? Sorry about that. They laughed and stood over her, massaging their crotches. You know, she must really like the scenery. Look at the way her eyes are bugged out of her head. Yeah, must be counting the stars. They chuckled and Fred massaged a tit with the sole of his shoe. Hey man, dont get it all dirty. I might want to bite on that later. Dont worry about it, she has another one. He watched her eyes bulge and her head roll back and forth as he pushed harder and scraped his shoe across her tit. Hey, whats that funny noise shes making? Is she singing a love song to you? Hahahaha. No. Shes just counting the stars. Hahahaha. Well, while shes counting stars lets get down to business. Looks like shes trying to keep the doors to the shop closed, looking at her legs tightly crossed. Krist honey, thats no way to run a business, shoving his foot between her thighs, her legs snapping apart as his shoe scraped and pinched her legs. He stood between her legs and shoved them apart with his feet. You know, I think shes just about the blondest broad Ive ever seen. Yeah, kneeling down close to her snatch, each kneeling against one of her legs, and shining a hooded flashlight on her bush. Krist, they are. Theyre almost as blond as her hair. Maybe we should take a few back to the boys. Yeah, thats a good idea. They plucked hairs from her bush chuckling as they watched her belly tremble. One thing you have to admit. Its more fun than plucking a chicken. Yeah, hahahaha. Goddamn it. I cant get this sonofabitch out. It keeps slipping through my fingers. Well, if at first you dont succeed, try, try again. Well, Im not going to give up until I get the sonofabitch out. There. There it is. You happy now? Yeah. O.K. I/ll flip you for first. No, thats all right. Be my guest. You may never have a chance to be first with stockings and a garter belt. Haha. Youre a real friend. Hold the light closer while I get it juiced up. They forced her legs further apart and Fred held the flashlight closer to her cunt while Harry prodded it with a stick. He poked and whirled and jabbed for a few minutes then told Fred to get her in the position. Fred grabbed her by the ankles and lifted her legs and straddled her head as he bent her legs and leaned heavily against the inside of the knees forcing her legs apart. Harry spread her skirt on the ground so he wouldnt get his uniform dirty then dropped his pants. He knelt then prodded her cunt a few more times with the stick then threw it away. Its still kind of dry. Im not going to take any chances on burning my joint on a dry snatch, wiping her cunt with spit. Now she should be ready. He hunted for her hole with his prick and let his body fall heavily on hers as it sunk in. She sobbed and moaned and tried to twist and turn as

Harry tried to bludgeon her with his cock, but the harder she fought the harder Fred leaned on her legs, spreading them so far apart she thought they would be torn from her body. Harry pressed hard and heavy on her body and face, telling her to move it. Comeon bitch, move it. Wiggle that goddamn ass, and she groaned and sobbed, fighting against the tearing pain in her legs, the weight of Harry on her body and face, fighting to suck air in her nose and let her muffled agony out through her taped mouth. I said move it bitch, reaching down and twisting the flesh of her ass between his fingernails. Thats it. Thats the way baby, continuing to twist her flesh between his fingernails as her body jerked from the pain. Harry continued to twist her flesh, twisting even harder as he felt her blood between his fingers, and thrust his cock harder and harder into her spit-lubricated hole, until he dropped his load.

He rested for a few seconds then jerked himself out and up. He wiped his joint with her pants then wiped the blood off his fingers. When he had fixed his pants he relieved Fred. O.K. I got her. Go to it. Shes all ready for you.

Fred kneeled on her stomach and massaged and squeezed her tits. I/ll be a son of a bitch, but you got some nice titties. Damn, you sure are crazy over tits. Why not? You like to pinch asses, I like to squeeze tits. Well, if you likem so damn much, why dont you get your old lady to grow you some big ones. That 2 peas on an ironing board bitch, she dont know what a tit is. Maybe I/ll just cut these off, twisting and squeezing with hands and finger tips, and paste them on the bitch. Hahahahaha. Paste them on her back then youll really be in business. Fred laughed as he straddled her and, as he continued to squeeze with one hand, he rubbed her nose

with the tip of his cock. Hahahahaha. Look at her squirm.
Youd better take it easy bitch or those cuffs will cut your
hands right off. They laughed and she continued to squirm
as Fred shoved his cock up her nose and crushed her tit
in his hand and her nipple between his finger tips, muffled
screams gurgling in her throat, her body jerking with terror
and the cuffs cutting deeper into the flesh of her wrists
until they felt as if they were sawing through the bone
and they continued to laugh as Fred continued to poke
his joint up her nose and Harry leaned harder and heavier
on her legs. Why dont you just lay still and enjoy it Mrs.
Haagstromm, hahahahahaha, but she continued to fight
the cuffs and the snapping pressure on her legs, her terror
forcing her to continue writhing and increasing the pain.
Fred gave a final squeeze and poke and positioned himself
between her legs. Get her ass up so I can shove it in her
nasty old hole. Harry raised her ass by leaning back while
holding her by the bent knees. Hows that? A little higher.
Yeah, thats good. Hold her just like that, her sockets feeling
as if they were going to snap and her hands feeling like
they were just about to be severed from her wrists. Fred
grabbed big handfuls of tits then leaned on her heavily
as he fucked her. I/ll be a sonofabitch if this aint the live-
liest piece of ass Ive had in a long-ass time. As he fucked
her he put his ear against her taped mouth. Speak to me
bitch. She choked on her screams and the wadded handkerchief and tissues. Now thats what I call beautiful music.
He leaned on her tits, digging his nails in deep, and raised
himself slightly so that his face was a few inches above
hers and let his saliva dribble from his mouth onto her
face until his mouth was dry then coughed up phlegm,
rolled it around in his mouth then let it splat on her face.
Hahahaha, how come youre coming so soon, hahahaha,

giving an extra tug on her torn legs. After Fred came he watched the heavy phlegm roll down her cheeks and neck before getting up.

Harry let go of her legs and they looked at her as she whimpered and struggled to relieve the pain in her legs, rolling them into different positions, trying to find one where they didnt still feel as if they were going to be torn from her body. Fred reached down and grabbed her nipples and tugged as hard as he could, lifting her off the ground. Goddamn if that aint one of the finest pairs of tits Ive ever seen, tugging, yanking and whirling then squeezing the crushed nipples between his finger tips, the pain and searing from the deep gouges continuing for many minutes, the pain so intense throughout her body that for the first time she simply lay still sucking air through her nose. Damn, you sure did a job on those tits. She looks like shes dripping red milk. Hahahahaha, yeah, I tried to get the motherfuckers off, but I guess theyre stuck on good. Too bad. Haha. I guess youll just have to go back to those 2 peas on an ironing board. They laughed and she remained still, her eyes bulging, her body still burning with pain, her limbs being torn from her body. She sure does like looking at the stars. Look at the way she stares at them. Shes probably had a lot of experience. Yeah, hahahahahaha. I think shes looked at them long enough, grabbing her ankles, crossing them, and twisting her over on to her belly, a gurgle gagging her as her arms twisted and yanked on the cuffs. I want to grab a handful of that nice round ass, grabbing a large lump of flesh with each hand and twisting as he tugged her cheeks apart. I/ll be goddamned if her ass dont make me hornier than a motherfucker. Harry got up and unlocked the cuffs from the bushes. Lets get her up on her feet. They each grabbed an arm and yanked her into a sitting position. She lifted her head briefly as a scream screeched at her ears, then let it hang forward. Come on bitch, on your feet, tugging and yanking as she stumbled and hung between them, her legs and feet being scraped along the dirt, throbbing pain and screams thrusting her head in bobbing arcs. They dragged her to her feet and leaned her against a tree. Goddamn if she aint a raggedy ann doll. Goddamn bitch, stand up, slapping her across the face and shoving her against the tree, the bark grinding into her flesh. There, thats better. Fred supported her by leaning on her stomach and shoving her against the tree while Harry cuffed her hands to her ankles. They looked at her as she leaned against the tree, her body bent at a right angle, her legs buckling. Now isnt that a pretty sight. Shes all doubled up with joy. Krist, look at those tits. They hang like a couple of sacks. Yeah, she looks like a cow. Why dont you milk her. Fred tugged and yanked on her tits while they both giggled. Steer her over this way so I can wipe the dirt off her back. I dont want to get my uniform dirty. Fred stood in front of her and supported her by wrapping his arms around her back, filling his hands with her tits, and backed her toward Harry. He wiped the dirt off her ass with her skirt. Fred held her tighter and tightened his grip on her tits as Harry rubbed his joint in the slime oozing from her cunt then slowly slid it up the crack of her ass until it reached her asshole then pushed it part way in and left it there and took a large strand of hair in each hand and wrapped them around his hands and as Fred shoved her against him he pulled as hard as he could on her hair and jammed his cock up her ass. She choked and her legs started to fold and Fred let go of her tits and locked his arms around her waist while Harry yanked on the hair reins and spurred his cock deeper into her asshole as her body was bent into a sharper angle, her head being yanked back and thrust into the back of her neck and down into her shoulders, her bent body hanging from Freds arms and on Harrys cock. The harder Harry rode his cock into her asshole the harder he tugged on the hair reins and the deeper the cuffs tore at her wrists and ankles the more impossible it became for her to withstand the agony of the cracking bones, the fiery pain and the horror of the struggle to get air to fight its way down her straining windpipe as her head was yanked back further and further with each thrust. When Harry finished he kept his hands wrapped tightly in her hair and his cock thrust deep in her asshole for a few seconds before unwinding his hands and telling Fred to let go. As Fred stepped back she slid off Harrys cock and crumpled into a manacled and muffled oval. She almost strangled as her head fell forward and the air jammed itself into her throat. She struggled to keep her face out of the dirt and not to choke on the rushing air as her head vibrated and shivered with panic. Her body tried to straighten itself so the air could flow freely into her lungs, but the cuffs yanked her back into the oval and the air fought its way down in huge, ragged chunks, feeling as though it would first rip through her face and head, her throat, and then tear its way through her chest, and then when it failed to rip its way through her chest it tried to fight its way back up her throat until another ragged chunk of air tried to shove it back down and they struggled and she swallowed and she could feel her stomach wrapping itself around her spine until the chunks of air jammed themselves into her lungs and the others following kept them there. As more and more air flowed into her she struggled less to breathe and the suffocating panic subsided and the pain in her body burned itself into her brain along with their laughter.

I/ll be a sonofabitch if she dont wiggle like a chicken

with its head cut off. I swear to krist, shes the best piece of ass we ever grabbed. Yeah. I guess thats why shes doubled up with joy. They laughed again as they bent over and picked her up. Youve rested long enough Mrs. Haagstromm. We dont have all night. Weve got to get back to work. She hung heavy on Harrys arms, her legs starting to collapse, and he jabbed her in the stomach with his finger tips. Comeon bitch, stand up. She retched and a hot lump slowly staggered its way up from her stomach and jammed itself in her throat as Fred tugged on her hair, her head snapping back, and Harry shoved her against Freds cock bursting into her asshole and up to her throat. Her body jerked and the cuffs tore and sawed at her wrists and ankles and when she tried to lower her body to relieve the pain she was jerked back and her body once again yanked against the cuffs. And when her legs started to crumple with each thrust of Freds cock, her body was forced up by Harrys hands twisting the flesh on her belly and shoving her stomach through her spine and Fred tugging on her hair and her body would bend and her legs start to collapse as the cuffs chopped at the bones in her wrists and ankles, the pain and agony increasing until there was nothing but pain and it got worse and worse each second after second after second after hour until nothing was supporting her and she slid from Freds cock and crumpled to the ground, the chunks of air fighting against each other, and somewhere there was laughter.

Goddamn if that aint the bleedinest bitch I ever fucked, wiping themselves off with her slip and pants. All you have to do is touch her and she starts bleeding. Yeah. Maybe shes a religious fanatic, laughing and fixing their uniforms. When they finished they took off the cuffs, wiped the blood off them, then grabbed an arm each and dragged her over to her car and dumped her on the front seat then tossed her clothes on top of her.

Harry leaned over her, pulled her head up by her hair and told her she had better keep her mouth shut or they would see to it that she was arrested for soliciting. Im sure Mrs. Haagstromms little girls wouldnt want everyone to know her mommys a fucking whore. He let her head drop then tore the tape off her mouth. They went back to their car and drove away

the ugly bastards. The ugly cocksucking bastards. Get away with anything. Any fucking thing. Probably laugh their fucking asses off driving around like king shit. Talking about my ass rotting in this fucking jail and laughing their fucking asses off. The ugly mothers cunts. The lousy cocksucking bastards. Jesus, I/d like to rip their eyes right out of their heads and just squeeze them. Just fucking squeeze them, the ugly cocksucking bastards, pounding across the cell from the wall to the door, the door to the wall, the wall to the door, to the wall, the door

then stopping in front of the mirror and looking briefly at the pimple then squeezing it as hard as he could, his eyes tearing and wincing from the needle-like pain in his cheek, crushing the pimple between finger tips until a few drops of fluid oozed out. God DAMN that hurts, squeezing his eyes shut and shaking his head. Just cant get anything out of the sonofabitch. Squeeze the shit out of it and still nothing comes out. The fucking thing will drive me out of my mind. Cant get rid of it. No matter what in the fuck I do I cant get rid of the sonofabitch. Its always there bugging the living shit out of me. Krist that stings. Maybe now itll come to a head and I can squeeze it and itll be gone once and for all. He tilted his head at various angles looking for a hint of white glaze on the pimple, then went back to the bed and sat on the edge.

The prowl car pulled up behind him and the cops got

out and asked him for his i.d. and all that shit and he banged their heads together and pinched a nerve on their necks and knocked them out then stretched them out on the sidewalk so that their cocks were in each others mouths and cuffed them in that position before turning on the red light and siren. He roared with laughter the next day when he read about it in the paper, especially the part about them being found in a strange and unnatural position. Hahahahahahahahahaha, strange and unnatural. Thats a good one. Strange and unnatural,

smiling at the gray wall, glowing inside, until his cell door clanged open and he went to the mess hall and nibbled at whatever meal it was and came back and stretched out on his bed.

HE paused dramatically before continuing. He looked down at his hands then into the faces of the Senators sitting behind the long table. He was unperturbed yet fully conscious of the many microphones, cameras, lights and eyes; aware that he was testifying before a special investigating committee of the United States Senate; aware of the fact that the entire country, and perhaps the world, would know what he said and would see him on movie and t.v. screens, yet he remained calm. The calm that comes with purposeful action. A resolve so strong and motives so right that you remain calm even though you know your very life is in danger, that the threat of death is with you every minute of every day, awake or asleep, on a crowded street or alone in your room. A threat that exists even in the special chambers of the United States Senate. Yet, fully aware as he was of this constant and ever present threat of death, he knew he had to, and would continue to pursue injustice no matter where it led him, no matter what the danger, no matter what the consequences. The gauntlet had been thrown at his feet and he had accepted the challenge.

Gentlemen, its not only for myself that I speak, but for the millions of victims that have gone before me and those who today, right at this very moment as we sit here in comfort and safety—I think I should add that for me it is only a relative safety as my life is in constant danger as evidenced by the many threats on my life that I have already related to you—those who are suffering, now, the cruel and harsh indignities of injustice. A blind injustice that has run amuck and poses a threat to each and every individual in this great country of ours. I speak not only for those millions, but for all those who may come after me. For all those who may not have to suffer the pain and misery that I, and millions have and are suffering, if we unfurl and hold high the banner of truth so injustice will be exposed whenever it exists, whether it be in the largest of cities or smallest of hamlets; in the brightest of spaces or the darkest of corners. Wherever, why and how long are not important. The only important thing for us to remember as responsible citizens of our country, and interested members of society, is that it does exist and that there is no such thing as a small injustice. What threatens the least of us threatens all of us. This malignancy must be ferreted out and exposed so it can wither and die in the searing light of truth. It must not be protected with lies and ignorance. It must not be allowed to be nurtured and grow in the darkness of apathy, lest it spread its venom of corruption until the very foundations of our country are infected and weakened. It is true that I am but one insignificant individual, but within me there exists the strength of truth, the strength of all men who have ever followed the banner of truth to the very gates of death.

He lowered his head and waited for the applause to stop, keeping it lowered as the huge, high-ceilinged room reverberated with applause. When it subsided he continued. I have already related my experience to you and you are aware of the suffering and indignities I was forced to endure. And as humiliating and terrible as they were, they were as nothing compared to the agony that others have been forced to endure. The plight of a young woman was brought to our attention—Mr. Lowrys, Mr. Prestons and mine—and we visited her, along with other interested parties, at a state mental institution. At the time we visited her she had been there almost a year and was still too hysterical to talk without heavy sedation. Up to that time she had had over one hundred shock treatments with no permanent results. She would be all right for a few weeks or so, but then she would gradually get worse and they would have to put her in restraint and eventually more shock treatments were necessary. As of last Thursday, the last time we contacted the hospital, the prognosis was the same. . .no hope. According to the doctors she will spend the remainder of her life in the institution, and most of that time she will be hopelessly insane. She is only 24 years old and will have to spend the rest of her days in a locked ward, half of that time in restraint.

She was only 23 when she entered the hospital, and had a 2-year-old daughter. I will tell you what we have been able to determine about the events leading up to her being committed, as briefly as possible. Some of her story is incomplete and confused, but enough was gotten by the doctors during lucid moments and while under hypnosis so we have a definite idea of what actually happened to her on the night of April the second of last year.

This young woman was like millions of others. She came from a good family, had a good education, never in any trouble of any kind during her entire life, and when she graduated college she married. A year later she gave birth to a girl and the three of them were extremely happy until the night of April second. Her husband was out of town on business and she left her daughter with her mother while she visited friends. On the way back to her mothers to pick up her daughter she was stopped by 2 policemen. They told her that her car matched the description of a stolen car and that they would have to check it out. One of the policemen drove her car while the other followed in the patrol car. They drove to a deserted, wooded area and gagged her, dragged her from the car and raped her, many, many times. I cannot go into too many details in public as they are too horrifying, but we do have copies of a detailed report of the incident to give to the committee. However, there are a few parts of her story that should be related now.

While they were raping her they had her handcuffed in such a manner that her wrists and ankles were cut so deeply that she will have large scars the rest of her life. The doctors said that the cuts were so deep that parts of the bone were actually exposed. They not only attacked her in strange and unnatural ways, but burned her with cigarettes over various parts of her body and beat her. And all the time they were doing these unspeakable and horrible things they were laughing. When they finished they left her, naked, in her car and she was not found until late the following morning. By the time she was admitted to General Hospital she was near death from shock, and her ankles and wrists were so badly mutilated and infected that eventually her right foot had to be amputated and the other ankle and her wrists took months to heal. It was only after months of intensive treatment that she was finally able to speak. Before that time she could only mumble while under heavy sedation. According to the staff who attended her at the hospital, the only thing they heard her say during this time was, please let me die. Over and over again. Please let me die. It was only over a long period of intensive and painstaking treatment that the doctors were able to piece together the events of that night. One minute she was a lovely young wife and mother, a good daughter, enjoying life and giving happiness to her family. Then 2 police officers decided to amuse themselves and now this young woman is hopelessly insane, sitting in the corner of a locked ward in a mental institution sucking her thumb, crying, unable to control the functions of her body, unable to feed herself, unable to do anything but sit in that corner, suck her thumb and cry. The direct result of a few hours fun of 2 police officers who had nothing better to do.

These events were brought to the attention of the police commissioner of that city and he provided the doctors with pictures of officers who were on duty in that area that night. During one of her lucid intervals this young woman was shown these pictures and when she looked at 2 of them she screamed and covered her eyes and yelled no, no, no. During other lucid moments she was shown other pictures with these same 2 pictures among them and when she came to them the same thing happened. There is no doubt in anyones mind that these are the two officers who attacked her that night, but there is nothing that can be done because there is no admissible evidence. They are still serving their community as officers of the law.

He once more lowered his head as people moved around on the chairs and the room hummed with excited comment.

And this is but one case. But one case in millions. But this one case could be anyone. Your wife, your daughter, your mother. Any helpless individual who may be victimized by insane and brutal authority.

And how many more policemen are there like these 2 who are still driving around in their prowl car stopping women and asking them for their license?

And she is but one woman. One woman out of millions who was driving home to her mother and little daughter and now she sits sucking her thumb and crying, or is perhaps in a strait jacket or padded cell waiting for her next shock treatment, doomed to spend the remainder of her life hopelessly insane.

And what of her family? What of her many loved ones?

What of her little girl who no longer has a mother to tuck her in bed at night and teach her her prayers? What of that little girl who is now forced to grow up deprived of a mothers love? And her husband who is not only deprived of her love and affection, but is forced to explain to his little girl why her mommy is not coming home, and who is forced to try to be both mother and father to his little girl.

And she is but one.

And I am but one. One that we know about. How about those thousands we do not know about?

And how about the so-called little things like traffic tickets and gratuities? Just little things. But one little thing ignored and then another and we have that poor wretched woman doomed to a life of hopeless insanity.

Goddamn right.
Let the bastards get away with anything and youre fucked.
And

what I have related of events on that night of horror is only the briefest and vaguest of outlines. The things they did to her made me sick when I heard about them. I couldnt possibly tell you about them here and now. They are beyond human imagination. Only a depraved and evil animal could conceive of doing such things.

He stood up and looked at the joint of wall and floor, then paced back and forth for a few minutes then stopped in front of the mirror. He studied the pimple, looking for evidence of a change, then shrugged his shoulders and turned away. He leaned against the wall for a moment and looked at the bed, feeling the cell and the heavy steel door. He was in here and they were out there. All he had was a lousy 50 sq. ft., and they had the whole fucking world to roam around in. All he had was a bed, a fucking shitter and a steel door and they had the whole world to fuck around in, to do any damn thing they wanted. If only he could get free of those bastards out there. All those rotten sonsabitches who keep fucking things up on him. Every goddamn time you get something going they come along and screw it up. No matter what it is they screw it up. They just cant leave you alone. Not for one fucking minute. No matter where you go or what you do some sonofabitch comes along and fucks it all up. Why cant they leave you alone. Why in the name of krist cant they just leave you alone. No. They have to screw it up. Every fucking time. They just wont leave you alone. If only theyd leave you alone for five fucking minutes everything would be all right. Thats all. Just five fucking minutes and everything would be all right. But they wont. The ugly motherfuckers,

going back to the bed and glancing around the cell. Concrete and steel. Yeah, and those 2 bastards are driving around like king shit. Probably laughing their asses off because Im sitting in this fucking cell.

He stretched out on the bed, let his eyes close and listened to the chairman of the special investigating committee of the Senate of the United States.

On behalf of the other members of this committee, and myself, I want to thank you gentlemen for appearing before us and making available to us, and the citizens of our country, evidence of misuse and abuse of authority. And especially to you, sir, who did so while your life was threatened. We have listened to your testimony and read the many documents submitted by you, and though what we have heard and read was not pleasant—but rather it was ugly and horrifying—we are indebted to you for making these facts known. We, too, agree that there is nothing more important than truth. It is only with the truth that we can make this country of ours truly free. And it is only by being scrupulously honest and diligent in defending truth by seeking out the guilty and exposing lies, that we can keep our nation free. This is not an easy task, but assuredly it is a necessary one. You have set a fearless example and it is now up to us, and the Congress of the United States, to follow your example. It would be more than cowardly for us to do less. It is an inspiration to us to have the privilege of working with an individual such as yourself who has set aside all thoughts of personal safety and stands exposed and vulnerable under the banner of truth, and it would be unseemly for us not to take our stand beside you under that banner.

He tried to walk normally, but couldnt because of his wet pants. His house was only a few houses away, yet it seemed like such a long distance to walk, especially in the bright sun with the buses and cars going by, and the people walking up and down the street. He had just learned to whistle, sort of, and tried whistling as he walked home, but the only sound that came from his lips was a muffled whoef, whoef. But at least it was summer and it wasnt cold. It would be impossible to try and walk normally with wet pants in the wintertime. But when his pants were wet in the winter it was from snow and ice and not pee, and he didnt have to walk as if they were dry. And he would be wearing lots of sweaters and a coat and even if his pants were wet with pee you couldnt see it. But he was wearing short pants and you could see the big wet spot and smell it and it was hard to walk as if his pants were dry. He could feel his legs staying apart even though he tried to keep them together like always. But he wasnt sure just how he did walk when his pants were dry. He knew he didnt walk like he was walking now, but just how did he walk? He tried to remember which way his legs should really go, but no matter how many different positions he tried none of them felt right. He tried squeezing his legs together, hard, but he almost stumbled and fell. With each step he tried a slightly different position, but none of them felt exactly right, and it seemed like such a long walk to his house. He could always tell his mother that he wet his pants. She would get mad, but maybe it wouldnt be too bad. But then she might ask him why. What could he say then? Something happened and he wet his pants? But she might ask him what happened and then what would he say? He could tell her he almost got hit by a car. That really happened once. On his way to school and he had to cross that big, dumb intersection where all the streets crossed each other and there were always cars going by one way or another and the traffic cop waved at him to cross as he stood on the island in the middle of the intersection and he darted across the street and a car slammed on its brakes because he had a green light too, and he got so scared he fell down and wet his pants. The car was real close, but he didn't get hit. At least he didnt remember getting hit, and the cop came over and the man got out and they asked him if he was all right and he cried and they examined him and made sure he was all right and they helped him up and they put him in the mans car so he could drive him home and tell his mother what happened and he was afraid to tell the man he had wet his pants and he knew he was going to get the mans seat all wet and he didnt want to get his seat wet, but he didnt know what to do, he had to sit on the seat, and he couldnt tell the man that his pants were wet so he tried raising himself by leaning against the back of the seat and pushing down with his feet, but he couldnt get very far off the seat and anyway he knew the man could smell him and it took forever to drive the few blocks home and all the time the man kept asking him if he was all right and if he hurt anywhere and he kept trying to keep himself off the seat and just stared through the windshield and jerked his head back and forth in answer to the mans questions and when they got home he ran up the steps yelling for his mother and put his arms around her and started crying and everybody was talking and asking and answering and she held him and reassured him and consoled him and when the man finally left he told her he wet his pants and she smiled and told him that that was all right, but if he told her now that he almost got hit by a car she would want to know why he was in the street and where was the driver and what was his name and where did it happen and he wouldnt know what to say. What could he say? How could he explain his wet pants? And anyway, it was all Leslies fault and her brother. If they didnt tell him to come down in the cellar with them it wouldnt have happened. He thought it was just going to be like the other times when he and his friends went in the cellar with Leslie and they took their pants down and Leslie lifted her skirt so they could see her thing and she spread it apart and then she bent over and he peed on her and then he bent over and she peed on him, but now his pants were wet and he just couldnt seem to walk right and soon he would be home and he would have to think of something to tell his mother. Unless, maybe, he could get into the bathroom before she saw him and he could take his underwear off and put it in the dirty clothes and maybe she wouldnt smell the pee. And then, maybe, he could sneak into his room and put on another pair of underwear and she wouldnt know and he could just sit around and listen to the radio until his father came home from work and they ate supper. But how could he get up the stairs without her hearing him, and in the door and down the hallway to the bathroom. Everything squeaked. The stairs, the door, the floor. Everything. And anyway, he couldnt walk right. Especially up the stairs. It was hard enough trying to walk right on the street, but going up the stairs was even worse. Each step seemed to squeak and groan louder and louder and his pants seemed even wetter. And he was colder now, now that he was no longer in the sun, and it was hard to adjust to the sudden darkness of the stairway and the cold wetness. As he worked his way to the top of the stairs the smell of pee became stronger and stronger and he shivered slightly as he opened the door and sort of shuffled into the living room where his mother was dusting the furniture. Briefly he was aware of the sharp, clean smell of furniture oil, but it was quickly overwhelmed by the smell of his pee. He wanted to look up at his mother and smile and then go trotting into his room or somewhere, or say something like, hi mom, or anything, but his body and lips wouldnt respond to the desire and he just sort of moved around where he stood with his face only half-tilted up, feeling wet and cold and burning all over. His mother looked at him and asked him what was wrong and he stammered a few muffled syllables and she walked over to him and looked at him more intently and asked again what was wrong and he tried to shrug and say, nothing, but he could only fidget and mumble, but only for a few seconds, and then he told her his pants were wet and Leslie peed on him and his mother kept saying what? what? and he showed her the wet spot and told her again, slowly, hysterically, that he had peed on Leslie and she had peed on him and his mother spanked him and he had to go to his room and wait until his father came home from work and then tell him what had happened and all the time he waited he just sat wanting to cry, hoping his father would never get home, and at the same time hoping he would hurry so he could get it over with, and eventually his father did get home and he told him what had happened and there was a lot of noise and confusion and eventually he was told to take a bath and when he finished his mother told him not to do that again and that he should stay away from Leslie and he was sent to bed early and at least the day was over, but he couldnt go to sleep because he was afraid they might say something to Leslie or her mother and father and they would know he told on her and she would tell his friends and they wouldnt talk to him and he wished he could fall asleep so the night would be over and it would be morning and maybe everything would be over with and at least now the smell was gone and he was warm and dry

and he couldnt figure out what fuck meant. A friend of Leslies older brother was with them and he kept saying he wished they could find a place to fuck and he followed them around trying to figure out what the word meant and wondering what they were going to do. They had on their skates and were walking through a dirt driveway and they were looking in bushes and cellar windows and that guy kept saying he wished they could find a place to fuck and he kept following them wondering why they didnt want to go roller skating or to the cellar where they usually went so they could look at Leslies thing and all the things she could do with it

and he wondered if Leslie and her brother still played games even after she got hair. His friend Jimmy had a sister a few years older than him and he used to peek at her and he said she had hair and he would tell them about it and how big her nipples were as they hid in the corner of the school yard at night all jerking off together. And sometimes in school he would take his out and wave it around under the desk and his friends would laugh and the teacher would always yell at them to stop laughing and every time she did he would laugh even harder and louder and then she would yell at him and make him write a demerit slip for laughing in the classroom

and he would wonder what it would be like to have a sister and if he did have one if she would let him touch it the way Leslies brother did and he wondered if she still let him and if Jimmys sister would ever let him touch it or look at it or if he would ask her if he could. Every day they would ask Jimmy if he had asked his sister yet and he always said no, so he never knew what it was like to touch there

mary, mary, quite cunttrary, how does your garden grow

and he couldn't pass the candy store without staring at the magazine in the window. It was called *Weird Tales* and there was a picture of a naked woman and all you could see was her terrified face and huge tits and there were martian monsters in the background and they were coming after her and her hair stood on end and her eyes were very big and she was pretty but the whole picture seemed to be her big tits and they were round like melons and stood straight out right under her face and many times each day he would stand there and stare and his stomach would start feeling funny and tight and he would start getting sick to his stomach and he would go home and jerk off

but just wait until he had his day in court. I/ll show those bastards. I/ll get them on the stand and tear them apart. I/ll makem look like the monkeys they are. I/ll crucify the bastards. I wont need any goddamn lawyer to help me hack them to pieces. I/ll do it alone. By the time I get through withem theyll curse their mothers for giving birth to them, the ugly motherfuckers. The fucking d. a. and the judge can go through all the stipulating shit they want, I dont give a fuck. All I want to do is get them on the stand. Thats all. Just let me get them on the stand and I/ll punish the stinking pricks. I/ll show them whose guilty, the rotten cunts.

mary, mary, quite cunttrary, how does your garden grow

all I want is a chance, thats all. Just give me my day in court with those mothers cunts and theyll be dead. That is right your honor. I wish to defend myself. And I realize, and am fully cognizant, of my rights to counsel and wish to waive those rights. Yeah, I/d waive anything to get at those bastards.

Q. AND *you say you and your partner were driving north on Hill St. when you saw someone in the doorway of the jewelry store on the north side of the 2200 block of Hill Ave.?*

A. *Thats right. Kramers Jewelry store.*

Q. *What time was this?*

A. *Approximately 2:35 A.M.*

Q. *I see. And I assume it was dark that time of the morning?*

A. *Yes. It was.*

Q. *And how fast were you driving?*

A. *Approximately 25 m.p.h.*

Q. *I see. About 25 m.p.h. And at this point is Hill St. a 1- or 2-lane street?*

A. *1 lane.*

Q. *And were there cars parked on the street?*

A. *Yes.*

Q. *I see. And approximately how far from the intersection were you when you noticed someone in the doorway of Kramers Jewelry store?*

A. *Well, we were fairly close to the intersection.*

Q. *Well, just how close is fairly close. 100 feet, 200 feet, 300 feet. Just how close were you?*

A. *Well, I guess we were a few hundred feet away from the intersection.*

Q. *I see. A few hundred feet away. I refer you to the diagram of the intersection on the blackboard and ask you to indicate how close you were to the intersection. (Defense counsel steps to blackboard and points with finger.) Were you here, or here, or just where were you?*

A. *Just about there.*

Q. *Here?*

A. *No. Closer to the intersection.*

Q. *About here?*

A. *Yes. About there. Or maybe even a little closer.*

Q. *I see. You were this close to the intersection and not further away from it?*

A. *Thats right. We were at least that close to Hill Ave.*

Q. *I see. In other words you were almost at the intersection itself when you suddenly noticed someone in the doorway of Kramers Jewelry store?*

A. *Yes.*

Q. *You are absolutely certain that you were that close to Hill Ave. and not a few hundred feet further south of the intersection?*

A. *Thats right.*

Q. *Theres no doubt whatsoever in your mind as to how close you were to Hill Ave.?*

A. *I said so, didnt I?*

COUNSEL *Just answer the question yes or no. Theres no need to shout. I can hear you plainly enough.*

A. *Yes. Im certain.*

Q. *And how fast were you going?*

A. *About 25 m.p.h. Ive already told you that.*

Q. *And is there a traffic light at that intersection?*

A. *Yes.*

Q. *And what color was the light facing you?*

A. *It was red.*

Q. *Are you certain of that?*

A. *Yes, Im sure.*

Q. *Are you certain youre not thinking of another intersection, perhaps the one you had just driven through?*

A. *Yes, Im certain.*

Q. *I see. And you say this was about 2:35 A.M.?*

A. *Yes.*

Q. *And what time did you start work that night?*

A. *We checked our car out at 9:03 P.M.*

Q. *And youre certain about that time?*

A. *Of course I am. You can check the records if you dont believe me.*

Q. *I dont think that will be necessary. But thank you for the suggestion. In other words you had been driving around your assigned area since 9:03 P.M., which would be a total of 5 hours and 32 minutes up until the time you saw someone in the doorway of Kramers Jewelry store?*

A. *Thats right.*

Q. *That seems like a long time to just be driving around. Dont you get a little bored or a little hungry?*

A. *Well, naturally we ate.*

Q. *O, I see. So you werent just driving around all that time?*

A. *Well, of course not. We ate between 12 and 12:30.*

Q. *Good. Im glad you did not go all night without eating. And how long have you been assigned to this particular shift?*

A. *For 6 months.*

Q. *And how long have you been a member of the force?*

A. *3 and ½ years.*

Q. *And all the time you have been assigned to driving a patrol car?*

A. *Thats right.*

Q. *And you had been driving without interruption from 12:30 to 2:35?*

A. *Yes, yes. I said so.*

COUNSEL *Please, just answer the questions.*

WITNESS *Well, I dont see what all this has to do with anything—*

COURT *The witness will refrain from arguing with counsel and just answer the questions.*

COUNSEL *Thank you, your honor.*

Q. *So you were driving from 9:03 until 2:35, with the exception of the half-hour from 12 until 12:30, and, I should think it safe to assume, you crossed many intersections with traffic lights during those hours. Is that correct?*

A. *Yes.*

Q. *How many intersections with traffic lights would you say you crossed that night?*

A. *I dont know.*

Q. *Well, about how many would you say. 50? 100? 500?*

A. *O, I dont know, maybe 100. I never thought of it.*

Q. *Naturally. Thats understandable. When a person drives as much as you do I imagine it would be very hard to say how many traffic lights they encounter during the course of a day or night.*

A. *Yes. Thats right.*

Q. *And I would imagine, at least its been my experience, that one looks pretty much the same as another. If you have seen one traffic light I guess you have seen them all?*

A. *Yes. Theyre all pretty much the same.*

Q. *But you do distinctly remember that this particular traffic light was green when you approached it?*

A. *No. No. It was red. Not green.*

Q. *Excuse me. Thats right. You did say it was red. You have a remarkable memory. You drive around the city night after night, month after month and are able to remember whether or not one particular traffic light was red or green, and not only that, you can remember even though at the time you saw something suspicious on the streets?*

A. *Thats right.*

Q. *I see. You notice someone in the doorway of a jewelry store at 2:35 in the morning and at the same time you are able to remember whether or not one traffic light, out of thousands, is red or green at the same time. That is truly remarkable.*

A. *Im trained to look for things like that. It makes no difference whether its day or night.*

Q. *Thats wonderful. And would you be kind enough to tell me, and the court, just how you can be so positive.*

A. *Because we had to stop before crossing Hill Ave., in case there was any traffic. We didnt want to run into a vehicle traveling on Hill Ave.*

Q. *Well, I think that is very commendable. And just who was driving at the time?*

A. *I was. Thats why Im positive about the light being red.*

Q. *I see. So when you drive you pay close attention to the traffic lights, and the speed you are traveling, so you wont cause an accident.*

A. *Thats right. Its part of our training.*

Q. *Fine. But if you were paying such close attention to the speed at which you were traveling, the traffic lights, and the traffic on the street, how were you able to also notice someone in a darkened doorway hundreds of feet away, notice that there was something suspicious, and study him so carefully that you were able to make a positive identification. Will you please answer that? I for one am deeply interested in how you managed to accomplish all this.*

A. *Because it wasnt all twisted up like you make it sound.*

COUNSEL *Please, answer the question.*

WITNESS *Im gonna answer the damn question if youll keep your mouth shut for a damned minute—*

COURT *The witness will not engage in a verbal contest*

with counsel and if I hear another outburst like that I/ll hold you in contempt of court. Now answer the question.

COUNSEL *Thank you, your honor.*

A. *It was my partner who noticed someone in the doorway and he told me about it.*

Q. *And then what did you do?*

A. *I brought the car to a stop, made sure there was no oncoming traffic, then crossed Hill Ave., parked, and got out of the car.*

Q. *I see. You both got out together?*

A. *No. Fred jumped out right away, before the car had come to a complete stop.*

Q. *And how much later was it before you joined him?*

A. *I dont know exactly. A few seconds I guess.*

Q. *I see. So Fred got out on the corner and was facing east, and you got out the other side and went around the car to join him. Is that correct?*

A. *Yes.*

Q. *And I assume you had to put on the brake and turn on the flashing lights so no one would run into your car, before you got out, went around the car, and joined Fred.*

A. *Thats right.*

Q. *And I assume this would take a few seconds.*

A. *Yes. Thats what I said.*

Q. *Well, that is not exactly what you said, but I will let it go at that. And what, exactly, did you see after you ran around the car?*

A. *You and Fred were standing on the corner and I heard him ask you for your identification.*

Q. *Youre certain that that is exactly what you saw?*

A. *Of course.*

Q. *Why do you say, of course?*

A. *Because there was a street light on the corner and I was only a few feet away.*

Q. *I see. We were just standing there engaging in polite conversation, is that it?*

A. *He was asking you for your identification.*

Q. *I see. We were just standing there like friends. He didnt grab me by the arm and throw me against the wall?*

A. *No. The 2 of you were standing on the corner when I came around the car.*

Q. *Then it was after you joined your partner that the defendant was thrown against the wall?*

A. *No.*

Q. *Then it was before you joined them?*

A. *No. No. I didnt say that. Goddamn it, you twist everything—*

COUNSEL *Your honor—*

COURT *The witness is in contempt of this court and if he doesnt stop these outbursts the court will have him confined. Now answer the questions.*

COUNSEL *Thank you, your honor. Now, where were we? Yes. Your partner and the defendant were standing on the corner when you came around the car?*

A. *Yes.*

Q. *Did you take your gun out before or after you got out of the car?*

A. *I didnt unholster my gun.*

Q. *Did your partner have his gun out?*

A. *No.*

Q. *I see. And he did not grab him by the arm or throw him against the wall either before or after you joined them?*

A. *No.*

Q. *Fine. Tell me, why did you arrest the defendant? No.*

Let me change that. Why did you stop the defendant?

A. *Because my partner said he saw something suspicious in the doorway of Kramers Jewelry store.*

Q. *And, actually, you did not see anything because you were driving and concentrating on that. Correct?*

A. *Yes.*

Q. *I see. And if I remember correctly you were traveling at 25 miles per hour and were only a few feet from the intersection when your partner said he saw something suspicious across the street?*

A. *Yes.*

Q. *Then you must have had to put on the brakes very suddenly in order not to go through the intersection and take a chance on hitting another vehicle?*

A. *Well, I didnt have to exactly jam them on.*

Q. *You did not? That is strange. I should think you would have to in order not to go through the intersection, considering where you say you were, and the speed at which you say you were traveling when your partner said he saw something suspicious.*

A. *Well, I cant say exactly where we were when he saw you.*

Q. *Saw me? How do you know he saw me?*

A. *Well, whatever he saw.*

Q. *How can you say what he saw?*

A. *Well, I mean—*

Q. *Just what do you mean? Did you or did you not see the defendant at that time?*

A. *What I mean—*

Q. *Never mind what you mean. Did you or did you not see the defendant at that time? Just answer yes or no, and never mind looking to the prosecutor for an answer.*

A. *Im not looking—*

COUNSEL *Answer yes or no.*

A. *No.*

Q. *You were just a few feet from the intersection when Fred said he saw something?*

A. *I dont know exactly—*

Q. *Just a few minutes ago you said, and indicated on the diagram, exactly where you were. Were you or were you not at that precise point when Fred said he saw something?*

A. *Yes.*

Q. *And you did not have to jam on the brakes even though you were just a few feet from the intersection and were traveling at 25 miles per hour?*

A. *I dont know ex—*

Q. *I dont know. What do you mean you do not know? You have already testified that you knew exactly where you were, and exactly how fast you were traveling, and that you did not have to jam on the brakes and now you tell me you do not know. Well, what do you know?*

A. *I know I/d like to kick the shit outta you—*

COURT *Order. Order. Take that man into custody and remove him from this courtroom.*

(WITNESS TO COUNSEL)

You sonofabitch, I/ll killya if I ever get my hands onya. Ya hear me? I/ll killya ya rotten sonofabitch. (Witness continues to scream and fight as the court officers drag him from the courtroom.)

COUNSEL *Your honor, in view of what has happened here this morning I would like to request that that officer undergo a psychiatric examination.*

PROSECUTOR *Your honor, I see no need for such an examination.*

COUNSEL *Your honor, I think my motion should be granted so it can be determined whether or not the witness is capable of giving honest testimony.*

COURT *Objection overruled. Such examination is so ordered. We will now recess until 2 o'clock.*

CROSS-EXAMINATION OF SECOND OFFICER CONTINUES

Q. *Now then, if I remember correctly, you testified that your partner was driving and you were sitting beside him in the front seat of the patrol car, and you were traveling north on Hill St., and as you approached the intersection at Hill Ave. you noticed something suspicious in the doorway of Kramers Jewelry store?*

A. *Yes sir.*

Q. *Just what do you mean by something suspicious?*

A. *I saw a man in the doorway.*

Q. *You are certain it was a man?*

A. *Yes sir.*

Q. *How can you be so certain it was a man?*

A. *Well, it was dressed like a man.*

Q. *It was dressed like a man? That does not sound as if you are certain. It?*

A. *Well. . .what I mean is it was someone who was dressed like a man and moved like a man.*

Q. *What do you mean by dressed like a man?*

A. *Well, pants and a jacket. You know, mens clothes.*

Q. *To be frank, I do not know. I have a difficult time telling a man from a woman by their clothes in the middle of the day, no less at night in a darkened doorway.*

COURT *Order. Order in the court.*

A. *Well, he moved like a man.*

Q. *Just how did this suspicious character move that made you so certain it was a man in a darkened doorway a hundred yards away while you were sitting in an automobile traveling at 25 miles per hour?*

A. *You know. He just moved like a man.*

Q. *No, I do not know. Please tell me.*

A. *Its just the physical mannerisms. We/re trained to know the difference. And anyway, we were stopped for the light.*

Q. *You were stopped for the light? Your partner testified that the car was traveling at a speed of 25 miles per hour when you saw this suspicious man in the doorway.*

A. *We were. When I first saw him. But I got a good look when we stopped. And I remember the light was red because I was leaning forward when Harry stepped on the brake and my head hit the windshield.*

Q. *He stopped so short your head hit the windshield and yet you were able to see in a darkened doorway well enough to tell it was a man?*

A. *I dont mean my head hit the windshield—*

COUNSEL *But that is what you just said.*

A. *Well, I dont mean my head—*

Q. *Well, what do you mean? It seems as if you do not really mean anything you say?*

A. *I mean the tip of my cap touched the windshield. I was just sort of jerked forward a little.*

Q. *I see. It was while your head was jerking forward that you were able to establish definitely that a man was doing something suspicious in the darkened doorway?*

A. *I didnt mean that I saw him then.*

Q. *All right. Now why dont we just take a minute to allow you to tell the court what you do mean. I, for one, am becoming a little confused as to what you do and do not mean.*

A. *Like I said before, it is part of my job to look in all the doorways of our patrol area for anything suspicious. Any sort of movement. On this particular night I was concentrating very hard because there had been a series of breaking and enterings that week between*

> the hours of 2 A.M. and 4 A.M. I saw a movement in
> the doorway and told Harry and kept my eyes on the
> doorway until we crossed the street and I got out of
> the car.

Q. I see. And you kept your eyes on the doorway even
though your head was jerking back and forth?

A. Yes, I did. I am trained to do that.

Q. I congratulate you on your powers of concentration.
Now, I would like to draw your attention to the diagram of the intersection of Hill and Hill. According to
the testimony given by you and your partner, your car
was approximately here when you noticed something
suspicious in the doorway. Is that correct?

A. Yes.

Q. And there were cars parked here, and here, and here?

A. Yes.

Q. I would like also to draw your attention to the position
of the street lights. One here, on this corner a few feet
from your car, one here on the opposite corner and
one here. And here is Kramers Jewelry store. As you
can see, Kramers is almost exactly in the middle of
those 2 street lights, except that the front of the store
is set back about 10 feet from the curb. You will also
note that there is an aluminum canopy measuring 8
feet by 4 feet over the doorway of Kramers Jewelry
store. Is that how you remember it?

A. Yes.

Q. Good. As a matter of fact thats wonderful. The training
program you underwent must be remarkable. Youre
driving 25 miles per hour, notice something in a darkened doorway, have your head jerked back and forth
by the sudden stopping and starting of the automobile,
are able to identify the suspicious movement in this
darkened doorway a hundred yards away as that made

by a male caucasian, seeing all this while inside a moving vehicle and being able to see through the many parked vehicles and at the same time, all in a matter of 2 or 3 seconds, you remember the position of the street lights and the size of the canopy over the doorway. I think that is remarkable. You must have graduated at the top of your training class. Just where did you graduate in your class?

A. *I dont remember.*

Q. *You dont remember. You, who have been so incredibly trained so as to be able to accomplish these incredible feats of observation and memory, and you do not remember where you were in your class? Come, come now. Do not be so modest.*

A. *Well, I think maybe it was around 30 or so.*

Q. *30 or so? And how many were in that class?*

A. *Im not sure. Maybe around 50.*

Q. *I see. Maybe around 30 or so, and maybe around 50 or so. In other words around the bottom 10%. Do you think maybe that might be accurate?*

A. *Well, I dont know. I guess so.*

Q. *I am really surprised. As remarkable as you are and you graduated in the bottom 10%. If that is the case I wonder what the top 10% are like. They must be absolute geniuses.*

COURT *Order. Order in the court.*

Q. *Now, to get back to the diagram. The doorway to Kramers Jewelry store is in the middle of the street lights, set back about 10 feet from the curb and has an 8 by 4 foot aluminum canopy over it which means there is less illumination in this area than in either direction to the left or right. In addition, there is the additional shadow of the canopy making the darkness almost impenetrable and you are sitting in an auto-*

*mobile under a street light which means you are look-
ing from the light into the darkness, through the
vehicles parked in front of the store and yet can definitely say, while your head is jerking back and forth,
that you saw a male caucasian acting suspiciously in
that doorway. Remarkable. Absolutely remarkable.*

A. I didnt say I saw a male caucasian in the doorway.

Q. *No, you did not. But you did arrest a male caucasian?*

A. *Well, you were on the street in the vicinity of the store.*

Q. *O, I—*

A. *And you were the only one there.*

Q. *How do you know I was the only one there? Did you
check the entire area, or even the immediate area?*

A. *Well, no. We couldnt.*

Q. *Why not?*

A. *There was no need to. We knew that the b and e/s were
committed by only 1 individual and we already had
our suspect.*

Q. *Really. Now that is very interesting. You knew that there
was only 1 individual committing the b and e/s as
you call them. And just how was this determined with
such certainty? Did he tell you or was the conclusion
a product of your magnificent training? But we will
not bother pursuing that. It is immaterial. We will
assume that you were told that it was only 1 individual
you were looking for. And I assume that you were also
told that it was a male caucasian.*

A. *We were told that it was probably a man. Thats all.*

Q. *Well, I wont bother pursuing the probability, for now.
What I am interested in right now is how you knew
the defendant was the only man in the area?*

A. *You were the only one I saw.*

Q. *I see. I was the only one you saw. That does make a
difference, doesnt it? In other words you cannot say*

that there was no other individual in the area, but only I was the only man you saw. Is that correct?

A. Well, yes, I guess so. But if there was anyone else there Im sure I would have seen him.

Q. Well, even considering how well trained you are, I think that it is open to question whether or not you would have seen someone who was hiding in any one of the many darkened areas in the vicinity. But I would like to ask you now exactly what happened when you got out of the patrol car?

A. I saw you walking toward me and approached you and asked you for your identification.

Q. Just one minute please. Lets back up just a bit. How far away from the defendant were you when you got out of the patrol car?

A. About 10 feet.

Q. I see. 10 feet. And he was walking toward you?

A. Yes.

Q. Not away from you, but toward you? Didnt this make you suspicious?

A No. Why should it?

Q. Well, if you were told to look for a man who had been committing crimes in your area and you noticed something suspicious in a darkened doorway of a jewelry store and you knew that this was the man whom you had seen in the doorway, why werent you alarmed when you saw him walking toward you? How could you know he wouldnt suddenly take out a gun and shoot you? Dont criminals usually run away from the police rather than walk up to them?

A. Well, it all depends.

Q. On what?

A. Well, whether or not they think they can talk their way out of it.

Q. *I see. Sort of brazen their way out of being arrested, is that the idea?*

A. *Yes.*

Q. *Well, I imagine that is possible. Now, as I remember your testimony, you got out of the car, approached the defendant and asked for his identification?*

A. *Yes.*

Q. *Fine. And as I remember the testimony of your partner, he stated that when he got out and joined you that you and the defendant were standing under the street light, talking, and that neither one of you had unholstered his gun or had in any way touched the defendant?*

A. *Thats right. There was no violation of constitutional rights.*

COUNSEL *Thank you. I appreciate your informing the court of that. I had no idea you were so well versed in constitutional law, but I keep forgetting the marvelous training you had and how well you did in your class.*

COURT *Order. Order in the court. We cannot have this trial continually interrupted by laughter. Proceed counselor.*

COUNSEL *Thank you, your honor.*

Q. *And because of your training you were able to keep the defendant in view all the time the car was crossing the intersection although you had to be able to do this with bright light in your eyes while he was in shadows and with parked cars obstructing your view, and be absolutely certain that there was not anyone else in the area who might be hiding or who may have run away from the patrol car when it was seen. Be certain enough that this was the man you had seen acting suspiciously in the darkened doorway of Kramers Jewelry store, if indeed, anyone was acting suspiciously in the darkened doorway of Kramers Jewelry store, know with certainty that this was the man and was one of the few, very few, criminals who do not run away from the police, but walk up to them and brazenly talk their way out of being arrested, you knew all this with certainty, and yet you also knew that this man was unarmed, even though you suspected him of committing many crimes in the area, you knew he was unarmed and was not going to attempt to harm you in any way. You knew this with such deep conviction that you stood on the street corner, under a street light, fully illuminated, as he walked out of the shadows, a man you believed to be a hardened criminal walked out of the shadows, and you just stood there and asked him if you might please see his identification. You didnt unholster your gun. Did not search him for a weapon. Did not touch him in any way. Did not so much as say, excuse me sir, but do you have a gun hidden that you might suddenly take out and shoot us as soon as my partner joins me here under the light? Do you expect this court to believe that story? Do you honestly believe that you can tell a story like that in this court and expect to be believed? You, who are so well trained you can tell the difference between a shadow and a hardened criminal from a hundred yards away in the dark of night? I am sorry. But I for one cannot, with the wildest stretch of the imagination, believe such a story.*

A. *Its the truth. We didnt—*

Q. *The truth? May I remind you that you are under oath?*

A. *I dont need you to remind me of that.*

Q. *Good. I am glad you do not have to be reminded about something. Or are you going to come up with another, I didnt mean?*

A. *It didnt happen the way you said.*

Q. *The way I said? I did not say it happened in any particu-*

*lar way. You are the one who said you stood under a
street light while a man whom you believed to be a
hardened criminal, whom you had caught in what you
believed to be a criminal act, walked toward you and
you waited for him with your gun in your holster and
asked him if he would please show you his identification.*

A. *I didnt mean I just—*

Q. *You didnt mean. Not again. Just what is it you didnt
mean this time?*

A. *I didnt mean I just stood there with my arms folded. I
walked over to him—*

Q. *Is that when you took out your gun?*

A. *Yes—no. I mean—*

Q. *Well, is it yes or no? When did you take out your gun?*

A. *He made a suspicious move and I took out my gun.*

Q. *What sort of suspicious move?*

A. *As if to pull out a gun.*

Q. *Now that is interesting. Would you mind explaining to
the court exactly how a person moves when he is about
to take out a gun? I am sure we would all like to know.*

A. *I cant explain it exactly.*

Q. *Why not? You know it so well there is no doubt in your
mind when you see this particular movement. Why
cant you explain it?*

A. *Its just the way a person moves.*

Q. *O, I see. You can only recognize it if you have been well
trained, like you?*

A. *He reached for his breast pocket.*

Q. *He reached for his breast pocket? You mean like this?
Is that the movement that means someone is going to
take out a gun, and use it?*

A. *Well, I wasnt going to take any chances. More than one
officer has been killed like that.*

Q. *But didnt you ask him for his identification?*

A. *Yes.*

Q. *Then why didnt you assume that that was what he was reaching for?*

A. *It was the way he moved, I guess. I dont know. Anyway, I wasnt going to take any chances.*

Q. *I do not blame you. I would not want to either. But why didnt you take your gun out right away? Why did you wait until you asked him for his identification and then take out your gun when he reached for it? Werent you taking a chance in waiting that long? Dont you think you waited too long? Wouldnt a well-trained police officer have taken his gun out right away?*

A. *I did take mine out right away.*

Q. *But you said you did not. That you waited until he reached for his pocket. Make up your mind.*

A. *I dont know—*

COUNSEL *You dont know. Again you dont know.*

A. *I mean I guess I took my gun out right away. After all, he was in the shadows and I couldnt tell if he was holding a gun in his hand or not.*

Q. *You couldnt tell whether or not he had a gun in his hand?*

A. *No. I couldnt.*

Q. *You were only a few feet away and could not tell if he had a gun in his hand or not, yet from a hundred yards, or more, you knew that he was in that darkened doorway and was doing something suspicious. So certain that you jumped from the car, with your gun out, and hit him with it.*

A. *I didnt hit him till later.*

Q. *Then you did hit the defendant with your gun?*

A. *Well. . . . I dont know.*

Q. *What do you mean you dont know? How can you not know if you hit him with your gun?*

A. *Well, yes, I guess so.*

Q. *I guess so. I guess so. Did you or did you not hit the defendant with your gun? Please answer yes or no.*

A. Yes. I hit him when he tried to get away.

Q. *He tried to get away?*

A. Yes.

Q. *First he walked over to you and then he tried to get away?*

A. Thats right. I guess he got frightened or something.

Q. *Before or after you asked for his identification?*

A. After.

Q. *I guess that would be when he made that suspicious move toward his breast pocket you told us about?*

A. Yes.

Q. *This gets more interesting as we go along. He walks over to you, you ask him for his identification, and he doesnt try to get away until he is so close to you that you can hit him with your gun?*

A. Yes.

Q. *Let me ask you, as a well-trained police officer, does this make sense to you?*

A. I dont know why he did it.

Q. *And just how did he try to escape?*

A. Well, he sort of moved as if he was going to run away.

Q. *He sort of moved as if he was going to run away? Now just what does that mean?*

A. Well, he kind of twisted his body like he was going to suddenly run.

Q. *And this was when your partner, Harry, joined you? As I remember his testimony he said you did not have your gun out when he joined you, so I assume he must have been there before you unholstered your gun?*

A. Yes, yes. Thats right. Our guns were still in our holsters.

Q. *But you had already asked him for his identification?*

A. Yes.

Q. *Then it was not as he was reaching for it that you took out your gun?*

A. *Yes. . .well, no. Not exactly.*

Q. *O, come now. You have already testified that that was when you took out your gun.*

A. *Well, it sort of happened together.*

Q. *What happened together?*

A. *He reached for his pocket and looked like he was going to run. At the same time.*

Q. *And Harry was with you by this time?*

A. *Yes.*

Q. *And that is when he looked like he was going to run?*

A. *Yes.*

Q. *And that is why Harry was holding him when you hit him?*

A. *Yes—I mean no. I mean he ran into Harry.*

Q. *O, now he ran into Harry. I thought he looked as if he was going to run away? Now you claim he actually ran. Not only did he run, but he did not try to run away from you, but ran into Harry so he could hold him while you hit him with your gun. Is that what happened?*

A. *No—yes—I mean—*

Q. *What do you mean? Will you please try to stick to one story and stop changing it every time you open your mouth?*

A. *Im not changing my story.*

Q. *Then what are you doing? Lying?*

A. *No. You just twist everything around and get me confused.*

Q. *I agree that you are confused. As a matter of fact I am surprised that so well trained an officer could be so confused. But maybe, just maybe, if you would stick to one story you would not be so confused.*

A. *Im trying—I mean I am.*

Q. *It might help if you would say what you mean the first time. Then, perhaps, we both would not be so confused.*

A. *If you wouldnt—*

PROSECUTOR *Your honor, cant we have a recess? Its late and I feel the witness has been badgered enough.*

COUNSEL *Your honor, I have no objection to a recess at this time; trying to ferret out truth from fiction is a trying task, but I do object to the use of the word, badgering. I am simply trying to ascertain the truth in the midst of confusing and contradictory testimony.*

PROSECUTOR *I will withdraw the word, badgering.*

COURT *Good. Im glad someone agrees on something today. Court will recess until 9 o'clock tomorrow morning.*

Just twist it around and shove it up their asses, treading the floor of his cell, nodding his head with strong approval, shove it up and break it off. Those ugly mothers cunts. I dont need no fucking lawyer to make those cocksuckers look like idiots. When I get through with them theyll wish to krist they never were born. I/ll fixem good. I/ll showem. The dumb sonsabitches. Krist, what a bunch of ignorant slobs. Filthy, fucking slobs and they can shove people around just because they have a badge. Ignorant fucking okies who dont know their asses from a fucking hole in the ground and they get away with murder because they have that fucking uniform and a crew cut, the flattop bastards. The fucking flattop bastards. Drive around like theyre king shit. Drink coffee and eat donuts like they own the fucking joint. Looking down their noses at people. Who in the fuck do they think they are. Nothin but a bunch of ignorant slobs and they look down their noses at people. Jesus, what a pair of balls they have. What a fucking pair of balls, pounding across the floor, waving his hands, take away their guns and they aint shit. They aint worth a fiddlers fuck. I dont know who in the fuck they think they are, but I/ll be goddamned if theyre going to get away with it. I/ll showem. I/ll be a rotten sonofabitch if I dont showem.

Q. *Lets see where we stand now . . . O yes, I think I remember. Because of your outstanding performance in your training program, you were able to see a male caucasian in a darkened doorway one hundred yards away, while the light was shining in your eyes, and determine that he was doing something suspicious—I assume by suspicious that you mean he was trying to break into the jewelry store?*

A. *Yes. Thats correct.*

Q. *And the reason for this is because you had been advised that there had been many such occurrences lately and you were to look for such things and because you are such a well-trained police officer that even though the circumstances were such that it might well be impossible for anyone else to come to such a conclusion, you were able to determine that this was a male caucasian in the process of committing an illegal act.*

A. *Well, yes. I mean it wasnt exactly that way.*

Q. *But you have already testified that it was that way.*

A. *I mean the conditions werent like that.*

Q. *O, I see. In other words we are to disregard all the testimony given by you and your partner because its not—shall we say—accurate?*

A. *No. What I mean—*

Q. *O, please, not again. For heavens sake what do you mean? Do we have to start from the very beginning again?*

A. *No. I mean—well, its just that its hard to describe.*

Q. *And its also hard for me to understand why such a well-trained officer should have so much trouble saying what he means. But let me help you. Was it or was it not dark in the doorway of Kramers Jewelry store?*

A. *It was dark.*

Q. *Were you or were you not approximately one hundred yards away and under the light of a street lamp?*

A. *Yes. Thats all true, but it was different.*

COUNSEL *Your honor. I truly do not wish to take up so much of the Courts time, but if the witness insists upon constantly changing his testimony it seems that I have no recourse but to go back to the very beginning and ask all the questions over again.*

COURT *Yes, the Court agrees. If the witness does not disagree with certain facts that he has already testified to he should answer the questions with a yes or no. Proceed.*

COUNSEL *Thank you your honor.*

Q. *I think it would simplify matters if I ask you if you wish to change any of your previous testimony, up to the point of your leaving the patrol car and approaching the defendant?*

A. *No.*

Q. *Fine. Now lets see if we can clarify a little of the confusion as to what happened when you left the car and stood under the street light, like a gentleman, and waited for a male, caucasian, whom you believed to be a dangerous criminal, walking toward you out of the shadows. And, because of your splendid training you knew he was unarmed and so did not unholster your gun. Is that correct?*

A. *Well—*

Q. *Please, yes or no.*

A. *Yes.*

Q. *Thank you. What color were his clothes?*

A. *Clothes?*

Q. *Yes, his clothes.*

A. *Well, I dont know exactly. They were dark.*

Q. *Dark?*

A. *Yes.*

Q. *All of his clothes?*

A. *Yes.*

Q. *Was he wearing a suit?*

A. *Yes. And a dark shirt and tie. I remember distinctly.*

Q. *Well, thats a pleasant change. But you are certain that he was not wearing dark slacks with a light jacket. Perhaps a light-blue jacket?*

A. *No. I definitely remember he was wearing a dark suit.*

Q. *Well, when you are certain, you certainly are certain. I guess it is that wonderful training. So, he was not wearing a light jacket with a light-blue shirt?*

A. *No.*

Q. *All his clothes were dark?*

A. *Yes. Very dark.*

Q. *Very dark?*

A. *Yes.*

Q. *You know, this training intrigues me more and more. As does your remarkable facility for observation. Here we have a man dressed entirely in dark clothes, very dark clothes, and you can notice him, under the unlikely conditions previously oulined by you, one hundred yards away. And not only notice him, but know exactly what he is doing. Remarkable. Most remarkable. Again, I commend you and your instructors. Now, lets see if we have the rest of the activities clear in our minds? You are confidently standing under the street light awaiting his approach, your gun still holstered, as your partner is coming around the patrol car, and as the defendant comes within arms reach of you and your partner he suddenly decides to try to escape. Is that correct so far?*

A. Yes. Our guns were in our holsters when he tried to escape.

Q. *Fine. Now, he did not try to turn and run, but suddenly ran into you when he was less than 2 feet away. Correct?*

A. Yes.

Q. *He ran into Harrys open arms?*

A. Yes. I mean he ran into Harry and Harry put his arms around him.

Q. *And that is when you hit him with your gun.*

A. I had to—

Q. *Just yes or no. Please.*

A. I hit him as he was struggling with Harry.

Q. *Please answer just yes or no to this question. Please. Was it while Harry was holding him that you hit him with your gun?*

A. Yes, but—

Q. *Just yes or no. And then you threw him against the wall?*

A. No.

Q. *Did he fall against the wall?*

A. No.

Q. *Then how did he end up with his face shoved against the wall?*

A. He didnt. We made him lean against the wall so we could search him for weapons.

Q. *Then this was after you had knocked him down and kicked him?*

A. No.

Q. *Then he was knocked down and kicked after he was searched for a weapon?*

A. No. We didn't knock him down.

Q. Then how did he end up on the ground?

A. He fell.

Q. I see. After you searched him and found he had no weapon he was so delighted that he fell to the ground and somehow managed to crawl under your foot?

A. No.

Q. Then exactly what did happen?

A. I dont know.

Q. You dont know?

A. I mean I dont know how he fell. He must have stumbled or something.

Q. I see. And then you dragged him to the car?

A. Yes. No. I mean—

Q. Please. Not again. Just tell the court what happened. Please, no more yes, no, I mean.

A. Well, we assisted him to the car.

Q. You assisted him to the car.

A. Yes.

Q. Just how did you do that?

A. We each took an elbow and helped him over to the car.

Q. You each grabbed an elbow and assisted him?

A. Yes.

Q. Well, that certainly was generous of you. Then, I assume, if you assisted him to the car he was not trying to es cape.

A. No, he wasnt.

Q. Was he handcuffed at this time?

A. No.

Q. In other words you were certain he was not going to escape or you would have cuffed him?

A. Yes.

Q. That is strange that a man tried to literally run over 2 well-trained police officers one minute and then is so submissive from just a light tap with a gun that he walks into a patrol car. Or could it be that perhaps he was incapable of running because he had been beaten with guns, fists and feet and was dragged across the pavement and thrown face down in the back seat of the car—never mind answering that question. I do not want to hear you stammer an answer. Just tell me, was it after you threw him on the floor of the back seat that you cuffed his hands behind his back?

A. Yes. I mean we—

Q. That is enough. Just yes or no.

A. But we didnt throw him on the floor.

Q. Then how did he get there?

A. Well, he sort of rolled off the seat.

Q. He sort of rolled off the seat?

A. Yeah, he must have stumbled or something.

Q. O come now, you do not expect us to believe that? The truth is that you shoved him onto the floor, twisted his hands behind him, cuffed him and kicked him, again, in the back.

A. We did not. We observed his constitutional rights.

Q. Yes. You observed them all right. And then you tore them to shreds.

A. We did everything legally.

Q. Yes, I am sure you did. And was it when you were cuffing his hands behind his back that you told Harry there was a smell of perfume in the back of the car?

A. No.

Q. Then it was after?

A. No. I mean I never said anything like that.

Q. Are you certain?

A. Yes.

Q. Absolutely certain?

A. Yes.

Q. *You never said anything to Harry about perfume on the back seat of the car and mentioned the name of Mrs. Haagstromm?*

A. *No.*

Q. *You are certain?*

A. *Yes.*

Q. *Absolutely certain that the smell of perfume did not come from Mrs. Haagstromm?*

A. *Yes.*

Q. *Here you are in the midst of apprehending a man you believe to be a hardened criminal, a man who has just tried to escape and whom you have had to subdue and you are certain you did not just simply mention something about the smell of perfume and Mrs. Haagstromm?*

A. *Yes. Yes. Im sure.*

Q. *How can you be so certain?*

A. *Because she was never in the car.*

Q. *How do you know? How can you be so certain she was never in the car?*

A. *Because I drove—I dont know who youre talking about. There was—*

Q. *Werent you about to say that you drove her car?*

A. *No.*

Q. *Werent you about to say that you drove her car to the deserted part of town and there you and your partner raped her?*

A. *No! NO!*

Q. *You didnt drive her car?*

A. *NO.*

Q. *Did Harry?*

A. *NO. I mean—*

Q. *You mean Harry was driving behind you in the patrol car?*

A. *No. I was—I mean I dont know what youre talking about.*

Q. *You mean after you had hit the defendant on the head when he was on the floor, and thought he was unconcious, you and Harry did not laugh about the woman you had just raped?*

A. *NO. NO.*

Q. *You mean the defendant just imagined the conversation?*

A. *He couldnt have heard anything like that.*

Q. *Why? Because he was unconscious?*

A. *Yes. No. I mean we didnt say anything like that.*

Q. *If he couldnt have heard it then he must have been unconscious.*

A. *I dont know.*

Q. *You dont know what he heard?*

A. *No.*

Q. *Where were you sitting?*

A. *In the back.*

Q. *With your feet on the defendants head?*

A. *No.*

Q. *On his back?*

A. *No.*

Q. *Then where were your feet?*

A. *On the floor.*

Q. *They were not on the back of the defendants head, shoving his face into the floor of the car?*

A. *No. No. Absolutely not.*

Q. *Did you notice a smell of perfume?*

A. *No.*

Q. *Did the defendant?*

A. *No.*

Q. *Was the defendant conscious?*

A. *I guess so.*

Q. *You guess so. Why dont you know definitely whether or not he was conscious?*

A. *I dont know. I just. . . . I guess he was.*

Q. *Was there any reason for you to think he might not be conscious?*

A. *We didnt knock him out if thats what youre getting at.*

Q. *I did not ask you to think about the reasons for the question. I repeat, was there any reason for you to think he was not conscious?*

A. *No.*

Q. *If that is the case you must have believed him to be conscious?*

A. *I guess so. Yes. Yes, I believe he was conscious.*

Q. *Then perhaps he was the one who mentioned smelling perfume?*

A. *No.*

Q. *You are certain?*

A. *Yes. Absolutely.*

Q. *How can you be so positive?*

A. *Because the defendant didnt say anything.*

Q. *Not one single word?*

A. *No.*

Q. *You mean this criminal who was so desperate that he tried to run over 2 armed and well-trained police officers just lay there, docilely, and let you take him into custody without saying so much as one single word?*

A. *Yes.*

Q. *He did not even inquire as to where he was being taken?*

A. *No.*

Q. *Isnt that unusual? I mean, doesnt a man usually say something when being taken into custody?*

A. *Well, sometimes.*

Q. *Only sometimes? Not most of the time?*

A. *Well, yes, I guess they usually do.*

Q. *Well, if such is the case, werent you concerned?*

A. *No.*

Q. *Why not?*

A. *He was safely cuffed. We knew he couldnt get away.*

Q. *I appreciate your efficiency. But I was referring to whether or not the defendant was alive or dead.*

A. *We knew he was alive.*

Q. *How did you know? Did you feel his pulse?*

A. *No.*

Q. *Yet you were certain he was alive?*

A. *Yes.*

Q. *Did you examine him in any way to ascertain whether or not he was alive?*

A. *Well, no.*

Q. *Then how could you be so certain he was alive?*

A. *I dont know. I just knew.*

Q. *You just knew? I realize that you are well trained, but I still find it amazing that you could be so confident. You have a man face down on the floor of your patrol car, a man whom you were forced to hit on the head with your gun because he tried to escape, a man you did not knock unconscious, a man who later fell against the wall, was unable to walk for some unknown reason and who then lay still, without making the slightest sound, and yet you were supremely confident that he was all right. It never occurred to you that he might have had a heart attack?*

A. *Well, no.*

Q. *Or a stroke?*

A. *No.*

Q. *Yet you did not beat him?*

A. *No. Definitely not.*

Q. And your feet were not on his head or his back where you could, perhaps, feel him breathing?

A. My feet were on the floor.

Q. Then for all you knew you had a dead man on the floor of the patrol car and you did not even bother to examine him?

A. I knew he wasnt dead.

Q. I ask again. How did you know?

A. I just knew. How should I know how I knew? I just knew he was alive.

Q. Even though he didnt utter a sound?

A. Yes.

Q. Then it must have been Harry who mentioned the perfume and Mrs. Haagstromm.

A. NO. NO.

Q. Then who did?

A. I dont know.

Q. Well, there was no one else in the patrol car. Or was there?

A. No. Of course not.

Q. Then if neither you nor Harry mentioned the smell of perfume and Mrs. Haagstromm, it had to be the defendant.

A. No. He didnt say nothing.

Q. Why? Was he silent because you had brutalized him and beaten him into unconsciousness? Is that why he couldnt have mentioned the perfume?

A. No. NO. There was no smell of perfume in the car.

Q. How can you be so certain? Wasnt Mrs. Haagstromm ever in the car?

A. No. I mean I dont know.

Q. Didnt she smell of perfume?

A. I dont re—a—

Q. *Didnt you tell Harry that she smelled like a rose when you threw her in the back of the car?*

A. *I didnt throw her in—*

Q. *Where did you throw her?*

A. *I didnt throw her anywhere.*

Q. *You left her in her car?*

A. *Yes—NO. NO. I dont even know her. I dont know what youre talking about.*

Q. *Harry drove her car and you followed. Didnt you?*

A. *NO. NO.*

Q. *Did you know she identified you by your name tag?*

A. *She couldnt. I took—YOU LIE. LIE. I DONT KNOW HER. I NEVER SAW HER IN MY LIFE.*

Q. *Then how could she identify you as one of the police officers who raped and attacked her—*

A. *You lie. NO. NO. Lie.*

Q. *Laboratory tests prove that you—*

WITNESS (*Leaping from the stand and trying to grab the defendant by the throat.*) *SHUT UP. SHUT UP. I/LL KILL YOU   KILL YOU   KILL YOU.*

The witness was then taken from the courtroom by the officers present.

COUNSEL *Your honor, I would like to suggest that counsel meet with his honor in chambers so I can clarify what has happened.*

IT was now time for a public performance. Obviously it would have to be before a select audience. An audience with whom his animals were familiar. Sometimes highly trained animals, such as his, get a little spooky in front of strangers, and he didnt want his dogs to be nervous. He wanted them to perform to perfection. They were going to prove that he was the worlds greatest dog trainer. Obviously they would be more relaxed in front of their families than anyone else. The perfect audience—parents, wives and children. They would be the pride of parent- and grandparenthood. My son the dog.

And every child should have a dog. . . . Yeah. . . . Hahahaha. . . . Look at Rover fuck. Fuck Rover fuck. Hahahahahaha. . . . Mans best friend.

He made sure the kennel was well lighted for the event. He wanted to be sure that every little movement, every little ripple of muscle, flare of nostril and twinkle of eye was clearly and unmistakably visible.

And against a wall he placed—built—stalls in such a manner that the invited guests would be unable to miss any of the performance and they, in turn, would be clearly visible to the dogs.

He thought of making a brief speech, a sort of ringmaster introduction, before the performance, but vetoed the idea. However, he did explain to the audience what the wires were for and demonstrated their use with a few tugs. When the howling subsided he warned the members of the audience that if they disturbed the show in any way he would yank the wires as hard as he could.

He also thought, briefly, of music in the background, but dismissed that quickly. He wanted nothing to distract from the primary purpose of the momentous event. It must be kept simple. The audience in their stalls, unable to avoid seeing clearly and completely; the room illuminated with a pleasant brightness; and an absolute stillness.

The wired dogs sat stiffly in a corner, waiting.

The audience stood frozen in their stalls, waiting.

He leaned against the wall, happy.

He didnt deliberately delay starting the performance to intensify the barbed and crushing pressure of time on his dogs and audience, but simply to feel and experience the joy of anticipation to its fullest. When, eventually, he reached the point of needing to put the anticipation into action he tugged the wires.

His dogs trotted to the middle of the kennel. They continued to stare at him. He tugged the wires. Dont you know you should always face your audience? They turned obediently. The eyes of the audience and the dogs collided then adhered. He watched the tender scene for many minutes and allowed them to do the same. Then, with another tug, the show began.

O.K. fido, beg. Stand up and beg. They stretched into action immediately and stood on their hind legs with their paws extended in the proper manner, staring into the faces of the audience. Thats the good boys. Here, catch. He threw them each a dog yummie and they snatched them from the air with their mouths and crunched them noisily before swallowing them. He smiled at the audience. Arent they good dogs. Im really proud of them.

Now show them how you can talk. Thats the good boys. Now bark. Good. Very good. Now howl. Isnt that good? Very good. Now yelp. No, no. You can do better than that. Comeon now. Dont embarrass me in front of our guests. Yelp. Louder, yanking on the wires and watching the faces of the audience turn stone in disbelief and terror. Now thats the way to do it. Very good.

As he put them through their paces he concentrated on the faces of their loving families and glanced at his dogs only from the corner of his eye. When they finished their preliminary tricks he told them to sit and rest for a moment, facing the audience. Then his face suddenly cracked with a sudden realization and he apologized to all present. Im sorry. I forgot how much little children love dogs and always want to pet them. Comeon fidos, go lick their rosy little cheeks and let them pet you. For a second his dogs froze, but only a gentle tug on the wires was necessary to shove them into movement. They went to the audience and licked the cheeks of the children. Go ahead kids, pet them. They love to be petted. Especially behind the ears. Thats the way. See that? See how they cuddle when you do that? O.K. fidos, now roll over so they can scratch your bellies. Thats it. Get those paws up a little higher. Good dogs. Now thats really good. Go ahead kids. Scratch them on the belly. They love it. They really do. They like that better than anything. O, dont let those things bother you. Theyre just a couple of dangling dongs of destiny. Hahahahaha. They wont bite you. Thats what they use to make cuddly little puppies. Hahahahaha. Thats it. Thats the way. See, I told you they love it. Look at the way they roll. O they really do love you. See how theyre licking your hands. Thats the good doggies. O.K. Thats enough. Sit up. The petting hands were withdrawn and the dogs sat up, a foot from the audience, awaiting the next command.

O.K. Now show them how you do your duty. They started trotting toward the post in the corner, but were stopped by a tug on the wires. Thats not the way I taught you to walk. Remember that you are show dogs and you should take pride in your breeding. Now lift your paws the way I showed you and keep your heads high and your noses in the air. Now circle the room and show them how well you have been trained. Thats it. Thats the way. Thats just fine. Good dogs. Good dogs. Now once more around the room. Good. Very good. You see how lightly they walk. Just barely touching the floor. Almost as if they were floating on an air cushion just above the surface. And notice how their noses are tilted upward, ever alert to the scent of danger. And notice how their tongues swing in unison with their breathing and tread. Im sure you must agree that a well-trained dog is a thing of beauty. O.K. boys. Post time. He chuckled as they jogged to the post and lifted hind legs in the prescribed and proper manner. Careful now. I dont want you to splatter each other. Good. Very good. Now continue. They sniffed at the ground for a few seconds, then, satisfied, they scratched small holes and gave them a final sniff before squatting and shitting. When they finished they sniffed the piles of warm shit before pawing the dirt over them. Very good. Did you see how well they did that? Most dogs just toss the dirt in every direction except the right one, but they completely covered their mess. I think they deserve a hand for that. He waited for a few seconds staring at the audience and waiting for them to applaud. They stared silently. Immobile. O come now. That isnt right. He tugged on the wires and the dogs yelped beggingly. Lets hear it for them. The hands of the audience moved like those of animated mannequins. Thats better. Now you guys give them a little bow to show them you appreciate the applause. Thats it. You people should keep in mind that a good performance deserves applause and is very much appreciated by the performers. Isnt that right boys? They nodded their heads. Thats my good doggies. O.K. Up. Up. They stood on their hind legs, begging. He threw them each a dog yummie.

Well now, I think its time to move on to bigger and better things. Why dont we show them how brave and stouthearted you are. As you people know there is nothing dearer to the heart of a dog than to be able to protect his masters and mistresses from danger. Especially children. How many times have we heard of cases where dogs have saved lives that were in danger from all types of disasters from a burglary to a fire. So I think its only fitting that I reward these wonderful animals by allowing them to protect you. Now I have not imported a cat burglar, nor do I intend to set fire to the kennel so they can lead you to safety, but I think what I have in mind will prove to everyones satisfaction, including my dogs, that what I have said about their bravery is true. Obviously to prove what I said I cannot have them simply go through a rehearsed performance such as has been done up to now. I feel that it should be a situation that they are basically equipped for, but one that is new and unexpected. In that way they can prove, or disprove, what I have just said about their instincts and bravery.

Now, I am sure that you are aware that you cannot move from your cozy little stalls, but perhaps you have not noticed that the 2 young children are in front, exposed, and that there are short, low sides protruding a few feet into the arena that form a sort of runway to where they are sitting. You see?

Now, if you will look directly across the arena—and this will come as a surprise to my dogs—you will see a flap of canvas that Im certain has not been noticed up to this point. Behind the canvas is a large, starving rat—screams from the audience stopped him and he yanked the wires angrily. Goddamn it. I dont mind hearing my dogs yelp and whine, but I cant stand that screaming. Now shut up. And you stop that howling. I hate being interrupted. He remained silent until his anger had subsided enough for him to be aware of the breathing of the others in the kennel. I hope I can continue without being interrupted again. As I said, this part of the exhibition is unrehearsed, but there has been adequate preparation. At least I feel that the preparation has been adequate. I have taught them how to catch mice, chipmunks and other little animals, and I feel they should be able to perform admirably against a starving rat. After all, theres only one of him and 2 of them. Also, they are so much larger and stronger than he is even if he hadnt been weakened by going days without food or water. O yes, incidentally thats why that little pan of water was placed in front of the children. It should make it much more interesting. And easier for the dogs. You see, in this way the dogs know the poor rats goal which should make it much easier for them to display their prowess and prove their bravery. Actually, I guess it is a little unfair to load this contest in favor of my dogs against that poor weak rat, but Ive always had a soft spot in my heart for dogs and children, and I am especially fond and proud of these animals. As a matter of fact, I was very worried about this and gave it much thought. I realized that my dogs couldnt take much pride in subduing 1 hungry and dehydrating rat, and I do want them to have a feeling of accomplishment after having worked so hard and so long to be able to entertain you properly by displaying their many skills to the very best of their abilities. I was also afraid that the poor, scurvy rat might be too weak from his imposed fast to allow them to put forth their very best efforts. So I sort of wired his cage so I can shoot a little ginger into him so he will be able to provide a little competition for my doggies. As a matter of fact, now that I think of it, I think I/ll go even further. I realize that this isnt very sporting of me, and Im sure that the poor little rat will not appreciate this, but I think I/ll give my dogs an additional advantage. I think you should be allowed to look him over and give him a good sniff before I turn him loose. Yeah, that sounds like a very good idea. Unfair perhaps, but I think you deserve it. Ive really enjoyed your performance up to now.

He pulled away the canvas cover and the eyes and teeth of the caged rat burst across the room. He looked at the rat, from a distance, and was pleased to see that it wasnt lethargic, but rather had the look of what he would call determined purpose. It was thin but obviously not subdued. It appeared to be quite capable. He observed the frantic twitching of his nose as it seemed to guide his eyes directly toward the water in front of him at the other end of the small kennel. He shot a burst of current into the cage and the rat jerked spastically and spit out a piercing snarl. The audience and dogs jerked back from the violent reaction and the squeals and groans from the audience were joined by the howls of the dogs as he jerked the wire. How many times do I have to tell you to be silent. I cant stand your goddamn screaming and the only way I can drown it out is with the howling of the dogs. And believe me, I can keep them howling just as long as you keep screaming. So shut the fuck up and let them concentrate on their jobs.

He glanced briefly at his dogs sitting and staring at the rat, their tongues hanging from their mouths. He looked at the rat hunched against the rear of the cage, his lips constricted in a beautiful snarl, the dull yellow of his teeth a perfect contrast to his searing eyes. His nose still twitching frantically, his skin tight, shiny and dry. He was a lovely rat.

As he continued to look he was calmed by the overwhelming fear in the room and the murderous demons that were seen by the eyes of the others.

O.K. boys. Go on over and take a good look at him. Go ahead now. Youd better take advantage of this opportunity. You dont have long.

They went over to the cage and looked, following the eyes that followed them.

Thats it, walk around and get a good look. Now give a good sniff. Dont forget, the more you know about your enemy the greater your advantage in the battle.

They slowly inched their way forward, sniffing. As they sniffed the rat smell was vague in their nostrils, but disgusting in their guts. Their throats burned with the acidy need to vomit, but their throbbing throats closed them off from that form of relief. Their bodies seemed to be composed of many separate parts each with a life of its own, each feeling the terror in its own individual way and all they could do was to experience the pain of panic.

They looked at the rat, but were unavoidably drawn to the endless length of stiletto tail that beat at them like a metronome, the roaring movement stinging their eyes. And the burning eyes of the rat throbbed in their ears. They couldnt hear their master urge them forward, but the tugging of the wires thrust them toward the cage. Their tongues hung dry. Foul slime chewed their mouths. Lice scuttled under their skin and a thousand rats gnawed their guts.

The huge, wiry whiskers waved blurringly as the rats

nose continued to twitch and the fire in his eyes became more and more intense. The long sharp teeth hung from his gums. His eyes followed the dogs as they moved yet his nose seemed to remain pointed toward the water. He suddenly snarled forward toward one of them, almost toppling the small cage. The dogs jerked back. Dogs and rat stared.

O. K. I think thats enough. Its time to get started. I/ll give you guys a few seconds to get into position.

He watched as they looked at each other, and then around the kennel, in complete despair. Then, their eyes on the rat, they backed their way, as far as the wire would allow them, between the rat and the water. They waited.

He looked at his beautifully repulsive rat as his dogs readied themselves, not seeing, but aware of their reluctant movements. He wondered if they were thinking of what the rat might do to the children if he got near them and they panicked and screamed and the rat felt threatened by them and attacked them with a cornered frenzy; or if everyone remained completely still and let the rat drink the water and go on his way. He wondered if his dogs were considering taking the chance of just stepping aside and letting the rat go to the water. Were they thinking of taking that chance?

He chuckled inside as he thought of the alternatives the dogs might be considering, and continued to stare at the rat. Everything about the rat was fascinating and attractive. The shiny dryness of the tight skin, the festering sores on the body, the twitching of the nose, and he could even feel the breeze from the fanning of the soft whiskers. He never particularly liked rats, but this was a good rat. Yeah, he was a good rat.

He pushed the button and the cage door was lifted and the rat was propelled by electric current and a crazed thirst toward the water at the childrens feet.

As the rat snarled forward the audience screamed and the dogs were thrust back until they hung from the wire for an endless precipitous moment until the strangling wire balled them together and they tumbled and rolled between the water at the childrens feet and the thirsty rat while their trainer screamed for silence and roared with laughter as he yanked the wires, then yanked again, and again as he experienced the exciting snarling of the rat, the yelping of the dogs, the screaming of the audience, the buzzing of flies, the scratching of nails and teeth, the piercing and tearing of flesh, the convulsions in stomachs and bowels, the terror, the beautiful terror of the game and the roar of his laughter and experienced the frustration of bones and muscles trying to move terrified bodies when movement is impossible, of frantic minds trying desperately to deny the existence of what they were seeing and feeling, experienced the panic of the minds and bodies of his dogs as they rolled and tumbled and wallowed in the path of a thirst-crazed rat who was propelled behind his twitching nose toward the water at the feet of the children and he yanked again and again to keep the beauty of the scene in motion as he experienced the deep joy of controlling everything that was happening to all in the room—all the movement, all the dread and terror that was shown and felt—controlling it all with simply some thin wire, a bowl of water, and a beautifully mangy rat.

Never had he experienced such infinite power and excruciating joy, and they increased and increased as the rat thudded into the

tumbling bodies and tried to squeal, snarl, bite and tear
his way through the interfering flesh that was kept in constant motion by scrambling terror and the simple yanking
of the wires as screams and howls now had to be forced
painfully through almost closed throats and he roared with
laughter and urged his dogs on to kill the rat, killim, killim,
getim by the throat, and one of his dogs fell back almost
pulling the wire from his hand as the rat tore his teeth into
the flesh of his stomach and clung desperately as he and
the dog jerked with panic and the more the dog tried to
shake the rat loose the deeper and deeper the teeth bur-
rowed into his body as the rat clamped his jaws on the
loosened flesh sucking the wet blood and he yelled at the
other dog to getim, get the sonofabitch you stupid fucking
dog, nows your chance, get on the neck, chew off his head,
and he yanked the wire and the dog suddenly felt the
tickle of the rats whiskers on his cheek and his head jerked
back and he tried to grab the rat with his paws but couldnt
because of the leather wrappings around them and his
voice screeched above the screams, biteim, biteim, chew his
head off, and he tried to get his teeth into the rat and the
rat jerked his claws across the dogs face again and again
and again and again and again and he howled and howled
and the claws scraped across his cheeks and eyes and finally
caught in his lip and the rat was stretched between the 2
dogs, the flesh of stomach and lip tearing and tearing until
the rat suddenly opened his mouth and hung from the dogs
lip by a curved claw, swinging back and forth as the dog
tried to shake him loose, then crunched his teeth into the
dogs nose and fiercely clung to it as he tightened his grip
until the force of his bite and the jerking of the dogs head
forced his teeth through flesh and bone and another yank of
the wire increased the rage of pain and terror and the other
dog whose stomach was ripped and bloodied howled and

leaped at the rat, clubbing it with his leather-wrapped paws and their trainer roared with laughter as he heard the thudding and splintering of bone and the rat was almost completely obscured from view as the dogs rolled and thrashed until finally it hung by its teeth from the wrist of one of the torn and bloodied dogs, and he swung and jerked his arm until the force tore the rat loose and he went flying across the room. The first round was over.

His laughter dropped to a low chuckle. The dogs panted heavily. The rat slunk in the corner, staring, his nose twitching. The audience was stiffly still. There was an air-sucking quiet. The bloodied and ripped dogs stared with crazed anger at the rat who was covered with their blood and whose thirst was now partially quenched. Now their eyes burned with pain and madness and they became the hunters reacting and acting on animal instincts. They didnt need to be told to attack. They didnt need to be thrust at the blood-slimy rat. They were not aware of defending anyone. They now had everything they needed to destroy the rat. To sink their teeth into the festered and diseased body. No wires, urging or threats were necessary. They had all they needed. They had the madness of pain.

He continued to chuckle softly, his face relaxed in a large soft smile, as he looked at the blood-splattered rat sensing, rather than really knowing, that the rat was unharmed and that the madness of thirst and hunger had been appeased with the blood and flesh of his dogs, and he was now simply a trapped rat. Nothing more. Nothing less. Just a trapped rat.

He looked at his
bloodied dogs and playfully toyed with the wires for no real
reason other than that he wanted to. They ignored the slight
pressure and continued to crawl very, very slowly toward
the cornered rat. His trainers pride filled his eyes as he
watched and observed. He saw the torn stomach of the one
dog, the small flaps of torn skin hanging from the gash, the
blood oozing out and flowing down the flaps and dripping
with a musical beat that seemed to be in harmony with the
movements, breathing and heart beat, onto the kennel floor.
He looked at his other animal but could not see the nose
that had been chewed, shredded and bludgeoned, as had
the rest of the face. The entire face was varying shades of
red with slashes, rips, chewed holes and lumps of pulp that
oozed and bubbled. He watched them move closer and
closer to the rat, their bellies and chests brushing the kennel
floor, their bodies forming a V forcing the rat deeper and
deeper into the corner. All teeth were bared, rat and dogs
alike. All bodies were ready to spring. There was nothing as
a reward. Only death or survival.

Suddenly the animals sprang
forward and for a moment the rat seemed to be locked between the huge heads of the dogs, but then he sank his
teeth in the cheek of one while the other snapped at him
trying to disembowel him with his teeth only to slide over
his slimy skin and as the animals jerked and swung and
butted the rat continued to gouge and rip with his teeth and
claws but the dogs never relented and continued to snap and
club at the rat and as he hung from one of the dogs the
other tore at the rats flesh with dull teeth until finally each
of the dogs had a portion of the rat in his mouth and tried
to yank him apart then finally pinned him to the floor and
gnawed and gnawed while the blood squirted in their faces

and they felt the rats bones hard against their teeth and they continued to gnaw until every little bone had been broken and crushed and all the entrails had been torn from the rats body and spread on their faces.

They stopped.

They raised their heads slightly and looked at the crushed and slimy mess a few inches from their eyes. They stared for many moments as if afraid that somehow the parts would come back to life. The glob was still.

Slowly they raised their heads, stared, then slowly turned their heads away and stretched out on the kennel floor, panting. Slabs of flesh and guts still clung to their faces.

BRAVO!   BRAVO!   THAT WAS GREAT! Really great! Did you see that? Did all of you see that? That was great. Really great. Now, thats what I call good dogs. A couple of good ratters. See, Ive been telling you all along that youre a couple of dogs. Hahahahahahahaha. You see, I was right, wasnt I? Youre a couple of dogs. Real good ratter dogs. Hahaha. He started to toss them a couple of dog yummies, then stopped. I think you should wash your faces before I give you a little treat. Thats the good dogs. Get those faces washed. You dont want to spend the rest of your life with rat gut hanging from your faces, do you? Hahahahaha. Rat gut. Thats pretty funny. Hahahahaha. He watched and waited as they cleaned their faces with their forepaws then tossed them each a dog yummie. Thats the good doggies. Now you rest for a while then I/ll give you some nice horse meat and some water before we continue. He continued to look at them and shook his head, almost sadly. You know, you look terrible. Even with the rat gut scraped away you look awful. How did you ever let one hungry, mangy rat do that to you? Krist. I can understand a few bites and scratches, but youre a godawful mess. You with your gut all chewed up and this poor guy with his face a bloody pulp. And your nose is missing. Well, I guess I cant blame you for that. You werent the one who was smashing it. Youll just have to blame your mate for that. O well, thats all right. You did a good job eventually. I must admit that I am very proud of you. Of course one little kitty-cat could have done a thousand times better, but you cant expect too much from a couple of dumb-ass dogs. Maybe youll do better next time.

But we/ll forget that for now. You just rest for a few minutes. I think our audience needs a few minutes rest too after that magnificent display of animal courage and savagery. Hahahahaha. And after we finish our little performance you can crawl into a corner and lick your wounds. Hahahaha. But now you just rest. We want the rest of the performance to be up to the high standards we/ve set. But now you need rest. Then we/ll show them what great lovers you are.

He looked at his dogs, the audience, the wet mess that was a rat, with only the long, thin tail intact, the tail in fact the only evidence that the mess was the remains of a rat and not that of some other animal or simply a pile of wet, gooey garbage. He continued to glance around the room and no matter how many times he looked at everything and everyone in the kennel, and no matter how carefully he investigated every little detail he could find no change, neither in the whole nor in any little detail. The audience remained stiffened, staring and silent. The dogs were still stretched out in the same place, in the same position, with their heads resting on their forelegs, the blood simply dripping from the many rips in their flesh, the face of the one dog transformed into a pulpy, bloody blob. The once-rat mess still just a glob of goo with a long thin tail. Everything remained still and unchanging.

Yet there was some kind of a change. Then, as he continued to look around the room, he slowly realized what the change was. It was within himself. The feeling of excitement and rapture that existed within him while watching the battle of survival and listening to the screams, the howls and snarls; the beautifully exciting sounds of agony and despair, all the sensations he experienced, the sense of accomplishment that had surged through him and burst forth with his bravos, the overwhelming happiness, was slowly draining from him.

He could not sustain it. All the vivid memories of terror in eyes and voice could not revive it to the point of intensity of a few moments ago. It had slowly built up through the performance, reached its apex and now, in spite of all he did to retain that intensity, it was slowly slipping away.

And as this realization grew he slowly became aware of the fact that he was tired. Physically tired. And as he went through his emotional withdrawal his exhaustion increased and he was content to lean against the wall and cease trying to sustain the intensity of excitement, but simply let it flow from him and enjoy the loosening of his body and the happy anticipation of rest.

And the more he surrendered to his feeling of exhaustion the more his disappointment with the changelessness of those in the kennel decreased and the more he enjoyed the relaxing unfolding of his body. And then the cause of his disappointment was realized with utter and complete simplicity. All the others were exhausted. The stiffened audience, the torn and bloodied dogs, and, hahahaha, that hopeless mess of a rat.

Now he was really exhausted. As a matter of fact he was so exhausted he fell completely apart. Hahahahaha. Yeah, he was so damned exhausted he was ready to be exhumed. Hahahaha. Thats a good one. He was really sleepy, sleepy bye-bye.

He stretched his body and mixed a low sigh with a soft chuckle as he glanced around the room again, this time looking differently. Everything was yet unchanged—the stares, the attitudes, the sounds, but he was no longer disappointed that the looks and sounds of a present terror were gone, or that the fear of apprehension was missing, because now he knew why there was nothing but apathy in the room. Hahaha. Yeah, especially the rat. He sure dont care about anything. The room was a big, quiet nothing simply because they were exhausted. It was that simple. They were beat.

He stretched out on the floor and put his hands behind his head and glanced a final time around the room. A little rest will change everything. Thats all we all need. Just a little rest. Of course he wasnt sure just how much rest the audience would get locked in their stalls staring at his bloody and noble beasts, but that was immaterial. The important thing was for the dogs to rest so they would be able to continue with the exhibition, and that he get enough rest to enjoy it. Thats all that mattered.

He adjusted his body until he found a comfortable spot on the kennel floor, made sure the wires were tight enough so that the slightest movement would awaken him, then completely surrendered to the peace and security of his exhaustion.

His sleep was calm and restful and his awakening was a warm drifting to consciousness. He could feel a smile on his face as he slowly opened his eyes and sat up. He could feel a change before his eyes were fully opened and focused. He looked first at his dogs, their positions only slightly changed, their bodies twitching in a restless and painful sleep. As he looked at their jerking bodies he became aware of the fact that there had been a great change in color. After the encounter they seemed to be entirely red of varying tones, now there was less red than any other color. There seemed to be more grayish white with splotches of dull red. There was also a lot of burning blues and purples. But what attracted his eyes the most were the crusty and caked browns. They completely fascinated him. They looked like deep tire-tread ruts in mud that had been trampled on. They seemed to pulse and grow and the longer he stared the more animated these areas seemed to be, the deeper and more jagged the cracks and furrows. And soon he could see new ruts forming and could hear the scabs crack and feel the pain throb through the bodies of his doggies.

Then, after many long and beautiful moments, he became aware of his heart beating in perfect unison with their throbbing pain and he felt the excitement once again start charging through him. He could feel his body tightening with the excitement and could hear the air rushing through his nostrils. The more animated became their pain the more his body became alive, the louder the cracking of the crusty scabs the more aware he was of the beating of his heart until he was completely involved with every throb and tick of their bodies, every sensation registered in their brains and the excitement charged through all of him until he tingled and vibrated with the old exquisite joy and he suddenly jerked his head toward the audience and instantaneously absorbed their horrifying apprehension and then his joy became sublime.

He
sprang erect and tugged his wired doggies awake. UP UP
UP. Youve slept enough my noble beasts. Its time for action.
Youve got to get with it. If you keep moping around like
that youll stiffen up and wont be able to perform. And we
wouldnt want that, would we? Hahahahaha. Not now. No.
Not now. We must save the stiffening for later. Hahaha.
Aint that right my lovers? Hahaha. What you need is some
action. Take your minds off your booboos. That nasty little
rat hurt my doggies and we have to take care of that. Later.
Hahahahaha. Right now the best thing to do is to take
your minds off it. Frolic and cavort and youll forget what
that mangy old rat did. Some good food, cool water and a
little fun and you wont even notice the throbbing pain thats
banging at your bones or the fires that are shooting through
you and burning your guts and your bowels. Will you? No.
Not in the least. So lets get on with the fun and games. But
we need energy to play. Dont we? Yeah. Good food makes
fido a peppy pup. Here you are my kay fucking nines. Some
nice fresh horse meat and a nice big bowl of water. That's
it, sniff it first. Make sure its good. Thats the way. Now lick
it a little bit before you take a nice big bite. O, you want
some water first. O.K. Go ahead. Wet your little whistles
first. Whats the matter little doggies, having trouble swallowing? Did that nasty little rat bite you all up and give
you a fever? Haha. You sure did get even with him. That
poor sonofabitch aint never going to swallow again. You
should be thankful for what you have. At least you can
swallow. Even if your throat does feel like its filled with
burning carpet tacks. You just take it easy and let some of
the water trickle down. Pretty soon youll be able to swallow.
But youd better not take too long. The show must go on you
know. We havent much time before the next scene. So youd

better hurry up. Thats it, force it down. It only hurts when you laugh. Hahahaha. And youd better chomp down some of the energy-giving horse meat. Dont forget, the audience is waiting breathlessly for the passion play. Hahahaha. Thats it. Get it down. Good doggies. Your throats arent being slashed with rusty razor blades. It only feels that way. Hahahahaha. And just think, pretty soon youll be in a lovers embrace. Now doesnt that make you feel better? Now doesnt it? Hahahaha. Thats a good title for the next scene of our little show. Love makes the world go round. Thats perfect. Absolutely perfect. Love makes the world go round. It also makes little doggies go woof woof and sniff sniff. Hahahaha. I really must admit that you dont look like lovers. You sure dont look lovely, anyway. What did you guys do while I was sleeping? You look like you got caught in a meat grinder. Hahahaha. But thats all right. Love heals all wounds. Or is it wombs. Hahaha. Look mommy, the poor doggie is wombded. Hahahaha. Relax before you get all wombed up. Hahahaha. Did you ever play tennis at womble-don? Hahahaha. I think my doggies are just wombderful. Haha. O.K., enough wombing around. Lets cut the umbili-cal cord and get on with the show. O.K. Lets nose those dishes out of the way. You take the food dish and you push the water dish. Thats the good boys. Thats it. Right there. Thats good enough. O.K. Lets get on with the show. And remember, its not loves labors lost. Its love makes the world go round.

And around and around they went. Without bene-fit of wired pressure. Nose and tongue sought out and thoroughly investigated asshole with complete acceptance. There was nothing to fight. There was no desire to fight. Through submission to pain and exhaustion they simply, automatically, did what they were trained to do. And they were trained to pursue their love-making with animalistic desire whether it was real or feigned. And so nose and tongue continued to pursue asshole with the required amount and degree of excitement and sound and sight.

Isnt that lovely? Isnt that just beautiful? You notice how the nose sniffs and quickly zeros in on the asshole? Its really quite remarkable when you think of it. When you think of how small the actual hole is. When you consider the fact that it is only a small part of the larger expanse of ass and is completely hidden from sight. Yet a few twitching sniffs and the nose is nestled in the unseen hole. And notice the technique with which the tongue explores that area between the cocksus and the cockbut. And keep in mind the fact that he has a pair of hairy balls to contend with. Yet love knows no boundaries or barriers. And theres something else you should keep in mind and that is that the tongue is used for more than one reason. Of course its obviously exciting. You can see that easy enough just by their reactions and their excitement. Having a warm wet tongue licking her ass and crotch is exciting to the bitch and certainly gets her twitching, but its also exciting to the male too to feel his tongue roaming around her ass and to feel her hole quiver around his tongue as he sinks it in deeper and deeper with relish. Hahaha. Thats pretty good, isn't it? With relish. Maybe theyd like it better with mustard. Hahahaha. Thats a good one. Musturd, custurd, and you you big shit. Hahahahahaha. . . . Well, anyway, you can see the joy it brings to both animals when he sinks his tongue into her hole.

But excitement isn't the only purpose this tongue in cheek serves. Hahahaha. From dancing cheek to cheek, its nose in cheek then tongue in cheek. Don't think it will go over in the ballroom too well though. Hahahaha. Always did wonder how you could talk with your tongue in cheek. Hahahaha. Speak boy,

speak. Thats a good dog. Did you hear that little bow-wow?
Very good. Thats called talking with tongue in cheek. But
theres more to it than dancing a fang dong go. There are
other considerations. Considerations of accessibility. You see
dogs are not civilized the way we are. They dont wipe their
asses after they shit and keep their holes clean with baths
and showers. The tongue is used for this. And when two
dogs love each other they like to wash each other. I guess
its basically a show of affection. But it also helps get this
hole ready for action. You know, gets those shit-matted
hairs out of the way and softens up those little balls of shit
that block the road to pleasure. And of course it helps juice
up the old shit chute

        suddenly one of the audience spewed
forth a river of puke that splattered on the heads of the
children and flowed and dribbled down their faces.

        Goddamn
it. Just when hes mounting the bitch. He yanked hard on
the wires and the stiffened dick was buried in the bitches
hole as they yelped and jerked and more vomit wrenched
itself from a gaping mouth and splattered on the little heads
and another mouth sprang open and the vomit shot out with
a groan and the bodies knotted and snapped with screeching, retching as the puke was followed with bile and snot
and phlegm dribbled from their noses and he watched the
gentle streams flowing and listened to the music of nature
as he yanked again on the wires—fucker. Fucker. Plow the
shit out of the bitch—and the exciting yelping and howling
joined the other woodland sounds and charged through him
exciting and animating him more and more and he screamed
with pure and absolute joy as he listened and watched and
yanked the wires—to the hilt. To the hilt. Turn the goddamn
bitch inside out. Shove it out the top of her head and flow
lovely rivers flow, and he waved his hands and arms urging

the gurgling brooks to flow and flow and his dogs to fuck and fuck and all the joy of life was his and he experienced it through all of his body, every cell of his being until it filled his soul and he could feel it, and see it, glowing with the brightness of a sun and he was aflame with warmth, a warmth that was pure and whole and grew warmer and warmer and ever warmer even as the rippling brooks became deep spastic groans and his spent dogs could only cringe as the yanking wires tore at their balls and they lay on their sides with their tongues and pricks limp.

OR maybe just stand there as Fred leaps off the witness stand and just sort of duck under his punch and let him have it right in the fucking gut. Yeah, and listen to him groan as he crumples then lift my knee in his face and let him have it on the back of his neck and look at him on the floor with his whole fucking jaw hanging from his cheek. And not stomp on his fucking head or kick his balls up into his gut, but just stand there and look at him. Not even spit on the sonofabitch. Just stand there and watch them drag him out of the court.

And maybe just turn my back slightly to the cameras so they can see me standing over the rat prick.

Too bad I cant put my foot on his chest and make like tarzan

mary, mary, quite cunttrary, how does your garden grow

or like David and Goliath. Yeah, with a slingshot in my hand and a rock in his head

and a huge two-handed sword raised over my head and I/ll smite the circumcised dog thus

No. Not like that. Stick the tip in his fucking gut and slowly twist the sonofabitch in until it crunches against his fucking spine

No, thats no good. Just stand there and look down at him.   Yeah, with my shadow across him. Yeah, with the camera over my shoulder and my shadow over his fucked-up face. The rat bastard.

But unfortunately there is nothing that can be done about this your honor. Mrs. Haagstromm has only brief moments of lucidity and she is the only witness to this outrageous crime. Legally there is nothing that can be done about bringing these men to trial. What I am endeavoring to accomplish is to prove that they are not fit, in any sense of the word, to be police officers and have the responsibility of enforcing the law. I feel it is my obligation to help bring this about. It would be simple enough for me to prove my innocence, but I believe I would be remiss in my duty as a citizen if I did only that without exerting all possible efforts on my part to have these men discharged from the force.

What does the district attorneys office know about this Mr. Stills?

Im afraid that I, personally, know nothing at all about the implications that these 2 officers may have been involved in the Haagstromm incident. I find myself shocked at the possibility.

Then you have no idea what the official position of the department is?

None whatsoever, your honor. Of course I can check if you would like me to.

Excuse me, but that may not be necessary. I feel confident that just a cursory psychiatric examination and evaluation will prove these men to be unfit to serve as police officers and as such they can be discharged from the force. I seriously doubt, in view of what has happened during this trial, that they will protest their dismissal in any way whatsoever. Especially if it is implied that no criminal charges will be pressed if they do not contest their dismissal. Of course, there is no need to tell them that there is no way that criminal charges can be brought against them.

Do you agree Mr. Stills?

Well, naturally I cant speak for the department, but I do think that, under the circumstances, it will be wise to ask for a postponement until the reports from the psychiatrists can be evaluated.

Do you concur?

Yes, your honor.

Yeah, you bet. By the time the head-shrinkers get through with those pricks they wont know which side is up or backward. What they should do is lock them in a cell next to the broad and let them listen to her whimper and cry all day and night. I bet that would drive them up a wall. Yeah, hahahahahaha, a padded wall. Those sonsabitches would be at each others throats in no time. Just like a rat at a dogs throat. Or a mongoose on a snake. Yeah, the fucking snakes. Rotten fucking snakes. But theyll get theirs. You bet your sweet ass theyll get theirs, the rotten—the cell door clanged open and he strode forth from his cell and down the corridor—mothers cunts

mary, mary, quite cunttrary, how does that fucking garden grow

and marched into the mess hall and took his place on line and stepped forward as the line shuffled along the wall

with silver fucking bells and cockle fucking shells

and picked up his tray and silverware and passed before the food dispensers then walked to an empty seat, deposited his tray on the table then sat in front of it and ate his fill

and empty scum bags all in a row

scraped the remainder of his food into the gar-

bage can, piled his tray on the cart and went forth into
the corridor and back to his cell

quite cunttrary

washed his
hands, splashed water on his face, patted it dry and inspected his pimple, looking for indications of its coming to
a head

how does it fucking grow

gave it a few tentative
squeezes, then a quick, short hard one, stretched the skin
around it

with those silver fucking bells

then splashed more
cold water on his face, patted it dry, then sat on the edge
of his bed, smiling and sucking his teeth. He crossed his
legs, propped his right elbow on his left hand and his chin
on his finger tips and looked toward the large crack in the
wall that eventually lost itself in the crack that joined the
wall and ceiling

and empty scum bags in a row

and waited until the steel door was clanged shut and
locked

then sat and listened to the court-appointed psychiatrists describe in technical and lay language the deep and
grave emotional disturbances of the two officers, how they
would not only experience extreme emotional elation from
committing cruel and abnormal acts, but would feel justi-
fied in committing such acts. He sat quietly and watched
and listened while inside he roared and screamed his approval as he watched the judge, the psychiatrists and officers, glowing as he heard the motherfuckers described as
unstable, immature, hostile, sadistic. . .unfit emotionally to
be police officers and skipped and danced as he watched
their fucking faces twist and their guts tighten and boil with

insane rage, knowing that there would be no defense made, no attempt to refute the testimony of the psychiatrists because orders had been given to their appointed attorney not to fight the dismissal for fear of bad publicity during an election year, for fear that more than just the unfitness of these two officers would be made public; for fear that many high public officials would be more than embarrassed, and so there would be no contest, but just a plea for clemency and when it was all over the judge would commit them to a state mental institution for an undetermined period and when things cooled down they would quietly be released one day, but he would see to it that that day would be a long time coming. A long time coming. He would keep a constant check on them and have them examined by independent psychiatrists and their opinions made public so the authorities would be afraid to release them. Not for a long, long, long-ass time. He would see to it that it would be many years before they walked free in the street. Or even walked free on the hospital grounds. He would make certain that they spent years confined in a locked ward with no privileges whatsoever. None. They would just sit and look at walls and each other. Thats all. Nothing else. Only walls and each other. Or other hopelessly deranged and violent cases. And they would hear the screams. Yeah, thats what they were going to hear. No music, chirping of birds or even the roar and rumble of trucks and cars. Just screams. And when the motherfuckers were turned into hopeless blobs and eventually allowed to leave, he would see to it that no matter where they went everyone would know who they were, and where they came from, and why they had been there.

And he would start with their families. He knew that right now they were in the process of moving, but no matter where or how far they went he would be certain that everyone knew who they were so when they walked the street and their kids went to school, everyone would point and whisper until they would be forced to move again and he would see to it that the pointed fingers, whispers and cold aloofness would force them to move again and again and again until they were so tired and filled with despair that they were no longer capable of moving but would simply sit in one place and wait to die. Or maybe some night when the kids were asleep they would turn on the gas and the next morning there would be nothing but death in the house. Or even pile the family in the car and drive off a cliff or swerve into an oncoming truck and be crushed. Yeah, others may think that this was the end of the case, but he would see to it that it wasnt. He would dedicate his life to the complete demoralization and destruction of those pricks and their families. O, how he wanted them to live. All of them. He wanted them to live a long, long time. And suffer. Suffer so bad that each second of each day will be an eternity. No matter where they go or how hard they try to hide he will see to it that the world knows who they are and where they are so they can experience the living hell of disgrace and despair, so they can all be crushed by endless time and see the children deny their fathers and eventually reach that time when they will long for death but be denied its gift. They will suffer—all of them—years of torment for every second of pain inflicted on him. Retribution, you sonsabitches. Retribution. And it will be mine. In my way, in my time, it will be mine.

When the brief proceedings were over, and the judge sentenced them, he was hoping the motherfuckers would fight or yell or something, but he didnt really expect them to. He knew they had been told to keep their mouths shut, that if they didnt they would be indicted for rape and if they were found guilty they could be executed. So he didnt really expect them to protest. And they didnt.

But it wasnt necessary. He knew what was happening inside them. He watched them squirm. He watched the reaction on their faces. And when it was all over and they were led from the courtroom he could see their fear and feel their panic. He knew it was starting. And he also knew it would get worse. Day by day, hour by hour, and then minute by fucking minute it would get worse, and he would be thinking of them every second of every fucking day of every fucking year. Yeah, he would be thinking of them. All of them.

He waited until the alleged mental incompetents were led from the courtroom before he stood, adjusted his jacket, shirt and tie and started walking slowly, yet firmly, from the courtroom. He knew the reporters and photographers would be waiting for him in the corridor. He knew that the families of the alleged mental incompetents were advised, very strongly, to remain in seclusion as long as possible, so all the cameras and questions would be directed at him simultaneously. As he approached the doors to the corridor he could see and hear the newsmen, and others, as he had so many times recently. He knew that when he stepped through the doorway he would have to angle toward the side and position himself away from the doors and lean against the wall in his usual leisurely attitude and answer the many questions as rapidly as possible. This procedure had become, by this time, automatic. He lit a cigarette as he angled through the doorway, and carefully put the burnt match in the ash tray on the wall.

Are you pleased with the decision, or do you think criminal charges should have been pressed?

No, I do not think a criminal indictment should have been sought. They are obviously sick men and as such I believe the decision is a just one.

Then you dont think they should be punished?

Well, in view of the fact that nothing has been proven to warrant punishment I do not see how they can be. In any event no matter how severely or long they would be punished it would not restore Mrs. Haagstromm to health.

As I understand the term, indefinite commitment, it is possible for those men to be released in a matter of months. Do you believe this is just, under the circumstances?

Yes, I do. As you say it is possible for them to be released in a relatively short period of time, but it also means that they must stay until competent authorities feel that they have recovered sufficiently to be *safely* released into society. This, obviously, may take a great deal of time.

What are your future plans now that this case is over?

To continue my—our—crusade.

What is the next phase of this crusade?

To determine why men such as these are given guns and the authority to use them. In other words a complete and thorough review of the procedures being followed at the present time that determine whether or not a man is the proper material to become a police officer so future incidents such as this can be avoided. You see, gentlemen, there is much more here than meets the eye. To begin with we have no idea what else these two sick men may have done during their time on the force. But just what we do know is overwhelming. A young mothers life destroyed. And it does not end there. What of her family? Think of how tragic it is to them. And what of the families of the men themselves? How will this affect them? What of their children, young and innocent? How will their future lives be warped and affected? And it even goes beyond that. What of the millions of people, young and old alike, who have been following these tragic events, how will their attitudes be affected? How will the institutions and age-old traditions of our society be looked upon by these millions of people? There is just no way we can calculate the damage done by these two sick individuals. It is tragic. Most tragic. But with effort it need not happen again.

Do you plan to take your crusade to other cities, or are you going to confine your activities here?

Well, as you know, I have already testified before the senate of this state and the Senate of the United States, as well as before various agencies in this city. In addition we have made the results of our investigations available to interested parties from all over the nation. To date, we have not only received requests for assistance from various civic groups, both official and unofficial, in all our major cities, but from many smaller municipalities. And I am certain that after the decision that was rendered here today these requests for assistance will increase many-fold.

Just how do you propose to handle these requests?

At the present time we are in the process of establishing a small office that will be devoted exclusively to this crusade. We have had many individuals offering their help in many different capacities. Basically what we propose to do is this: arrange the results of our investigations in chronological order and have them bound in as many volumes as will be necessary—with depositions and carefully indexed. In addition we will issue a separate volume outlining the procedures we followed and what the results were. This will provide a foundation upon which these other organizations can proceed with their own investigations. In addition, we will be available for consultation and assistance should any situation arise where our procedures volume is not applicable.

It sounds like you have a lifes work cut out for you.

It is the least I can do for Mrs. Haagstromm. . . .
Now,
if you will excuse me gentlemen, I really must go as I have
a great deal of work to do.

He nodded and shook hands as flash bulbs
exploded and cameras ground. He walked briskly and pur-
posefully down the corridor and through the doors into the
sunlight. He stood momentarily on the top step looking up
at the blue, cloudless sky, then descended the steps and
walked through the parking lot toward his car feeling the
clear blue of the sky, hearing the cameras and flashing
lights and reliving the scenes in the courtroom and caressing
the solid, unshakeable strength in his gut and the joy of
being alive that vibrated through his being as he saw with
absolute clarity the purpose of his life and the goals and
rewards that wait at the end of the clearly defined road,
knowing with absolute and complete confidence that nothing could deter or prevent him from following that chosen
path

and when the teacher pointed to the denominator of
the fraction and asked him what it was he said, the plural,
and the other kids laughed and the teacher frowned and
asked again and his head burst into flames and he stared
at the fraction on the blackboard hoping and waiting
for the answer to leap at him and come out of his mouth and
he stammered as his head shook and the chalked figures became blurred and floated gently and the teacher asked someone else and he sat in his seat and burned as the teacher
continued the lesson,

the rotten bitch. One fucking minute
shes teaching spelling and the next shes with the fucking
fractions. The fucking asshole. And anyway, who gives a shit
what its called,

jerking himself off the bed and stomping to

the door and looking through the window at the fucking signs then continuing his journey from door to wall and wall to door,

and fuck you and Pee Wee too. Big fucking deal. I missed a tackle and he made a few lousy yards. So fucking what? Who needs it? Who needs anything. Dumb fucking cunt.

how does your cocksucking garden grow

Rotten bitch.
There was more than 1 number. I wasnt really wrong

stopping in front of the mirror and attacking his pimple, his eyes watering as the pain of ground glass stabbed him until he had to lower his hand and stomp back to the bed and drop on the edge and hold his head with his hands and stare at the huge pimple on his cheek. It looked like a snow-capped mountain glazed with ice and was so swollen it looked as if it would burst. And even without touching it he could feel the piece of wire twisting itself inside. He bathed it with hot water for many minutes then patted it dry, then maneuvered his fingers around it, tentatively prodding with the edges of his fingers until he found the proper position then started squeezing, his face twisting and his eyes closing from the pain. He stopped, keeping his fingers in their position, and breathed deeply wishing he had a pin or needle he could lance it with so he could get the fucking thing started, but there wasnt a fucking thing in the cell he could use so he attacked it again with the edges of his fingers until he once again was forced to stop and catch his breath. He attacked again, determined to continue to squeeze the sonofabitch until it burst no matter how much it hurt, and when he was about to stop because of the pain he pressed his eyes shut tighter and squeezed harder and harder until he could hear it cracking then opened his eyes and watched the white, wormlike pus wiggle and crunch its way out then suddenly lowered his hands and leaned on the sink, his head lowered, his eyes tearing, and panting. He blinked his eyes clear of the tears then raised his head and looked at the twisted tail hanging from the white lump on his cheek. He wiped it off with a piece of toilet paper and inspected it before squeezing it, gently at first, feeling its firmness and substance, pressing a little harder and harder until it was flattened. He looked back in the mirror and once more positioned the edges of his fingers and squeezed with short, hard jabs and heard another one crackling out, watching it grow longer and longer as the tears dropped from his eyes, and continued to jab at the huge, white lump as it gave birth to another wiggling tail that slithered along his cheek until it was a couple of inches long and he stopped and gently removed it from his cheek before it broke. He looked at it stretched across the toilet paper for many moments before testing it with his finger tips and once again attacking the parent body relentlessly. His eyes were jammed shut and he could hear the crackling and crunching turmoil, and feel the needle-like pain pricking him, and could visualize those thin, white bodies crawling away from the constant and increasing pressure, and he wanted to scream as the pain jabbed deeper and he squeezed harder until he heard a sharp crack and a whooshing explosion and he heard the core of his festering lump splat against the mirror. His hand grabbed the sink and he shook his head trying to clear his eyes and get them to open so he could look at the fruits of his victory. He blinked many, many times, and continued blinking as he raised his head and looked at the twisted and mangled mess on the mirror. For many minutes he just looked and enjoyed. Eventually, when his eyes dried and cleared, he could see the endless convolutions like a miniature brain. He continued to stare and study the twists and turns until he noticed the light reflecting from a thin, almost invisible hair stuck in the middle. It was so small and thin that he could only see it when he held his head at a particular angle, yet that little sonofabitch was the cause of that festering lump stuck on the mirror, and all the fucking pain and misery he had to go through to get rid of the sonofabitch. All the fucking bullshit just because a little fucking hair had to grow in instead of out. If the fucking thing had grown like it was supposed to he could have just cut the fucking thing with his razor and it would have been no different than any one of a million hairs that he had cut while shaving, but this motherfucker had to grow in and fuck him all up and put him through all that fucking misery

and pretty scum bags in a motherfucking row

and pain and he had to walk around with a fucking golf ball on his cheek, unable to sleep on the side because the fucking thing hurt so goddamn much, all because some little fucking hair fucked him up. Just like everything else. Theres always something fucking you up. Or someone. Krist. Same old shit, all the time. Just cant be left alone. If its not some dumb cunt of a teacher its a lousy fucking hair. Fuckem. Who needsem. I got the sonofabitch out anyway.

He carefully slid the core off the mirror with toilet paper then held it in the palm of his hand while he looked and poked. It was hard. It felt as if there were a piece of gravel in the middle. Even the outer layer was hard. Not as hard as the center, but hard. When he squeezed it with his finger tips he could feel the resistance. Jesus, how could a fucking thing like that grow. Its incredible. A little hair fucks up and a fucking lump like this grows and his face is a fucking mess. He looked at his face and the hole in his cheek. He put his pimple down on the sink and began prodding the infected area, squeezing here and there, making sure everything was out, making sure that there wasnt the slightest bit left. He continued to squeeze and mop up with toilet paper until only blood and water came out, then picked up his pimple and studied it from various angles and distances, prodded it, squeezed it and rolled it around with his finger tips. After a time he dropped it in the toilet bowl and stared at it for many, many loving minutes before flushing it and watching it swirl around and around in smaller and smaller circles until it disappeared with the gurgle of the water.

He dropped his hands and raised his head then walked over to the mirror and looked at his blemish. He started to poke at it, but stopped. There was no point to it. It wasnt ready yet.

He leaned against the wall and glanced through the window in the door, through his reflected face at the hallway, the laundry baskets and signs with their little arrows; yellows here and greens here and blues here and who cares about north and south, its all the same. North could be south, or green or wood or anything. Its all the same. A big nothing. Everything is nothing. Cops or robbers, robbers or cops. Its all the same. A big nothing. Its never like it should be, walking as slowly as possible back to the bed, never. Never really comes out right. Going to camp. Or anything. It was O.K., but there was something missing. Shit, I dont know. It just should have been better. Those shithouses sure did stink. Or whatever they called them. What the hell did they call them. Johns, or something like that.................o yeah, willies. Johns, willies, elmers. The same thing. Anyway, they sure did stink. I guess it was all right. I dont know. But it should have been better. Talking for months about it, about getting out of the city for 2 weeks and going swimming and hiking and all that shit and then youre there and its not all that great. I guess it was O.K. though. I mean we did go swimming and hunt around for salamanders and turtles and things and go on hikes, but it was never what it should have been. And what can you do at camp when it rains? Sit around and talk I guess. I dont know. But I guess I liked it. It must have been fun. But it seemed like there was something missing. Maybe I should have stayed another 2 weeks that first time. It was better than the other times. I guess. It seems like that was the time we had the race in the war canoes. Sure did get wet. Wonder if anyone won that race. It was a lot of fun though. I guess there was a lot of things like that. I guess I had fun. But not enough to stay. Funny, but I can still remember how the mess hall smelled. Seems like it always smelled of hot cereal. That wheat cereal. And that rotten prick looking at me like I was some kind of weirdo or something because I licked my spoon clean before taking some plums out of the bowl. Shit, big fucking deal. What the fuck did he think I had, leprosy or something? The rotten mothers cunt. Looking at me like that and making a big deal out of nothing.

Like the time I found that book and took it to school. Somebody always making a big deal out of nothing. Found it on the street on his way to school. It was a small cartoon booklet and it started with a woman getting undressed and a burglar watching her outside her window. He comes through the window and a huge penis bursts through his pants and they say and do a lot of funny things he didnt understand. He showed it to his friends and eventually gave it to someone. The next day the entire school was marched out to the yard and they stood there while a few teachers and a couple of the older boys walked up and down looking at everyone and all the rest of that day and the next morning all the kids wondered what was going on and they talked about spies and somebody stealing something and the police were going to come and maybe some kid had a gun or something and there were so many stories it was impossible to keep track of them all. The next afternoon he was sent down to the principals office and the assistant principal showed him the booklet and asked him if he had brought it to school and he said yes and she told him it was a naughty book and a few other things and he panicked and told her he found it and started to cry and she told him it was all right, not to be upset, but that if he ever found another one he should either throw it down a sewer or give it to her.

Hahahahahahahahahaha. I wonder if she had a collection? Wouldnt mind having one now. Might help pass the time. Seems like all those guys had 2-foot dongs. Shit, they didnt have dongs, they had clubs. Wonder what youd do if you had a rod like that? Guess you could always shove it up some cops ass. O fuck it. Its all a bunch of dumb shit.

> *one, two, three, upsa daisy*
> *i dont care if i go crazy*
> *just so i can beat my daisy*

As the days of the trial progressed he couldnt help but notice that the wives of the cops were glancing at him. At first he averted his eyes and continued to concentrate on the proceedings, but after their glances had met many times he became more and more aware of the fact that the glances werent hostile. When the trial ended he called them and after they had spoken for a few minutes he knew he had them. As he waited for them to get to his apartment he set up the hidden cameras and made sure everything was ready for their visit. When they arrived he took them to the bedroom immediately and let them undress him, then watched as they undressed each other. They made love to him, he made love to them and they made love to each other, following his directions. When they left he developed the pictures and laughed aloud with joy and excitement as he looked at the endless number of beautiful photographs. The angles and lighting were perfect on hundreds of them. Their faces were clear and distinct, their activities obvious. It was a shame he didnt have a big dog they could have fucked, but that wasnt important. The pictures he had were perfect. He hung them up to dry and went to bed happy and relaxed, looking forward to the morning when he would select the pictures he would send to their husbands and families. It was an exciting sleep and awakening the next morning. He also sent copies to their friends, the principal of the school their children attended, and to the church of their choice. His heart sang with gladness when he heard their hysterical voices on the other end of the phone, and he listened in silence as they told him of what had happened to their children and themselves. They sobbed and pleaded and begged. He smiled and his body tingled as he felt their world coming to an end and he could see the tears streaming down their faces and could feel the marrow draining from their bones, see them on bended knees, washing his feet with their tears and begging him for their lives. It was a lovely scene and he loved the music, and when he had heard enough he gently cradled the phone and let the joy flow through his body.

The story of the incident in the mental institution was on the front page and he stretched out in his easy chair as he read the account of the two police officers, who had only recently been committed, running amuck and attacking hospital personnel and leaping through an office window and trying to claw their way over the fence. They were finally shot with a tranquilizer gun as they attempted to escape and returned to the hospital, still screaming incoherently—I/ll kill the bitch. I/ll kill the rotten fucking bitch—. They both had multiple lacerations about the body and face from the glass, and their hands were ripped and torn from their attempt to climb the fence. No explanation was given for their behavior. After their wounds were treated they were put in restraint and locked in the maximum-security wing of the hospital. The 2 officers were committed after a trial. . . .

Hahahahahahahahaha. Theyll never get out. If it worked once it will work again. There are plenty of copies of the pictures and more can be gotten any time. Any time. And they wont even be able to kill themselves. Just sit in that padded cell and wait. Wait for nothing. He dropped the paper on the floor and went for a walk in the sun.

The officers each found an envelope on their beds when they returned from the dining room. The envelopes were opened and the pictures dropped on the bed.

The pictures were looked at one at a time, many times, then placed next to each other on the bed and stared at with an exciting fascination at first and then a growing and rumbling nausea as the pictures were studied more and more carefully, each position and action absorbed deeper and deeper until their flesh started to tremble then their entire bodies roar with rage and they screamed as they attacked the pictures with their fists, pounding them into the bed, then crushing them, throwing them against the wall, trying to pulverize them with their feet, picking them up and tearing them and throwing the pieces with all their strength onto the floor, screaming that they would kill the cocksucking bitches, the no good fucking cunts, and pounded on the door and screamed and pounded and it was nice walking in the sun

and he sat on the edge of his bunk, a small piece of string in his hands, trying to remember how to tie a bowline. He looped the string this way, that way, positive that that was the way to do it, yet it never came out right. He closed his eyes trying to imagine the illustrations in the boy scout manual, yet he couldnt seem to follow them no matter how carefully and slowly he tried. He stopped for a second then very methodically tried it another way and still he couldnt get the goddamn thing tied properly and he strangled the string with his hands and screamed at it and threw the son-ofabitch on the floor and stared at it for many long minutes wishing the fucking thing was alive so he could kill it and tear it to shreds, his body trembling, his head shaking and burning, staring at the motherfucker and trying to make it disappear by focusing all his hate on the fucking thing. Finally he picked it up and squeezed it as hard as he could, his stomach sucked back to his spine, his eyes fused shut, a furious groan rumbling through his chest and throat until he finally heaved it into the toilet bowl and kicked the handle and watched it whirl around and around as it descended to the hole in the bottom and gurgled out of sight and down into the sewer with the rest of the shit where it belonged.

Jesus fucking krist, how in the hell can you be expected to tie a fucking knot with a fucked-up piece of string like that? You gotta be crazy. Its impossible. Like those stupid knot-tying contests. Lining up and running to the pole with the pieces of rope hanging from it and picking up the stupid piece of paper with the name of the knot youre supposed to tie on it and the stupid fucking rope gets all stiff and wont bend and gets all fucked up. What a dumbass fucking thing that was. I wonder what asshole came up with that fucking idea. Like that asshole of a teacher having an arithmetic lesson right after the english lesson. Shes gotta be out of her fucking mind. But theyre the boss and you have to do what they tell you. If only one of those fucking assholes knew what they were doing it might not be so bad, but theyre all the same. Every fucking one of them. Theyre the boss, but they dont know their ass from a hole in the ground. Dumb fucking assholes,

pacing the floor and waving his arms,

krist, what a bunch of dumb sonsabitches. And the fucking world is full of them. Always fucking something up. Always. And always telling you what to do. Jesus, what a bunch of dumb shit,

briskly pounding across the floor of his cell from wall to door, from door to wall,

six times seven is forty two
one more whack and I/ll be through

striding up to the door, snapping around and pounding his way back

to the wall in a few quick strides, then snapping around
again and bulling his way to the door,

> *I dont care if I go crazy*
> *Just so I can beat my daisy*

back and forth until he stopped in
front of the door and glared through the window then
jerked around and stared at his fucking cell and spit as
hard as he could, watched it scream through the air and
splat on the floor. He stared at it for a period then stomped it
and ground it into oblivion.

> *and scum bags all in a row*

Theres
always somebody bugging you. They just wont leave you
alone. No matter how simple things are theres always some
sonofabitch complicating things and fucking with your life.
Jesus, this fucking world stinks. People are nothing but a
bunch of shits. A rotten bunch of shits. They always want
to screw you. You go in to buy a pair of shoes and tell the
guy what kind you want and the exact size and everything
else and he sticks something on your foot and when you tell
him it doesnt feel just right he tells you its your size and it
looks great on you and all that shit and by the time you get
home your feet are blistered and all fucked up and you cant
even kill the sonofabitch or shove the fucking shoes up his
motherfucking ass.

> *rotten fucking scumbags in a motherfuck-*
> *ing row*

A simple fucking thing. All you want is a pair of
shoes and some rotten mothers cunt makes you buy a pair
that chew your fucking feet all up. But this is your size.
They look very good. Its the best shoe in the house. And
all that fucking horseshit. And the old bullshit about break-

ing them in. I/d like to break his fucking head the four-eyed slob.

Like that prick Mr. Rose of the Ridgeway movie. Another four-eyed slob. Going to give all the kids in the neighborhood a xmas present and you wait on line all fucking day and they run out of presents. For hours you wait on that dumb fucking line while they take their own sweet time handing out the presents, patting the kids on the head and blabbing a merry xmas and all the phony shit and then, when its almost your turn, they hand you some shit about running out of presents and its too fucking bad if you didnt get one. King shit. He really thought he was king shit because he was the manager of a fucking movie house, the rotten bastard. I hope he rots in hell.

> *I love you*
> *you love me*
> *hang my balls*
> *on a cherry tree*

Theres always somebody who will screw things up for you. Always some ballbreaker rubbing your face in shit. And anyway, it wasnt my fault she was standing there in the pew in front of us. So I looked at her ass during the lords prayer. Big fucking deal. And if anybody saw me thats tough shit. They shouldnt have had their eyes open anyway. Its none of their goddamn business anyway. Thats the trouble with this fucking world, people just cant mind their own fucking business. What the fuck business is it of theirs if I look at some dames ass? And anyway, it was right in front of me. Its not like I went searching around the church looking for an ass to stare at during the lords prayer. It was just there in front of me. And I probably wasnt the only one looking at some dames ass. I bet plenty of those fucking do-gooders do plenty of

staring too. Maybe even cop a little feel once in a while. Theyre all as full of shit as a xmas goose. They probably spent saturday night fucking anything that was still breathing and then come to church with their pious bullshit.
I shouldve shoved it up her ass. Krist, I bet they really wouldve got their bowels in an uproar. If all those phony bastards really kept their eyes closed during the lords prayer i couldve shoved it up her ass and nobody would have known the difference. I could just stick my hand up her skirt and diddle her twat and nobody would know a fucking thing. And she could just lean on the pew in front of her and I could get my hand under her pants and diddle the shit out of her and when the services were over we could wait until everyone was gone and we could go up in the choir loft and I could stretch her out behind the organ and lift her skirt and shove my holy pole up her hole and we could really say the lords prayer. . . . . . yeah. . . . . . we could really do a fucking job on it. Hahahahahahaha

Our Father
                andshoveitin,rightuptothehilt
                                who art in heaven
and wiggle your ass bitch
                hallowed be
                        my holy pole is in your
hole
        thy name
                sowiggleyourassandsaveyoursoul
                                thy kingdom
come
        o baby, dont come. Its so good. Its so good.
                                thy will be
        done

deeper, deeper. Its so good.

on earth as it is

And suck the
nipple off her fucking tit

in heaven

and dig my fingers in her
juicy ass

give us this day

o god its good. Its so good.

our daily
bread

fuck me bastard, fuck me!

and forgive us

and shove my finger
up her shit chute

our trespasses

and tickle the lips of her cunt
with the head of my prick

as we forgive

o jesus, jesus, jesus.

those

hail mary full of cock

who trespass

and the fucking organ blasts
hallelujah

against us

around, and around, the lips of her cunt
goes the head of my big fat joint

and lead us

until I get a few
fingers up her asshole and shove my holy pole in that juicy
hole

not into

and shove my prick and fingers in until they meet

and i can tickle the head of my prick with my fingers
                                        temptation
o jesus, jesus, jesus jesus jesus
                            but deliver
                                    o god youre
killing me
            us from evil
                        and just twirl my cock and fingers around
and around and watch her eyes
                        for thine
                                roll around and around,
HALLELUJAH, HALLELUJAH
                            is the king
                        and flop back and forth
                                    dom
                                        and
have her arms and legs wrapped around me
                                and the power
                                        and
my fingers and cock shoved deep into her gut
                        THE FUCKING POWER
                                    and pick
her up and HALLELUJAH HALLELUJAH with the fucking
                                organ blasting
and spread her on the altar rail
                        AND THE GLORY
                                and watch my joint
get sucked into her hole
                    THE GLORY THE GLORY GLORY
                                and put the
eucharist on the head of my joint
                    GLORY GLORY
                        HALLELUJAH HALLELUJAH
and give her communion

AND THE POWER
                    and fill her snatch with bread
and wine
        FOREVER
                and take holy communion
                            AMEN
                                o god
in heaven, o god, o god *AMEN AMEN* and fuck until the
fucking church shook *AMEN AMEN AMEN* o krist, o jesus
jesus jesus HALLEFUCKINGLUJAH o baby, baby baby
AMEN AMEN AMEN come in me come in me *AAAMEN
AAAAA MEN   AAAAAAFUCKING MEN   oooo
OOOOOOOO AAAAAAMEN AAAAAAAMEN AMEN
AMEN AMEN AMEN AMEN AMEN AMEN AMEN AAA
AAAAAAAAAAAAAAAAAAAAAAAAAAAAAAAAAAAAAAA
AAAAAAA   MEEEEEEEEN*
                            and he rolled and groaned
as a glowing warmth swelled its way through him, the
pressure increasing and increasing, his eyes trying to
struggle from their sockets, and burning as a sun brightness
burst into minute comet-like particles that screeched across
his minds sky until he thought he would explode and he
lunged at his painfully stiffened prick and tried to strangle
it or bend it or break it off but could only clutch it and cling
to it desperately as it continued to swell and burn as the
pressure throbbed through it and he pitched and rolled on
his bed feeling the swelling pressure increase until he could
no longer contain it and his body twitched and jerked as
he felt the heat splatter over his hand in slowly decreasing
sputters until his body stiffened then crumpled as the last
of the warmth dribbled onto his fingers. He slowly turned
his face into the pillow. His sobbing groan was a silent,
no.

Still clutching his penis he gently brushed his face deeper

into the pillow. For a moment he felt as if he would drown
in his own juice as he heard words gurgling in his throat.
Eventually they fell from his lips. o god.   o god.
    no.   no,
                brushing his face deeper into the tear-
wet pillow. When he couldnt get his face any deeper into
the pillow he stopped, then slowly turned his head until his
cheek rested on the dampness. He continued to keep his
eyes clamped shut but the bursting comets were gone and
the brightness was now an almost completely motionless
gray, an undefinable, almost nonexistent, gray.

                          The gray
hung before him. Pain pierced his ears as his jaw clamped
tightly against an unseen threat, his hands strangling and
wringing the limpness between them, trying to squeeze the
life out of it, tugging at it, yanking at it, yet all it did was
to hang limp and unresisting. He continued to cling and
grasp waiting and hoping to feel the life of resistance
threaten him so he could renew the fight with the energy
of fear and anger, to give them a purpose, to be able to
concentrate everything on this one object, to obliterate all
with the annihilation of this single threat, to be free of
everything with the destruction of this one single object.
To twist, to throttle, to clobber and thrash all aggressiveness
into submission, to pry open the cell door, to twist apart the
bars, to club the bricks on the wall   yet still it
only hung limp and unresisting. The battle had to end without an opponent, without bones to break or flesh to sink
teeth into, without entrails to be gored and spewed about.
No victory. Only submission.

His hands remained stiffened and clenched until they relaxed with the decreasing of the force, then nails withdrew
from flesh. He slowly unpeeled the fingers from the sticky

and slimy skin and his hands fell on the bed, still partially curled like dead spiders. He rested in the grayness.

Or

hung suspended in what rest would come. He remained motionless on the bed vaguely aware of himself, of the dulling pain from his jaw to his ear, of the straining pain in his chest, of aching joints and muscles, of the conspicuous warm wetness of his hands, the sticky presence resting on his thigh. He felt exposed and vulnerable.

He wanted to curl his body into a ball, to roll into a corner where he would be safe, to find something to protect him, yet he couldnt turn the thought into energy. The more conscious he became of his exposure the more frantic were his thoughts of seeking some sort of defense, of tucking his head between his knees and burying his head under the pillow, of wanting desperately to find some sort of cover to hide behind and still his body refused to move. His head raged at him to RUN, RUN, RUN and find a cover. HIDE. HIDE. And the thoughts were hammers clubbing his head, relentlessly pounding away at his skull to move his body, move the body, move your body, and still he remained motionless on the bed suspended in the grayness and his mind screamed and howled at him to move yet all he could do was clamp his jaws tighter against the threat and the barking in his head until the inexorable pressure created its own release and he groaned his body into movement and he sobbed as he tediously raised his knees to his chest and curled his throbbing head into himself and clutched his knees with the wet, sticky hands and rocked gently, tears dropping from his eyes and sobs from his throat, cradling himself deeper into the bed as the tears gently dropped onto his cheek and softly rolled down into his mouth, the rhythm of the rocking and sobbing, the caressing of the tears, slowly darkening the grayness until all light was shut out and he could sink into a sleep.

A dark yet shallow sleep. A submission to exhaustion. A loss of consciousness and an avoidance of light. Yet not deep enough to avoid the turbulence on the surface while deep enough to feel the pressure from the bottom. Whatever or whoever he was sought to find that finite area where all pressures are equal and constant. To find that small pocket of weightlessness where no pressure is felt, where there is no tugging in opposite directions, no straining for a painless balance, where all of him was suspended and cushioned between the 2 crushing and yanking pressures where no pressure existed. Where no light existed. Where no time existed. Where no need or desire existed. Where there existed no blackness. There, where there existed nothing, not even a void.

Yet the harder he fought to find this the more distant it became. The more he struggled against the pressures the more imprisoned he became. The more enmeshed he became in their conflicting directions. The further he was tugged in opposite directions that kept him immobile. And the harder he fought for movement, any movement, the more stationary became his position, the more painful his existence.

He fought despairingly to go deeper into the blackness of a sleep, any sleep, even the sleep of death or some form of nonexistence, but even with the loss of consciousness he dreamt he was awake, lying on the bed trying desperately to sleep. If he could find some way to prove that time had passed, no matter how short that time, he could tell himself that he had slept and perhaps then, just perhaps, he would feel rested. But there was no way of knowing if time had passed. Even if he could open his eyes there was nothing to be seen that would prove that time had passed, that it was now hours, minutes, or even seconds later than it had been. There was nothing. Even if his eyes would open everything would look, and feel, as it had. There would be no change. Nothing tangible that he could clutch and caress as proving that it was now later than it had been.

Time seemed stationary, yet the painful pressure of time was constantly felt. If only the pressure would crush the life out of him and allow him simply to sink into the inviting blackness he could then stop struggling and rest. Or if he could see the movement of clock hands or feel the passing of time he could then feel he was getting closer to something or at least further away from something, it didnt really matter which. Nothing really mattered. If only there were some kind of movement. But everything remained motionless, the body not even moving on the bed, while feeling the tearing pressure from all sides in all directions. Feeling deep within him in that pit where there lived the violent and contorting pain of maggots crawling through your guts between the rusty tin cans and broken bottles and the screaming urgency to get time to move, to just move before every FUCKING GODDAMN PART OF YOUR BODY SCREWS UP INTO A FUCKING BALL AND YOUR WHOLE FUCKING BODY DISINTEGRATES, JUST SHATTERS
and
there was no escape, even with the lack of consciousness, for with it came dreams of wakefulness. There was no escape from the past. The struggle against it only entangled him deeper in the fear of the future. There was no place for him to go. No place he could hide. No place where his enemy didnt exist. No escape from unconscious wakefulness. There was no rest.
And so he just lay there with the nauseous pain of exhaustion, his entrails contorted from

conflict, his eyes aching and burning as if the lids had
been torn off and the huge, swollen eyeballs exposed to
the heat of light. No matter what he did he couldnt rid
his eyes of the huge, incomprehensible weight pressing on
them, nor be rid of the writhing in his gut, the twisting ache
in his muscles or the searing pain that shot through his
bones like electrical current.

Yet it was this constant and all-
pervading pain that seemed to allow him to survive for
without it the overwhelming anguish and terror of his
mind would have destroyed him. He somehow seemed to
sense this and tried to concentrate on the pain in his body,
trying to clobber it into submission, the energy put into
the struggle increasing the pain. He fought and it grew and
all the while there was the specter in his mind of going
off to some far place and never returning. Off into some
dark area where that specter would never allow him to
return, from which there was no return, not even to his
present painful existence. And so in spite of himself, and
beyond his will, he fought the pains in his body with a
fury that allowed him to stay just this side of that border
of that unknown, praying only for the passage of time.
Wanting to get out of this now. Each and every second
seeming like his last. Every atom of energy seeming to be
his last.

Then, at last, time did move and his cell door was
clanged open with the yell of chow time. His eyes somehow opened, but there didnt seem to be too much of a
change with the exception of more light. He knew he was
looking at something, seeing something, but he didnt know
what. He continued to look until he realized that what he
saw from the corner of his left eye was the wall and the
dimness of what was visible was the pillow. It was only
after moments of consciousness of the fact that that little

sliver of gray was the wall that he realized his face was almost completely buried in the pillow. He then realized the pillow was damp, vaguely aware that it was caused by his tears. He continued to stare at the gray sliver trying to react to the continued command of chow time..

He moved his head, then raised it and lifted himself on an elbow, becoming more and more aware of the fact that he would have to move the rest of his body sooner or later. If only they would just let him stay in his bed. Not make him move. Just let him rot away until he wasnt even a spot on the sheet. No stain. No dust. Nothing.

But he knew they wouldnt. He knew he had to move. To get up. To walk to the mess hall. To stand on line. Get a tray. Move. Then stop. Stand. Move. Stop. Stand. Get the food. Walk to a table and sit. Then get up. Scrape his tray and put it on the cart. Then go back to his cell and lie down on the bed. He had to do all this. There was no choice. It had to be done. But first he had to move. He had to get his legs over the side of the bed. Raise his body. Then stand. This had to be done first. He had no choice.

He started to move his legs, trying to do what had to be done, while squeezing his eyes, tightening his mouth and fighting the nausea in his stomach. He had to move those legs but it was so hard to do when all he was aware of was the limp stifIness of his crotch. Jesus Krist, how could he move with that damn thing stuck to his legs and covered with stiffening slime? Goddamn those rotten, fucking bastards. Why in the hell wont they let me just stay here. Why do I have to go and get a tray of that rotten shit? I cant eat that rotten garbage, that stinking horsemeat.

CHOW TIME. Up your ass with your fucking chow time, and the legs groaned their way to the side of the bed, fighting their way free from the restraining stiffness and cold wetness. It seemed to be an insurmountable obstacle. It was a chore he didnt seem to have the energy to complete. Yet it had to be done and so the legs slowly inched their way away from the restraints toward the edge of the bed until they were extended over the side and the rest of his body started moving. He sat on the edge for a moment, the covers wrapped around his legs. LETS GO. LETS GO. CHOW TIME. LETS MOVE IT. He clutched at the covers. Move your ass you rotten pricks. Who the fuck needs your rotten food. . . . . o shit. . . . . shit

throwing the covers off and standing. He looked down at the blatant stain on his pants, feeling the cracking streams down his thighs, wanting to splash water on them, but unable to. His legs were so weak he almost fell back onto the bed. He braced himself then leaned against the wall. His legs were trembling. So was his gut. He moved a leg. Then the other. The pants clung to his crotch and thighs. The pants started to tear loose as he moved but he could still feel the stiffness of both. He continued moving one leg and then the other. The stiffened streams continued to crack and chip. A cold wind seemed to blow between his legs. He could feel the wet, gooey tip of his penis and could think of nothing else as each leg was slowly moved and that wet, sticky limpness bumped and rubbed against one thigh and then the other. Back and forth it swung in sickening exhibition. It was as if thats all there was to him. As if that was all there was to be seen. Just a limp, sticky, scraping penis floundering around between his legs. And he had to walk behind it, slowly moving one leg and then the other, and follow it wherever it led him. It wasnt a part of him. He was a part of it.

The corridor was unbearably bright and long. The floor seemed slippery and sloping and far too wide. If only it were narrower, much narrower, he wouldnt have to worry about falling or being propelled from one wall to another, his knees buckling and legs crumbling, trying to cling to the hard smooth surface of the wall, frantically trying to keep from collapsing into a disjointed blob on the trembling floor. If only he didnt have to walk down the middle of the corridor. If only he could slide along a wall and drag his legs behind him over the springy floor. If only he could flatten himself against a wall and shove his face in the dull grayness and somehow tug or pull his body behind him. Or if only the corridor would narrow so he could stretch out his arms and brace himself against both walls and inch his way down the long corridor. If only he could close his eyes.

He tried closing his eyes slightly, but they were immediately yanked open as his body was almost slammed down on the floor. He could feel his eyes bulging from his head as he struggled and staggered down the corridor. And he could see. He could see the floor and walls with their splotches and cracks, the signs and doorways, the many bodies moving, the entrance to the mess hall and the lights.

And he could feel the light and staring eyes.

He approached the end of the line as it slowly shuffled into the mess hall, but it always seemed to be just a few feet away until it finally stopped moving and eventually he was able to join the end of the line. He tried to fold himself into the wall.

There was the noise of movement, voices, tin trays and cups, but all he could feel was the light and eyes. And the limp stiffness.

He pressed into the secure wall and closed his eyes. He could still feel the light and eyes all around him, but at least the dimness of closed eyes was soothing. He could feel his body panting for something, for some sort of life. For some sort of relief from the aching nausea that churned in his stomach and throbbed up his spine to his head. Ice-pick pains stabbed his ears, his neck and shoulders and he wanted desperately to be back on his bed, safely locked in his cell, curled up in a tight ball hidden from himself. Yet he feared collapsing into that little ball on the mess hall floor. He knew he had to go through certain motions. He had to accept a tray of food. He had to sit at a table for a safe length of time. He had to scrape the food from the tray into the garbage, put the empty tray on the cart then make his way back to his cell. This he had to do in spite of the nausea. In spite of the pain. In spite of the weakness and fear. In spite of the light and eyes.

He was suddenly prodded forward as the guy behind him told him to move. He fought to keep from falling while keeping himself pressed into the wall and inched behind the moving line.

He clutched a tray in his hands and wanted to ask for just a small amount of food so it would be easier to carry, but was afraid to speak. He slid his tray along the counter, watching the food being plopped onto the tray in wet piles. When he reached the end of the counter he lifted the tray and slowly, painfully turned, trying desperately to prevent the food from sloshing over the sides of the tray. He carefully twisted a foot to the side, fraction by fraction, until he found the position where he could slowly twist his body around without falling, feeling his way into the safest position, his eyes always on the sloshing food. Eventually he completed the turn and he lifted his head and eyes just enough to look for an empty seat.

Then he realized where he was, that he was standing in front of the mess hall with his tray held in front of him and everyone could see him. Even the men with their backs to him could see him. He wanted to lower his tray while twisting his body and closing his eyes and backing his way to a seat, any seat, and hiding himself under the table. Yet all he could do was remain motionless with the tray extended before him, his body trembling, his mind screaming until he was once more prodded forward. Comeon buddy, moveit. Whatta yathink ya doin, posin for holy pictures?

He stumbled forward, the warm water spilling onto his hands, feeling the many, many pairs of eyes staring, feeling the fingers pointing with disgust, until his legs scraped against a bench and his body started to fold from pain and his knees banged on the empty seat and the tray clanged on the table. He twisted his body onto the seat, continuing to stare at the food on the tray, lowering his head even further, wanting to rub away the pain in his knees and shins and keeping his mouth clamped tightly shut and breathing through flared nostrils to keep from puking.

He knew he had to pick up the spoon and make the motions until he could safely leave the mess hall. He moved his spoon among the food wanting to feign disgust at the rotten slop on his tray so he could just get up, dump it in the can, toss his tray on the cart and leave, but the most he could do was to dip the tip of the spoon

in something on his tray. He tried to gauge the time so
he would know when he had been sitting long enough to
leave. Or maybe he should wait until the others left before
he stood up and walked past them to the door and down
that goddamn corridor to his cell. If only he could move
the fucking spoon. But at least he was hidden under the
table. But how long could he sit here? If he waited for
them to tell him to get up and leave then there would
be no way he could avoid their eyes. If he just got up
now, slowly, quietly, maybe no one would notice him. But
how in the name of krist could he get up so they wouldnt
notice him. Suppose he toppled forward, or some damn
thing, and the shit spilled all over the damn place or someone and they started yelling at him. If only the goddamn
floor wasnt so fucking slippery he wouldnt have to worry
about shit like that. Some sonofabitch probably spilled
some of the rotten slops on the floor and it would be just
his luck to step in it and slip and fall on his ass. The
goddamn shit was so rotten it wasnt fit for a fucking dog
anyway. Why in the hell do they have to pile so much
of it on your fucking tray? The cocksucking bastards. Somebody should shove it in their fucking faces. He continued
to twist the spoon in something on his tray, watching it
move along the top of the pile, still feeling the lights and
the eyes.

    He had to move. There was no choice. He had to.
The longer he sat the more he became a part of the bench.
He could feel the cement getting harder and harder. He had
to move. Some fucking how he had to move and seek the
freedom of his cell.

    The guy sitting across from him belched
and stood up then picked up his tray. He slid to the end
of the bench, clutching the tray, and faced the wall before
standing. He stood close behind the guy that had been

sitting across from him and shuffled his way to the garbage can, let the food slide off the tray then put the tray on the cart. He kept his body twisted toward the wall as he walked down the side of the mess hall and through the door, turned stiffly so his body remained twisted toward the wall and pulled one leg behind the other, his hand ready to lean against the wall, and worked his way down the corridor feeling the light and the eyes. He could see the soft gray of his cell door and he wanted to run to it, through it, but it was more important that he keep his body twisted toward the wall and not fall on his back.

He slowly got closer and closer until his hand felt the warmth of the cold steel. He leaned against the door jamb for a brief second, looking at his bed, then tilted forward until he bumped into it. He scrambled onto it and let his body unbend in the soft warmth of the mattress. His body remained twisted, twisted into the mattress. His right eye was buried in the pillow, the left peered at the wall. The left lid blinked when necessary. His lungs functioned. His arms hugged the body of the pillow, his hands gripping the edge. It seemed like a toe moved. He could smell and feel the warmth of his breath as it flowed into the pillow then billowed into his face. It was his breath. It was good to feel. And it was all he could hear. It flowed into the pillow, then billowed around his face. He could feel, too, his heart, and it seemed like he could hear it, but he only felt it. Could only feel the unheard beating. And he could feel his chest. His lungs functioned, but he felt his chest. He could feel the pressure on his right ear pressing into the pillow, and could feel the left exposed to the cooler air. He could feel the beat of his heart in his shoulders, could feel it beat down his arms and hands, into the cheek buried in the pillow. Warmly buried in the pillow. The other out in the air, quiet, still, seemingly cool, and free from the beating of the heart and the flowing of the blood as if the flowing and beating stopped at the neck and that cheek was just there, a companion of the other yet completely unattached even to the exposed and cool ear. Air was forced, almost thrust, into his chest, yet it was done silently. Everything was silent. The bodies moving in the corridor. The trays being piled on carts. The flies buzzing around the commode in the corner. The only sound was the sound of his breath flowing into the pillow and filtering into his face.

He remained twisted into the mattress, silent and motionless, save for the needed blinking of an eyelid.

The door clanged shut. He heard it clearly, distinctly, over the sound of his breath flowing into the pillow. And he felt it. Felt it over the beating of his heart, the flowing of his blood, the pain in his chest and the functioning of his lungs. He could feel it over the stiffened limpness and the light and eyes. He was safe.

His head moved slightly and he looked at the door. Thick, heavy steel. It was smooth and gray. It looked warm. It was impenetrable. It had a small window of thick, unbreakable glass. Wire-mesh glass. Outside were people and lights and baskets and signs, and rooms, and cells, and hallways, and walls and ceiling and floor, but the door was impenetrable. He was safe.

He moved his head a little more, then his shoulders, and loosened his hands on the edge of the pillow, and his left arm, then hand, crossed over his chest until he was leaning on his elbows, his face looking directly at the door, his head nestled down between his shoulders. He looked at the door. On the other side were baskets and signs. His body moved. A foot, an ankle, a leg, then the thigh. His shoulders moved a little more and then a hip. He was on his back, propped on his elbows, his legs crossed. Blues here. Yellows. Blankets. The door was locked. The huge bolt was shot.

He straightened his arms slowly and as his body and head were lowered to the bed he watched the window sink from sight and the wall came into view and then the joint where wall and ceiling met and as the back of his head went deeper into the pillow there was only the ceiling with its cracks twisting and winding their way to the corners and fading from his sight. He stretched his body and keeping his head still he followed the cracks with his eyes into the corners. He stretched his arms and legs toward the end of the bed and the sticky coldness made the door transparent.

He rolled over on his side and raised his knees. He squirmed around on the bed for many moments trying to find a secure position, but he couldnt hide. And each and every movement demanded the greatest exertion of energy as if he were glued in his present position and had to crack loose then move his body and tug his crotch after him. He knew he should simply get under the covers but thinking of all the necessary moves forced him into trying to find some other way to get comfortable even though he knew that each attempt would prove futile. He tried adjusting his body in various positions, his head, his legs. . .his knees raised to this level, to that level, his body at various angles and the various parts of his body at different angles to the others, yet long before he settled in any one of the countless positions he knew it would have to be changed to another, and so he continued to squirm and burrow until his despair forced him to try to get under the covers.

He
rolled over on his left side, keeping his knees bent, and
reached behind him and pulled the covers down as far as
he could. Then he raised and moved various parts of his
body, moving the covers down an inch at a time until he
was finally able to work them under his soggy ass. Then
he reached back with his left foot and shoved with his
hand while continuing to move his body, until he got the
covers hooked with his foot then yanked and tugged until
he could get both feet under then rolled quickly over on
his other side and yanked the remainder of the covers from
under his body, feeling the sheets resist him, his fingers
almost tearing and shredding them, until he was able to
whip them over his body.

Then
he simply lay quietly for a few moments, his hand still
clutching the covers.

Eventually he loosened his grip on them
and put his left arm on top of them and adjusted his body,
looking for the most comfortable position, but every move
was so tiring and impossible that he finally stopped. Moving
was more painful than any position he attained. It was like
trying to move when your pants were wet and it was cold
and snowing, only worse.

He tried adjusting his position to relieve the pain in
his groin, but no matter how high he raised his knees he
couldnt find any relief. There was a painful weakness in
his legs that seemed to force him to think of having to
walk and he knew he couldnt, that if he tried he would
simply double up and crumple to the floor, and no matter
how hard he tried to change the image in his mind he
could only think of being forced to walk and ending up
in a crumpled ball on the floor. It seemed like the only

thing that would get that image out of his mind was to
concentrate on the cramping pain in his gut. It felt as if
his balls were being squeezed and twisted by a huge hand
and the piercing pain shot through his gut and tugged at
his asshole. He tried to shove everything out of his mind,
but the pain increased and his chest and head swelled with
nausea. He could feel the foul bile in his chest and throat,
he could feel it swelling his head and burning his eyes. He
thought of kneeling in front of the commode a few feet
away in the corner of his cell, but he couldnt move.
He couldnt get his arm to move, to throw off the covers.
Or his legs to slide off the side of the bed. He knew he
couldnt make it anyway, that he would simply end up on
the floor curled up in a little ball until someone looked
through the window and saw him there and came in to
drag him out. He could only swallow and swallow with
his teeth pressed against each other, and try to force the
sourness down against the pressure in his knotted and
twisted gut. He could smell the rotten stink as it continued
to bubble up and he fought to swallow again and again.
He couldnt stop twisting and turning on the bed. His knees
were up to his chin and still he felt as if he were stretched
on a rack with some fucking sonofabitch kicking him in
the balls. If only he could get his hands around the throats
of those fucking bastards who put him here. If he could
shove a lit cigar in their fucking eyes or shove an ice pick
in their ears. Or if he could just get to the commode and
hang his head in it and just let the fucking puke come out.
If he could only relieve the pressure. But he knew he
couldnt make it. Even if he could get the fucking covers
off or slide out from under them in some way, he knew he
would never be able to cover the few feet from the bed
to the commode without crumpling and then some rotten

sonofabitch would see him on the floor and drag him to his feet. . . .

Jesus fucking krist, what the fuck could he do? His body and head throbbed and burned with the constantly swallowed puke. He kept his mouth jammed shut as his body jerked with spasms and fought the vomit down between retches. He fought and swallowed over and over and his body jerked on the bed like a puppet whose strings were being jerked. The contortions increased until he felt as if his balls were being shoved and yanked into his gut and no matter how hard he fought and swallowed the pain and pressure increased and he bobbed around on the bed as his body was bounced about by the contortions until he clamped his hands over his mouth and felt the bitter slime ooze through his clenched teeth and lips and crawl around his face and between his fingers. It was warm and wet and sticky. It stank. A few drops dribbled out of his nose and slid over the knuckles of a hand. He pressed harder and harder with his hands yet still it oozed from his mouth and spread further on his face until soon he felt it bubbling from his breath and felt it spreading over his cheeks and into his eyes until he felt as if he were going to drown and he had to move his hand from his face and he tried to catch the puke in his cupped hands as it seeped through his lips and dribbled from his nose and he could feel it flowing over his hands and wrists and saw the long thin strings of mucus stretch thin and shiny as a spiders thread as he lowered his hands from his face. He fought so hard against the spasms and pain that soon he was no longer capable of resisting and his lips and teeth parted and the puke jerked from his mouth into his cupped hands until there was nothing left to come out and his body con-

vulsed with the dry heaves. His eyes burned and he felt
dizzy as he stared into his hand filled with the warm, sticky
bile. He couldnt keep his head still. It rolled around, back
and forth, and everything was cloudy, but even if he
couldnt see his hands distinctly, he could feel them. And
he could feel the window. And the hundreds of people in
the corridor. The glass was thick and wired, but transparent. The door was thick and indestructible, but there
were keys to the lock and it could be swung back on
hinges. And he lay on his side staring at his cupped hands
filled with phlegm and vomit oozing from between his
fingers, flowing over his hands and dripping onto the bed;
and his nose stung and burned from the sour, acid stink
and agonizingly tickled as little bubbles of mucus and bile
burst and gurgled in his nose and throat. His head jerked
viciously as the fucking snot just hung on the edge of his
nose and tickled until he wanted to scream his fucking
head off and claw that fucking nose off his face but his
hands were jammed together with the scummy puke and
he clenched his teeth and his lips crawled from each other
and his body knotted in a fucking growl and the rage
flooded his eyes as his head continued to thrash the air
and he shoved his nose into his shoulder and rubbed it
back and forth, back and forth then lifted his head and
squeezed his eyes shut as his lips twisted further back on
themselves and in his head he wailed and screeched and
a snarling, trapped-rat aaaaaaaaaarrrrrrrr gurgled in his
throat as his body screwed itself tighter and tighter and
his head trembled and the screeching in his head pierced
his ears, the snarling flooded his throat and his spine was
shoved deeper into itself between his shoulders and his
knotted stomach rose higher into his chest, pushing his
breastbones apart until he could no longer breathe and the
screeching and snarling ceased and his flesh and eyes felt

as if they were being scorched and his spine as if it would snap and his head be thrust down into his chest.

Then his body suddenly slumped and his head fell forward, his eyes shutting, and he once more felt the warm, wet slime dribbling over his fingers.

It trickled onto his thighs.

He shook his head slowly from side to side with a low, pleading, no   no   no

His body slid from the bed, his hands cupped tightly, protectively, close to his chest, and fell against the opposite wall then he inched his way to the commode in the corner and opened and lowered his hands and watched it slide into the clear, quiet water. He leaned heavily into the corner and watched the ripples in the water as it continued to drop from his hands, splash, bobble, then jerk up and down before it started slowly sinking or just spreading across the surface.

As he stared he could feel the nausea growling in his stomach, but all he could do was shake his head and dryly cry until his body was folded by a spasm and he fell, sobbing, to his knees in front of the commode and let his head hang in the opening as the spasms pumped pain and tears through his body. He clung to the sides of the bowl, his head shoved against the valve until the spasms subsided, then leaned his arms on the sides and his head on his crossed hands and let the saliva drip from his lips. He stayed on his knees, with his head bowed and eyes closed, for many, many long minutes. His eyes ached, felt hot and wet, but it was so good to have them closed and have his face buried in his hands. His body existed but was only an empty weakness and there only to join and support his head. In his mind he kept shaking his head, no, no, but it remained still, pushed into his crossed hands. God it felt good to have his eyes closed and just to drift with the exhaustion. He could still feel the pressure on his eyes as if two large thumbs were pressing against them, but it felt good having them closed, seeing nothing but a grayness and drifting deeper and deeper into his exhaustion. And the further into it he drifted the more aware he became of his stomach and legs and shoulders and the twisting ache in the back of his neck, and he continued to sink and drift until his head slid from his hands and banged into the wall.

He jerked his head up and moved his eyelids slightly. He started to lower his head back onto his folded hands, then stopped and shook his head and leaned on the commode and pushed himself up, then straightened his legs until he was standing, supported by the wall. He slowly turned his body around until he was in front of the wash basin, then turned on the water, his head hanging from his neck. Leaning against the wall he let the water flow and flow and flow over his hands, cupping them and letting the water flow between his fingers and over the sides, and as he continued to stare at the water he slowly lowered his body, then bent it and lowered his head further until it was close enough to try and flip some water on his face. He lifted his cupped hands, lowered his head, but the water flowed up his arms before he could get it to his face. He filled his cupped hands again with water and labored his hands up as far as he could without spilling it, then dropped his face into it and staggered and almost fell. He leaned against the wall with one hand and splashed water on his face with the other until he was too tired to lift his hand any more.

He leaned against the wall, his forehead on his arm, his other hand in the water. It was cold. Wet. It streamed into the palm of his hand. He leaned against the wall and stared at the water. At his hand, wet and cold.

He could see through the stream of water. He could see his hand, the white porcelain, the stainless steel drain and the tip of the shiny faucet, and the water flowing from the shiny tip onto his hand, into the basin and down the drain. It all happened at once and kept happening. Over and over and over again.

He shook his head, but again, only in his mind. He just leaned against the wall, his forehead on his arm.

And the water continued flowing and his hand got colder and wetter.

He watched his hand turn off the water and hang over the basin as the last drops of water silently pinged into it. His body shuddered with a sigh as the final drops fell from his hand.

He raised his eyes and looked at the bed a few feet away. He could place his body on it. He could cover himself with the blanket. It was all so fucking simple. Cover the few feet to the bed, lie down, cover himself and rest. Perhaps even sleep. Yeah, just that simple. But what was the use? Why bother? Why not just stand here with his forehead on his arm, propped against the wall. Whats the difference? Why go to all the trouble of going all the way from here to there. For what? Just to lie down under the covers? Why bother? Only have to get up again sooner or later. Why not just stay here against the wall. Just freeze like this. Petrify. Turn into a fucking statue. Why not? Whats the difference? There. Here. Anywhere. Theres no difference. Only the positions different. Lean here. Lie there. So what? So fucking what? Who needs a bed and covers? Who needs anything? Everything

is nothing anyway. Whos going to do me anything? Them?
Those pricks? Who needs them? Just lean and twist your
back. Get the fucking knots out. Get them out and put them
back in. Yeah. In an out. In an out. In an out. Fuck it.
Who needs it? Its all bullshit anyway. Same old shit over
and over. Up an down, in an out. Drink an piss an eat
an shit. Who gives a shit?

his hand bumping over the edge
of the sink and hanging at his side. He leaned toward the
area of the bed and his body went forward. A foot moved
and somehow the other moved in front of it and he
stretched out his arms and his body continued to move
further away from the wall and the first foot got in front
of the other and his hands touched the end of the bed
and slid forward and his feet dragged themselves behind
the bending body and then his arms were on the bed and
he pushed himself forward so the top of his body fell on
the bed, his face buried in the woolen blanket, his legs
hanging and waiting to be pulled up to join the rest of
his body.

The blanket scratched his face and his breath burned
his face as it warmed itself in the long, stiffened fibres.
But what the fuck was the difference. It was all the same.
Lean against a wall, hang from a bed. What the fuck was
the difference? Everything is nothing anyway. Just wait.
Just hang here and wait. Eventually it will move. Eventually you will be stretched out on the bed and you can
squirm your way under the blanket. Why rush? Fuck it.
You lean. You hang. You stretch. Whats the fucking difference? The blanket scratches your face or it scratches
your ass. So what? So fucking what? Its all the same. Just
wait and sooner or later it will move or youll just freeze
here. Its all the same.

His
arms stretched slowly forward, his hips wiggled and his
toes pushed against the floor. He crawled forward on the
bed until his hands gripped the edge of the mattress then
he pulled until slowly all of his body was firmly on the
mattress. He rested. Sniffed the blanket. It smelled. All
kinds of smells making 1 blanket smell. Its own smell just
like any armpit or asshole. All different, but all the same.
All their own. Their own fucking stink.

He squeezed the
pillow under his head and thought briefly of getting under
the covers. No. Screw it. Rest first. Just rest. First rest. Get
under the blanket later. Just rest for now. Rest.

He replaced
the gray of the walls with a darker shade by closing his
eyes. It felt good to shut out some of the light. Not all,
just some. Just enough so there was a gray without images
or threatening corners. Not the blackness that gives birth
to those sudden flashes of stinging light that slash your
eyes, or the velvety darkness that thickens and becomes
animated and flows and somehow moves around and over
you. Just a soothing gray. Nothing to see.

But he could feel.
He could always feel. There was a sense of security in
old, familiar feelings in spite of their discomfort. He felt
the nausea tugging at the back of his throat and he automatically swallowed repeatedly and rapidly, and the more
he swallowed the more his sickness seemed to flow through
his body until it nestled in every part of him, every cell,
every breath, until they were one.

He knew he didnt have
to worry about throwing up. Not now. That was done with
for now. There would be a time, as there had been from

time to time, when he would once again be hanging over the bowl, his face puking on his reflection as he hung desperately to the edges of the commode his body once again jerking and writhing with dry heaves, his face breath-close to its shattering reflection. But not now.

For now his sickness was more friend than foe. His sickness, now, was persistent and constant, but it wasnt threatening to burst from his mouth. It was just there—in him, through him—everywhere. And he knew it would always be there. That it would never desert him. That no matter what happened, no matter where he might go or what the world might do to him, he could always rely on his companion. He was as constant as the northern star. That was the one thing he could always rely on.

And he could always curl around his little ball of sickness and share his pain of loneliness, of shattered dreams, of tears on saddened faces. Tears that he may have caused and that made it necessary to curl himself around his friend so he could live with the knowledge of these tears, knowing that no matter how bad the pain was that it should be worse, that it wasnt really equal to the tears.

He snapped his eyes open and stared into the commode corner, then slid from the bed and stumbled to the corner. He very, very carefully examined the wall, the floor and the gleaming white porcelain. He tore off a long piece of toilet paper and got on his knees and inspected the area from various angles, dabbing and wiping at any spot that looked wet. When he finally finished he dropped the paper in the bowl, watched it flush out of sight then looked at the bowl for many minutes to be certain it didnt somehow work itself back up. He nodded his head approvingly and staggered back to his bed and checked the corner once more before kneeling beside his bed and managing to push the blanket down far enough to allow him to squirm under it as he climbed onto the bed. He lay quietly for a moment catching his breath and thinking of the easiest way to get under the blanket. Eventually he searched around for the edge of the blanket with his feet, worked them under it then reached back and grabbed the edge of the blanket and, curling up, pulled the blanket over him.

He felt the hard coarseness of the blanket against his body and neck, and his little ball of sickness deep within him tantalizing the back of his throat. His eyes were fixed on the corner and he felt quiet. He knew that soon his eyes would start to burn and ache and then they would close. Everything seemed to be quiet and still. His comfort was logical.

His eyes slowly drifted from the corner along the junction of wall and floor and the tributary cracks until the lids closed and he could be closer to his friend. The coarseness of the blanket was soothing. He started feeling weightless, as if it were possible for him to simply drift away from wherever he was to some place as yet unknown, unimagined, and he hugged the blanket tighter around him, rubbing his cheek with its edge, experiencing the same tremor as usual when the drifting started, but knowing that his friend would not allow him to stray too far, and soon, very soon, he would be back where he belonged. Back to the safe and known.

He felt the blanket on his cheek and the mattress under him. He curled his knees up closer to his chest and clasped his hands between them. He could feel the spirit of his friend flowing through his body, reassuring him, and having finished his journey he returned to his place and nestled deep within his host.

The drifting ceased and he was once again fully aware of his body and his friend. The gray got darker and more soothing, more comfortable. He was once again in a familiar place, the place to which he always returned. No matter where or how far he might go in any direction he always returned to his friend. There was a time, it seemed, when he traveled great distances for long lengths of time, but the journeys continually became shorter and more frightening and he would hasten home to his friend. And, unlike the past when he would start his journeys often, he now found very little desire to attempt to leave the security offered by his friend. A step or two was enough to convince him now that whatever might be out there wasnt worth the effort so he simply stopped trying and remained where he belonged. And if he had ever felt any different he could no longer remember it, and even trying to remember seemed pointless. He knew how it felt now, and that was the way he always felt and would always feel. There was no other way. Thats simply the way the world is and always will be. A pair of tight shoes and blistered feet. If you get a pair that dont hurt youre a winner, but you cant expect it. Its just a freak. The next pair will cut you to pieces. Theres no point in trying. Its all a game. Thats all it is, a fucking game. You just have to try and screw them more than they screw you. Make them pay. Right through the nose. And make them keep paying. . . .

Yeah, like their kids. Send copies of the pictures to the school principal and pass them out to the kids. Make them keep paying. I could get envelopes in a five-and-dime store and print the address with one of those cheap ball-point pens. They could never trace that. Just be careful of fingerprints, thats all. And just drop a few envelopes with pictures where the kids will see them and theyll be all over the school in no time. And what could those bitches say? Theyd have to deny it and claim they were fakes or something. And if they admitted they were real and told them about the night with me their old men would really go crazy. Theyd never get out. Theyd be as crazy as Mrs. Haagstromm. I could just deny it anyway. Just hide the cameras and the rest of the stuff and they couldnt prove a thing. Nothing. And before it was over theyd all be on the funny farm. The kids too. Spend the rest of their lives locked up, a bunch of blithering idiots. And maybe they could meet each other, once a week, in the basket weaving class. And there would be no way they could prove anything. They wouldn't be able to touch me. And they could just rot away in there, smelling their own stink,

    mary, mary, quite cunttrary

                           and let them eat breakfast with each others stink. . . .

                    Screwem, the bastards.

                          Like

that rotten sonofabitch Joey. He must have washed and gargled with garlic the way he stunk of it all the time. The lousy wop bastard. He sure did screw me. I know goddamn well he did. You couldnt get a marble, any fucking marble, in the holes in his cigar box. The sonofabitch clipped me for a whole bag of marbles. Maybe more. I shouldve broken that fucking cigar box of his over his head and taken my marbles back. And his too, the rat fucking bastard.   O fuck it. I guess its not important anyway, some other sonofabitch wouldve cheated me out of them anyway.

                    I shouldve just dried myself off with Leslies handkerchief, or something, then nobody wouldve known anything.

Like that
goddamn kid at the beach that time. Screamed and hollered
like he was dying because I hit him on the head with a rock.
His own fucking fault for suddenly coming around the
corner of the house. How in the hell was I supposed to know
he was going to turn around the corner. I couldnt see him.
Asshole sonofabitch. Walking right into the rock. No matter
where you go theres some fucking asshole screwing things
up.

But its going to be my turn now. I/ll get those fuckers in
court and really tear them apart. I/ll make them jump
through hoops. I/ll make them beg for mercy. I/ll fuckem
up so bad theyll have to crawl out of court. I/ll get that
d.a. so confused he/ll have to go back to law school. I/ll
teach him a few tricks he never even heard of. I/ll teach
them tricks that havent been invented yet. And I wont let
them just dismiss the charges and throw the case out of
court. I/ll make them go through with it and let the jury
bring back a verdict of not guilty. Theyre not going to trick
me with any of that legal bullshit and throw the case out
and then refile the charges. Not me. I aint falling for that
shit. I/ll see to it that it goes to the jury so they cant get
around the double jeopardy. The rotten pricks. Theyd just
love to pull that shit on me. They think they can get away
with anything, but they wont get away with it this time.
I aint buying it. They can peddle that shit somewhere else. I
aint having any. Theyre going to find me not guilty, and
then Im going to shove it up their ass.

Q. IN what direction were you traveling as you approached the intersection?

A. North.

Q. And what was the time?

A. Approximately 2 A.M.

Q. And you were driving?

A. Yes sir.

Q. And your partner was sitting next to you?

A. Yes sir.

Q. In the front seat?

A. Of course.

COUNSEL Just answer—

PROSECUTOR Your honor, I object. Theres no need to continually ask the same question 6 different ways.

COURT Sustained. It is not necessary to repeat the same question after it has been answered.

Q. And how fast were you driving?

A. Approximately 25 miles per hour.

Q. And how far from the intersection were you when your partner said he saw someone in the doorway of Kramers Jewelry store?

A. About one hundred feet.

Q. And how far from Kramers Jewelry store?

A. Approximately three or four hundred feet.

Q. Dont you know exactly how far you were from the doorway?

A. No. Not exactly.

Q. And were there cars parked on the avenue?

A. There were a few, further down the avenue.

Q. There were none parked near Kramers Jewelry store?

A. *No.*

Q. *And how was the visibility at that time?*

A. *Good.*

Q. *There were no visual obstructions?*

A. *None.*

Q. *Was the area well lighted?*

A. *Yes.*

Q. *And was the weather clear?*

A. *Yes.*

Q. *There was no fog or haze?*

A. *None.*

Q. *And you are sure the street light was burning?*

A. *Absolutely.*

Q. *But didnt that cast a shadow in the doorway making it difficult to see?*

A. *There were lights on in the store window.*

Q. *Are you—*

PROSECUTOR *Your honor, all these facts have been previously testified to and proven by expert witnesses. The Department of Water and Power has testified that the street lights were burning; the burglar alarm company has testified that the alarm would have sounded if the lights in the window were not burning; we have the report from the United States Weather Bureau and I see no reason why the witness should be badgered with these superfluous questions.*

COUNSEL *Your honor, I was just try—*

COURT *The court agrees that this line of questioning is unreasonable and unnecessary. I would also like to remind the defendant that he insisted on acting as his own defense counsel in spite of the contrary advice of the court and the availability of a public defender. I will make an exception in this case, for obvious reasons, and ask the*

*defendant, again, at this time, if he would like to be
represented by counsel for the remainder of the trial.*

DEFENDANT *No, your honor, that will not be necessary.*

COURT *Then I will advise the defendant, for the last time,
that the proper trial procedures will be followed or the
court will hold the defendant in contempt. Proceed.*

I

shouldve just bashed their fucking heads together and
walked away

and dont give us any of your lip buddy. Just
get in the car. We'll tell you why later.

Just shove you around

like you were nothing.

Thats a good doggies.

Beg. Beg you flattopped bastards.

Q. *And you say you saw someone, or something, in the doorway of Kramers Jewelry store and told your partner to
stop the car?*

A. *Not exactly. He was in the process of stopping for a red
light as we approached the intersection. It was then
that I saw a man in the doorway.*

Q. *How can you be sure it was a man?*

A. *From the way he was dressed and his features.*

Q. *And thats the only reason?*

A. *Well, I didnt undress him if thats what you mean.*

COURT *Order. Order. Order in the court.*

All they want to do
is railroad you. Thats the way they operate. No matter how
hard you fight them the rotten bastards knife you in the
back and then laugh in your face. They dont care. Like that
poor sonofabitch that stole forty dollars from the govern
ment and they sent him away for a year and a day. A lousy,

stinking forty dollars and they gave him a year. It could have been forty cents. Its all the same to them. Yeah, like that poor slob who stole a couple of boxes of cookies and they kept him in jail for a couple of years waiting to go to trial. The poor bastard may still be in there for all I know. Or anyone knows. The only way you can beat them is if you steal millions, then they love you. Then everyone respects you for being a smart businessman and a success. And if you get caught you get a whole roomful of smart lawyers and you go free. Or maybe they fine you a few dollars and slap you on the wrist. But if you dont have the money for a lawyer youre s.o.l. And thats it. Youre just shit out of luck. You bet your sweet ass that none of those big-time lawyers are going to help you if you dont have thousands of dollars to give them for a few days work. Theyd rather see you rot in jail the rest of your life and laugh while they sit around their swimming pools sipping their goddamn martinis. I could just see some lawyer like Stacey Lowry defending someone like me. Yeah, I could just see him stooping that low. Fat chance. Hes too high and mighty to bother with me. That would be beneath his dignity. He wouldnt want to soil his hands. Suppose he lost the case. He wouldnt have fifty thousand dollars to comfort him. Theyd rather let someone else lose the case. They dont care who, and they dont care who goes to jail. Just as long as they dont lose the case.

And they wont let you defend yourself. They know you could do a better job than a public defender. You bet your sweet ass they do. But they pull that legal mumbo jumbo because theyre afraid you might do a better job than the jerk they appoint to defend you. So they throw all their technicalities at you whenever you get them on the ropes. They have their own rules and thats it. They dont care about anything else. They just wont give you a chance to prove theyre wrong. No matter how far back in the corner you shove them they throw another one of their rules at you. You just cant win. No matter what you do its not what they want. Krist, what in the hell do they want from you. Why do they do this? Over and over again. Jesus. And its always the same. Over and over again. You do this, you do that, and its never what they want. And theyre always hounding you about it. I dont understand it. I just dont understand. I try. Krist, Im always trying, but something always happens. Some screwy thing is always happening to me. No matter how hard I try, no matter what I do, I always end up sucking hind tit. Every goddamn time. And they dont even try to understand me. What do they want from me. No matter what I do it isnt good enough. Im always wrong. And theyre always telling me how to do it. Always the same smart-ass bullshit. Well, if it didnt work that way, why dont you do it this way? They can never mind their own business. Theyre always telling you how to do it. No matter what in the hell it is, they always want to tell you how to do it. They wont just leave you alone and let you do it your way. No. Not them. They always have a better way. Well, Ive always done it this way and I never have any trouble. What a crock. Over and over again. They never change. Always telling you to do it their way. They get you so damned screwed up that something always goes wrong. Every damn time. They always manage to ruin everything and you end up with a big nothing. Over and over again, everything ends up nothing. No matter what you do it always ends up like this. I tried. I always tried. I know I did. Always. But somehow everything I touch turns to shit. There just doesn't seem to be any point to it. To anything. Whats the use in trying? Its just going to get all screwed up anyway. Theres always someone hanging over your head telling you youre not doing it the right way. Always. I know I could have

those cops begging for mercy if the judge would leave me
alone. But he wont. In five minutes I could have those cops
so confused they wouldnt know which side was up, but the
lousy d.a. would be objecting all over the place and the
judge would be telling me I cant do this and I cant do that.
Its not the proper procedure, or some damn thing. No matter
what you do youre wrong. Its weird. Like its a crime to
breathe or something. Krist, its not my fault. I was just
a kid. I didnt know. All I knew was I wanted a new over-
coat. I didn't know about money. Yeah, yeah. I know she
was probably all torn up inside because her son was crying
for a new coat. But I didnt know. Not then. How was I
supposed to know they couldn't afford it? I said Im sorry.
What do you want from me? O.K. O.K. Im sorry. Forget it,
willya? So I didnt really need it and Im a hard on. What do
you want from me? I cant open my mouth without someone
jumping down my throat. Just leave me alone. Krist, youd
think I was asking for a million dollars or something. All I
want is to be left alone. Is that too much to ask for, to just
be left alone

       sitting on the edge of his bed, his hands clasped
between his thighs, head hanging,

               and not be bugged all the
time. All I know is that it stinks. Everything stinks. It smells
so bad you can taste it. And it tastes so bad you can smell it.
Like something is rotting inside. And you cant just spit it
out. No matter how hard you try you just cant spit it out.
Theres always that foul taste in the back of your throat and
you hack and hawk and spit and gargle and still the sonofabitch is back there somewhere. You clear your throat and
cough over and over and think its gone and then all of a
sudden its back there again and no matter how many times
you think its gone it comes back. It always comes back and
lodges itself in the back of your throat where you can taste

it and smell it. Your nose always burning from the stench of rotting flesh.

And for krists sake dont smile. Whatever you do dont smile. Then theyll really get bugged. Youll really bring them down. All over you. Theyll find out whats making you smile and yank it away from you. Just as sure as krist made little apples theyll yank it right out of you. Theyll yank and tug and twist until your gut is in your throat and your insides feel like they have a rat chewing on them and you retch so hard youre afraid youre going to turn inside out. Yeah, dont smile. For the love of krist dont you dare smile or youre in serious trouble. You have no right to smile. Theyll burn you at the stake and point the finger at you. Yeah, youre goddamn right they will. Just try walking down the street smiling and see what happens. Just try it. Jesus, why wont they let you live. Is that so much to ask for. Just to live. Just to be left alone and live the way you want to. So what if you screw up. Its none of their business. Why do you have to try it their way? They think their way is the only way, the fools. Theyre so goddamn hardheaded they think their way is the only way and if you try it your way they make sure it screws up. Theyll make sure you end up holding the same old bucket of shit. Theyre afraid you might make it your way and then theyd have to admit they were wrong. But they make sure that doesnt happen. Theyd rather see you spend the rest of your life with your guts all tied up in knots and that foulness lodged in the back of your throat. They dont care. They really dont care how much you suffer. They really dont know anything about pain. They laugh at it. They really cant feel other peoples pain. Yeah, sure. I know. Im not denying that. We all hurt people sometimes, but they think its funny. They just pass it off. They hurt someone and they forget about it. They just forget about it. It doesn't even bother them. They just toss it out of their minds. It doesnt faze them at all. They dont suffer because of it. They dont relive it. Over and over again. With them its just a big so what. What happened, happened, and they let it go at that. They just go home, get laid and go to sleep, just as if nothing ever happened. And the next day they go walking down the street with a big shiteating grin on their face. Happy as a lark. They dont suffer a minutes pain. Not one single minute. They dont live with it and suffer from it. They dont feel flooded by other peoples tears. They dont hear and feel them sloshing around inside them, their tongues arent burned by them. They just go on as if nothing happened. The operation was a success, but the patient died. Yeah, thats all. Bang the gavel. Next case. They dont know what it is to feel the sorrow of the world. To feel the hollow, lumpy pain of hunger. Or loneliness. That terrible, overwhelming feeling of loneliness that makes you unaware of crowded streets and noisy rooms. That terrible loneliness that makes simple movements gigantic chores and weighs so heavy inside you that you cant answer a simple question with a yes or a no, or even shake your head. You cant even stare into inquisitive eyes. You can only feel the heavy loneliness flowing through your body and hanging wet and heavy on your eyes. They know nothing about these things. To them tears are tears and nothing more. They dont feel them. They just dont feel. Thats what it is. They just dont feel. To them a kid with torn sneakers shining shoes is just a shoeshine boy. Thats all. They dont care about what may be going on inside him. They think he likes it. They really believe he likes to shine shoes and dont even think of the torment and misery that may be gnawing at his gut. They just sleep and get up and go to work with that some old grin stuck on their face. They dont lie there and feel the air getting heavier and heavier. They dont wake up in the middle of the night sweating, feeling the darkness pressing on them. Just lying there listening to the ticking of the clock, feeling it get louder and louder and wrapping itself around you tighter and tighter with each tick of the clock and you know if it gets any tighter you will be crushed out of existence, yet, somehow, it does get tighter and tighter and still just a little tighter as you struggle to suck air in, quietly, afraid to move, wanting to just turn over and grab the clock and throw it against the wall, but you cant move. Youre frozen under the weight of the darkness and the ticking of the clock. And you wait. For it. You wait for it to shatter its way through the window or suddenly splinter the door and you wont be able to resist or run. And so you just lie there, paralyzed, straining to hear whats outside the door, whats outside the room, feeling the pounding of the clock and the immobility of time. But they dont know these things. They dont know the terrors that go through your mind as you lie there in that pit waiting for a hint of light to tell you that the night is over. That time did pass and another night is over and you move and somehow manage to sit on the side of the bed and look at the clock and stare at the second hand as it ticks and tocks its way around past the five and then the six and then the seven staring deep into the face of the clock, watching time move outside you and forcing thoughts of the day upon you. Another day to get through, somehow, one sweeping, endless minute at a time, and then it would once again be night and you go to bed hoping to sleep, simply sleep, until daylight, but it never happens that way. Youre suddenly awake and the blackness is impenetrable and you feel the ticking of the clock and once again there is the torture and agony of immovable time squeezing the life from you and the despair of surviving another endless night. But they dont know this. They just sleep. Unaware and unconcerned. Oblivious to the pain and misery in the world.

Insensitive to the suffering around them. They just dont
know. Theyre insensitive to everything. Every thing. They
just dont know. They seem to think its all a game, like
making fun of the kid with the glasses, or laughing at you
when you get a haircut. They just jump around and point their
finger and sing, haha, you got a haircut, you got a haircut,
and make you cry. Theyre always doing things like that. A
little kid may save his money for days, or weeks, to buy an
ice-cream cone and when it falls on the ground they laugh.
The kid may have shined shoes or collected bottles to get
the money and they just laugh. And make fun of him if he
picks it up and eats it anyway. Or laugh even harder if he
doesn't pick it up. Yeah, sure, I know. But thats different. I
just laughed because the other kids did. I didnt really want
to hurt him. Not really. It was just something that happened. Its not really the same. None of those things were
deliberate. Yeah, I know, but even that was different. She
had no right blocking the doorway. How could people get
on and off the train with her blocking the doorway like that.
You know how many people almost got hit with the door because she wouldnt get out of the way. And anyway, I didnt
really hurt her. I just sort of bumped her a little. O.K., O.K.,
maybe I did lose my temper sometimes, but everybody
does that. I didnt plan to hurt anyones feelings. Not like
them. They get pleasure out of hurting people. And anyway,
I said I was sorry. At least most of the time. God, what do
you want from me. I said I was sorry. A thousand and one
times I said I was sorry. Isnt that enough? Youd think I
was some kind of animal or madman or something. At least
I never went around hitting people on the head with an ax
or something. God, how about all the people who beat their
kids, or starve them and lock them in closets and that kind
of thing. Like that kid Pickles. He was always stealing
pencils and pens and things in school because his old man

used to hit him on the head and knock him down the stairs and that kind of thing. I never did anything like that. And the people who start wars and millions of people get killed. I never did anything like that. And anyway, I was always sorry. I really was. Honestly. You dont think they are, do you? Do you think they care? I tried not to do those things again. I honestly and truly did.

Sometimes I feel like a motherless child

Its not really my fault things never seemed to come out right. They just seem to come out that way. Yeah, like that time. And that was a long time ago. A long, long time ago. And it was an accident. It was just something that happened.

Sometimes I feel like a motherless child

We were just playing and somehow he fell and got a bloody nose. He wasnt really hurt and I told his mother I was sorry. And anyway, it wasnt even my fault. I didnt do anything, but I told her I was sorry anyway. We were just playing. Thats all.

Sometimes I feel like a motherless child

God, I dont know how it happened or how any of those things happened. They just seemed to come out of nowhere. One minute everythings all right and the next its all fallen apart. Just crumbled. And I don't know how. Or why. But it always seemed to work out that way. And I know I tried. I tried not to do those things. Im sure I did. Yeah, maybe I could have tried harder. But how hard do you want me to try?

A long way from home

And anyway, whats the use? Everything will fall apart eventually anyway. Everything always ends up nothing eventually. I cant win. I just cant seem to win. There just doesnt seem to be any point to anything. It will end up being wrong anyway. Everything I do is wrong. Even if Im right Im wrong. Been wrong so often so long I guess I wouldnt even know if I was right. Its not important anyway. Ive been wrong enough to last me the rest of my life anyway.

A long way from home

And I guess I always will. Really doesn't make any difference where I go or what I do. May just as well stay here, or anywhere. Its all the same. And always will be,

his legs hanging over the side of his bed and swinging back and forth slowly, rhythmically, his hands still clasped between his thighs. His head hanging from his neck. His friend tugged at the back of his throat and he swallowed automatically. His friend flowed caressingly through his body and closed his eyes with a wet ache. He felt his friend sing to him and he could taste him. At least he wasnt alone. He would always have his friend. He didnt have to seek him out. And he knew that his friend was right, that there was no point in trying anymore. How many times had he tried? Endless and countless attempts, but the result was always the same and he always had to return to his friend and automatically swallow rapidly and repeatedly as his friend tugged at the back of his throat. Yes, his friend was right.

The door clanged open and a set of blues was tossed on his bed. A voice yelled court time. He didnt move, but stayed with his friend, his legs swinging slowly back and forth, ignoring the open doorway.